A NEW BEAU

McNally Men #2

MOLLY McCARTHY

Copyright © 2022 by Molly McCarthy

All rights reserved. No part of this book may be reproduced in any form or by any electronic or mechanical means, including information storage and retrieval systems, without written permission from the author, except for the use of brief quotations in a book review.

To request permissions, contact the publisher at mollymccarthybooks@gmail.com

Paperback: 978-1-7376276-3-0

E-book: 978-1-7376276-2-3

Edited by Jenn Lockwood

Cover art by Red Leaf Book Design / www.redleafbookdesign.com

This is a work of fiction. Names, characters, businesses, events, and incidents are the products of the author's imagination. Any resemblance to actual persons, living or dead, or actual events is purely coincidental.

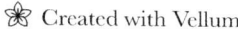 Created with Vellum

CONTENT NOTE

This book contains strong language, sexual content, and themes of human trafficking and physical and verbal abuse.

For survivors of all kinds. You are stronger than you know. Do not be afraid to let softness coexist with your strength.

PROLOGUE

Heavy footsteps from the hallway echoed throughout the empty room. *Clunk. Clunk. Clunk.* Emma cringed at the familiar sound. Each thundering step brought whoever was coming that much closer to where they kept her. The room was her own personal prison, devoid of windows and with only one entrance, kept locked up tight from the outside.

The footsteps increased in volume as they approached. Emma braced herself, sitting up straight against the concrete wall and balling her hands into fists. At the tail end of a deep breath, the footsteps continued right on past her door. Her shoulders slumped with relief.

Safe. For now.

A large, silent yawn escaped her mouth as she allowed herself to relax. Sleep had been nearly impossible to come by at this place, and when she *had* managed to fall asleep, she'd been rudely awakened—most of the time by pain. A kick in the side, a heavy boot pressing down on her chest, or a fist in her hair, yanking her to sit up, were not unusual occurrences.

She guessed it was nighttime, given her lethargy, but that could also be in part due to the lack of food weakening her body. As if goaded by her thoughts, Emma's stomach rumbled, the sound ricocheting off the concrete walls and floor. The last thing they'd given her was a single slice of bread that she'd nibbled on around the molded parts. That had been hours ago…or perhaps even a full day. Before that, it had been half a rotten apple. The absence of nutrition coupled with the lack of sleep had left her weak—just the way they wanted her. The chilling thought sent a shiver down her spine.

Sinking back into the cold concrete, Emma allowed her eyes to drift shut. She estimated that she'd been there for four days, but without a clock or a watch, it was impossible to really know. There was no furniture, no mattress, not even a stray pillow to offer a reprieve. The one blanket she'd been given was now completely drenched in blood. She shivered again, the sound of her own breathing filling her ears in the otherwise silent room.

Moments later, a quiet noise at the door caught her attention. A barely perceptible *click*.

Her eyes popped open, and she bolted upright. She'd been sure those footsteps had passed by, and it wasn't like the men to approach her room quietly. They liked her to know they were coming to build her anticipation and dread.

Suddenly, the door swung open, revealing a large, hulking figure she didn't recognize. He looked nothing like the Latino men who'd been in and out of her room incessantly for the past few days.

This man was white with a short, military-style haircut. He wore all black—black cargo pants, t-shirt, bulky vest, and scuffed work boots. And he was holding a shiny black gun… pointed straight at her.

1

4 *hours earlier*

Beau blew out a breath as he sank into the leathery bench of the booth. Dropping his overstuffed duffel beneath the table, he nudged it toward the wall with his foot, away from any prying eyes.

Roger, who'd been filling in as his partner since Diego went on leave, sat beside him. Two other fellow police officers sat on the other side of the booth. Beau couldn't even remember their names. Thing One and Thing Two, he'd call them. They were on their second round of beers, but Beau was still nursing his first. He couldn't risk being drunk or even tipsy for what he had planned tonight.

It wasn't unusual for him to hit the pub after a shift to decompress and let loose a little. He never minded imbibing—it wasn't like he had anyone counting on him for anything. He could drink, and party, and pick a woman to take home, if the mood struck him, with no consequences.

But tonight, he was only at the bar for appearances. He'd just worked his last shift as a police officer, and it might have looked weird if he just took off and went home alone. He figured he should at least make some sort of final appearance.

It was a bittersweet ending. He'd always wanted to be a cop, following in his father's footsteps. Other career options had never even crossed his mind. As soon as he graduated high school, he'd left his hometown on the island of Nantucket and headed to Boston to attend the police academy. After graduating with flying colors, he'd headed straight into the job.

Eight years on the force had taught Beau a lot, and he'd done a lot of good, but lately, there had just been too much shady shit going on that he wanted no part of—misconduct, abuses of power, priorities that were in the wrong places. And after what happened with Sofia… There was no way he would stay in an organization that had failed her so epically.

He wasn't entirely sure what would come next for him beyond his one lingering obligation. And he hoped to take care of that quite soon…tonight, if he was lucky.

Tipping his head back, Beau took a slug of lukewarm beer. Despite its lack of decent lager, Paddy's Pub had become the local watering hole favored by most police officers in Boston. The atmosphere was just right with a slew of pool tables, a wall of dart boards, and a vintage jukebox stationed in the corner. It helped that there was never any shortage of beautiful women ready to be taken home.

"Are they making these smaller these days?" one of the men across the booth—Thing Two—asked as he tipped his glass in his hand to test the weight.

"That's what she said," Beau muttered under his breath. Roger guffawed and slapped him on the back. Thing One frowned and furrowed his brow. Beau couldn't tell if the joke had gone over his head or if he was just a prude.

He wished Diego was there.

Diego was the only person he would miss from the force. They'd been partners since graduating from the academy together and had grown as close as brothers. The past few weeks without Diego, while he was out on personal leave, had been the worst of Beau's career.

Looking away from the Things, he scanned the pub. A group of rowdy young men was playing darts, tossing surreptitious glances toward a table of young ladies and raising a fit of giggles each time. A couple of hulking bikers with beards longer than most women's hair sat in their usual stools at the bar. Their leather jackets gleamed under the spotlights above the bar.

The bikers had been going to Paddy's every Friday night for years. At first, they had made Beau uncomfortable. He was conditioned to scope out potential risk, and the bikers looked like the epitome of danger. As it turned out, though, they were totally harmless. The bigger of the two actually volunteered at a dog rescue in his free time and had tried to talk Beau into adopting more than once. Beau could never commit to something like that, though. Too much responsibility.

A buxom blonde sitting at the bar caught his eye. *Damnit. Becky. Or was it Betty?* He couldn't recall the correct name. They'd hooked up a few weeks prior, and she'd gotten…clingy.

Beau didn't do clingy. He preferred one-night stands, though he could be coerced into a continuous hookup as long as the woman understood that it wasn't a relationship. Becky/Betty didn't fit that bill at all. After their first night together, she'd turned into a stage-five clinger—calling him all the time, showing up to his apartment late at night, asking his fellow officers about him… He'd finally had to threaten to file a restraining order. Thankfully, she had taken the hint and backed off on her own.

Now, though, she was sitting just across the room and watching him with googly eyes. Her lips were stained bright pink, the color rubbing off a little more each time she sucked on the straw of whatever fruity drink she had in front of her. Beau shifted in his seat. He couldn't help his physical reaction to the sight. Not when he could still remember how those lips had felt around his—

"Hey, anyone want to play some pool?" Thing Two's voice tore Beau from his thoughts. Breaking his gaze away from B— he was almost positive that was the first letter of her name— he returned it to the men at his table.

Thing One nodded and threw back the rest of his beer. "I'm game."

"Sure." Roger turned to him. "Beau?"

"Nah, I'm gonna knock back the rest of this beer and get going."

"You sure? It's your last pub run as a member of law enforcement."

Beau grimaced as a sour taste filled his mouth. At this point, the idea of being a member of law enforcement turned his stomach. "Not really. I turned in my badge and gun this afternoon."

Roger shrugged. "Semantics. You just got off a twelve-hour shift. Whatever your title—or lack thereof—is now, that doesn't change that you've worked your ass off today. You deserve to let loose a little."

"I'm exhausted," Beau lied. "But I appreciate the offer."

Roger clapped him on the back. "Well, it's been great working with you these past few weeks, man. Wish you all the best."

"Thanks," Beau replied, watching as the three men took off toward the pool tables and feeling supremely grateful that he'd never have to deal with them again.

Slugging back the rest of his beer, he was just preparing to rise when Becky/Betty trotted up to his table, sliding her sweet little ass right into the booth beside him and blocking his exit.

"Hey, officer," she said in a breathy voice. Reeking of

desperation and cheap perfume, the woman attempted to bat her eyelashes, though it seemed the alcohol had dulled her reaction time, so it just looked like she was blinking oddly. Up close, Beau noted that her mascara had rubbed off a bit underneath her eyes, and her lipstick was smudged. Had she always been so sloppy, or was he usually just too drunk to care?

"Not anymore," he grunted. "Today was my last day."

One of her blonde, manicured eyebrows drew up. "Did they at least let you keep the cuffs?"

Normally, Beau would've chuckled at the innuendo, but he didn't want to encourage this particular interaction. "Nope," he replied.

"I've missed you," Becky/Betty whined, running a finger over his exposed forearm. As he watched her sharp, hot-pink nail drag over his skin, he considered the fact that she could probably slice him open with that thing.

"I've been busy. And we're not together, remember?"

The woman scooted closer, pushing her chest out in what was probably supposed to be a provocative way. Instead, it just made her look desperate. "I know we're not together, silly," she said, her finger drawing higher up his arm. "But we could still have another fun night, couldn't we?"

Beau scowled. Apparently, the threat of a restraining order hadn't worked quite as well as he'd previously thought. "Not tonight," he said. "Not ever."

Her hot-pink lips snagged into a pout. "But why not?"

"We've been over this. I'm not interested."

Her pout pulled into a full-on frown. "But…but…"

"Look," Beau interrupted. "I'm getting out of here. Please get out of this booth so I can leave."

She opened her mouth to argue but got cut off by a woman at the bar.

"Beth!" she called, gesturing wildly. "I'm here!"

Beth. That was her name. Beau shook his head. At least he'd been close.

"Look, Beth," he said. "Go enjoy your night with your friend. We're never going to happen."

Beth cocked her head to the side, looking undecided for a fleeting moment. Luckily, her friend came bouncing over and took her by the elbow. "Come on!" she said. "I have another round of cosmos coming!"

Beth allowed herself to be hauled out of the booth, apparently unable to resist the allure of more cosmos. She shot Beau a longing glance as her friend dragged her back to the bar. He quickly averted his gaze and stood, grabbing the duffel and slinging it over his shoulder. Without a second glance, he made his way out to the parking lot and hopped into his black pickup truck. One upside to stopping after a single drink was the ability to drive himself home.

When he arrived back at his apartment, Beau dropped the duffel on a kitchen chair. He'd have to go through the contents sometime soon, but for now, it could wait. There was a more pressing issue he had to take care of first.

Heading for his bedroom, he pulled on black cargo pants and a black t-shirt, glancing at himself in the mirror to make sure he was as concealed as possible. Satisfied that he would blend seamlessly into the night, he strapped himself into his Kevlar vest and tugged on his black, steel-toed work boots. Though scuffed and worn, they'd held up like a charm.

Next came the weapons. He slid a knife into the ankle strap beneath his pants and tucked another into his belt sheath. Those were just for back-up. The pistol he shoved into his side holster would be his main form of protection. It wasn't his service weapon, of course. He'd turned that in. This was his own personal Glock 19. One of the most popular guns in America, it would be near impossible to trace any stray bullets he discharged back to him.

Feeling confident and prepared, Beau headed back to his

truck and drove toward his destination, satisfied when he was able to make it there without using his GPS. He probably could have driven there in his sleep with the number of times he'd mentally mapped the route over the past few weeks. As he neared the building, Beau flicked off his headlights and slowed to a crawl, then parked just beyond the parking lot behind the cover of a row of bushes.

Silently exiting the truck, he took a moment to get his bearings. There didn't appear to be any guards outside the building, which was sloppy, but not entirely surprising. Mason was one lucky son-of-a-bitch that he hadn't been annihilated yet. That fact was about to change if he had anything to do with it.

Sticking toward the edge of the parking lot where he could more easily blend in with the bushes, Beau crept toward the building. He passed a few doors as he searched for a more clandestine entrance. Around the back of the building, he discovered a rusty, unmarked door. Jiggling the handle as softly as humanly possible, Beau released a silent sigh of relief when he found it unlocked. He placed his hand on his gun before pushing it open, prepared to shoot first and ask questions later.

Quiet as a church mouse, he prowled through the dark room he'd entered, silently cursing when his foot banged sharply into something. He bit his lip to contain a groan and carried on a little slower. A faint light came into view as he made his way farther into the room. Following the light, he eventually came upon a hallway where he finally found signs of life. Empty liquor bottles, candy wrappers, and cigarette stubs littered the floor. Unholstering his gun, he held it loosely in his hand, ready to defend himself if needed.

A quarter of the way down the hallway, a noise caught Beau's attention. Ducking into an alcove, he slid as far as he could into the shadows and listened as the sound got closer. At some point, he identified it as footsteps. Not a light *pitter patter* of feet, but more like the *clunk clunk clunk* of heavy boots.

Holding his breath, he waited for the owner of the footsteps to discover him, but they never reached his hiding spot. They stopped—probably fifty feet away, Beau guessed based on sound alone—and a door opened then slammed shut.

Peering around the corner, he found the hallway empty and continued on down it. The walls on each side were full of closed doors, and he had no clue what he was looking for. Which door would house his target? It was like a game of Russian roulette.

One door in particular caught his attention due to the amount of trash that had accumulated outside it. There was shit strewn throughout the hallway, but the mountain of it sitting outside this door rivaled Everest. That had to be the one.

As he approached it, Beau realized the room was locked from the outside. *What the fuck?* That didn't make any sense. Mason wouldn't be imprisoned—he was the head honcho. But the litter outside the door indicated that it was the most well-used room in the hall. Where else would Mason be? Maybe his own men had turned on him and were holding him hostage. Wouldn't that be a hoot?

Bewildered, Beau tiptoed toward the door and slid the lock out of place. Tightening his hold on the gun, he slowly turned the knob and swung the door open.

2

Emma's eyes widened at the sight of the gun. She let out a blood-curdling shriek, unable to contain her pure panic. Scrambling backward, she collided with the concrete wall and slid down to the floor, sinking under the realization that there was nowhere to run.

"Fuck," the man growled. Almost as scary as the gun itself, his imposing figure had her recoiling. Dressed in all black, with his eyes narrowed to slits, he looked dangerous and ready to kill. His menacing gaze darted quickly to the hallway, then to the bloody blanket in the corner before returning to Emma. "Fuck," he said again as he strode toward her.

"Please don't," she begged, her gaze trained on the shiny metal weapon as she huddled herself further into the corner. Her back fought with the wall as she tried to get as far away from the man as possible. "Please!"

"Shh!" the man hissed, stopping halfway across the room. He holstered his gun, giving her a slight sense of relief, but his furious frown had her hugging her arms tighter around her knees.

That was when the footsteps started up again. Those loud,

clunky footsteps that meant he was coming for her. Emma's gaze darted between the man and the now open door.

"You have to come with me right now." The man loomed above her and stuck out his hand. She automatically flinched away, conditioned to expect pain.

"Please," he said, his frown deepening. Reaching forward to pull her up off the ground, the man grunted when she tried to wrench his hand off her arm.

"Let go!" Emma screamed, pain lancing down her arm as his fingers pressed against the dark bruises there.

"Jesus," the man grumbled as she wriggled about, desperately trying to escape his firm grasp. Releasing her momentarily, he readjusted to grab her by the hips and hoist her over his shoulder with ease. Her legs dangled over the front of his body while her arms flailed helplessly at his back.

The footsteps were so close. He'd be there any second.

"What are you doing?" Emma screeched as she was carried toward the hallway. She kicked her feet blindly and managed to connect with some part of the man's body—a knee, maybe? He let out a small grunt but kept on, undeterred.

"Angel, please," he pleaded. "Stay still so I can get you out of here."

Angel? Get me out of here?

Emma only had a moment to process those confusing words before finding herself face to face, albeit upside down, with the man with the clunky footsteps. She screamed, and the man carrying her cursed yet again. Still balancing her over his shoulder, he skillfully kneed her captor in the groin. The man doubled over and received a swift kick to the chest, knocking him to his back and effectively diffusing his threat.

The man in black took off with Emma, running down the hallway with both speed and grace. Her weight didn't seem to slow him down one bit.

Some of the others must have heard the commotion, because two more Latino men rounded the corner, chattering back and forth. One turned around and ran back, plausibly to get more backup or grab a weapon, while the other charged toward them.

"Hold on tight," the man carrying Emma warned. She fisted her hands in his shirt, holding on for dear life. He chose a slightly different fighting tactic with this new opponent, going for his legs first to knock them out from under him, then kicking him hard in the side once he was down. The man curled into a fetal position, clutching his side in pain.

"Two down," the man muttered as he raced toward the exit. Emma thought they just might make it out when the second Latino man returned, waving a gun and yelling in Spanish.

"Put it down," the man demanded, tightening his hold on her legs.

Instead, he pointed the gun straight at them. Emma barely had time to scream before the man carrying her swiftly unholstered his own weapon.

"Put it down!" he shouted, his tone lethal in itself. Clearly sensing there was no chance of that happening, he quickly aimed his gun at his opponent and pulled the trigger.

The sound of the gun firing sent Emma into shock. Adrenaline shot like ice through her veins, and she choked on air, barely able to breathe, let alone speak. Bile crawled up her throat as the man who'd been shot fell backward, clutching his leg in pain. Blood already seeped through his worn jeans. She was close to gagging when the man carrying her spoke.

"Come on. Let's get out of here."

Emma opened her mouth to respond, but only a strangled sound came out. Her entire body had started shaking, and she felt faint.

"Don't give out on me now." The man barreled toward

the door at the end of the hallway. He flung it open, and fresh air greeted them—the first time she'd felt it in days. It was pitch black, and nearby crickets had the audacity to chirp as if this place wasn't the depths of hell.

The man carried her to a pickup truck behind a row of bushes. Before she knew it, the passenger side door had been thrown open, and she'd been dumped into the seat where she sat stunned.

Her liberator hopped into the driver's seat beside her and put the car into gear, quickly buckling his seatbelt and throwing the car into reverse. He glanced over at her quivering body.

"Seatbelt!" he ordered. When Emma failed to respond, he reached over and deftly fastened it himself while she sat shaking. After a quick look out the rearview mirror, he backed out of the bushes and began driving like a bat out of hell.

Still trembling, Emma pulled her legs up onto the seat and hugged them. "You…you shot him."

"He got what he deserved," the man replied, his eyes skillfully scanning their surroundings while both large hands remained steadily on the wheel. Defined muscles and tattoos peeked out from under his shirtsleeves. His biceps bulged, threatening to burst through the cotton t-shirt.

She imagined that he could probably break her neck with one flick of his wrist.

The man remained no-nonsense until they reached the highway. Then, his shoulders visibly relaxed as he announced that no one had followed them. Finally glancing over at Emma, he took in her curled-up form and frowned. His hard gaze softened, and he reached behind him for something in the backseat.

"Here, take this," he said gently, his tone markedly different from before as he offered her a large leather jacket. When she didn't reach for it right away, he gently placed it on the seat beside her, then returned his hand to the steering wheel.

Emma slowly uncurled her body enough to shrug the jacket on, wrapping it around herself for both warmth and modesty. All she wore beneath it was the wretched white dress she'd been in for days. It had once been one of her favorites, but it was now filthy and covered in blood, the trauma she'd endured practically woven into the fabric of the garment.

"How are you feeling?" the man asked, his eyebrows drawn tight with concern.

"I'm...confused."

He let out a grunt. "I'm sure you are."

She sat silently as he ran a hand over his head, smoothing out his short brown hair.

"You're safe now," he said. "You can ask me anything you want."

"Wh-what's your name?" she stammered, asking the first question that came to mind.

"I'm Officer—I mean, I'm Beau."

"Officer?" she asked, not missing his blunder.

Beau swallowed. "I was Boston P.D. up until this afternoon."

"Oh," she whispered, unsure what to make of that.

"What's your name?" he asked when she didn't reciprocate.

"Emma," she answered quietly.

"Emma," he repeated, letting the name roll off his tongue. "It's nice to meet you, Emma. Wish it was under better circumstances." He seemed so calm and collected, and yet, their circumstances were anything but.

She frowned, asking the second question that came to mind. "Where are we going?"

"I'm heading to my apartment right now, but is there somewhere I can take you that would make you feel safe?"

Emma's mind flashed to her father's house, and she hugged her legs tighter. "No."

"That's fine," Beau said, his tone soothing. "You'll be safe at my place."

Though she wasn't sure whether or not to believe that, she figured his place couldn't be worse than where she'd been.

Beau sighed wearily as he ran a hand over his face. "Before we go to my apartment, do I need to take you to a hospital? I can tell you're a bit battered, but sometimes there are worse injuries that you can't see."

"No," Emma replied quickly. "No hospitals." She knew what he was referring to. Injuries you couldn't see because they were inside of her. But no. She didn't need a hospital, and she definitely didn't want to leave any form of a trail. There was no way she was letting any of those men find her again.

"Good," Beau said with a nod, "because I don't want any trail of your name anywhere until we get this all figured out. It could put you in danger again."

It was as if he'd read her thoughts. It seemed unrealistic that going to a hospital could be unsafe, but in light of recent events, Emma realized the world wasn't as safe a place as she had naïvely believed it was.

"How did you find me?" she asked, more questions emerging as the shock wore off.

Beau was silent for a moment before answering. "I was hunting down a criminal—the man I believe was keeping you there. He's a human trafficker I've been trying to catch for weeks."

Having assumed the men holding her were traffickers, Emma wasn't surprised, but hearing the words out loud still made her cringe. Equally upsetting was the fact that she was the reason Beau hadn't been able to stay and track down the leader.

"I'm sorry you couldn't get him today."

"Don't be sorry," Beau said, a frown marring his brow. "I'm grateful I found you when I did."

Emma picked at the sleeve of the leather jacket tucked around her. "You said you'd been hunting him for weeks. I must have gotten in the way of that tonight."

"I've been hunting him for weeks, and I'll keep hunting him." Beau's tone left no room for second-guessing. "My priorities all changed when I saw you in that room. No way could I have left you in harm's way while I tried to find him."

"But what about all the other women that could get hurt before you're able to get to him again?" Though she hadn't actually seen any other women during her time in captivity, she was positive there were plenty of other victims out there.

Beau's grip tightened on the wheel. "I'll do my best to help those women, too. But they're no more important than you, Emma. Sometimes you have to take care of what's right in front of you before you can think about the hypotheticals."

Though she was obviously grateful to have been rescued from that awful place, she couldn't shake the feeling that it would have been better for the greater good if Beau had spent his time catching his criminal rather than saving her. Nonetheless, she was eternally grateful he had. "Thank you for getting me out of there," she whispered.

Beau sighed. "Angel, it was my pleasure. We have a lot to go over, but it's late, and you're in bad shape. Why don't you rest until we get to my place?"

"Okay," Emma conceded, shutting her eyes and laying her head back against the seat. As the shock wore off and exhaustion crept back in, she willed herself to stay alert. Beau seemed like a decent guy, but her days of trusting people implicitly were long gone.

A few moments later, Beau began talking, and Emma realized he'd made a phone call. She listened attentively to the one-sided conversation.

"Hey, dude," Beau said. "I know it's late. Sorry. Are you

sleeping at Christa's tonight?" He paused for a moment, presumably listening to whatever the person on the other end of the line was saying. "Great. Listen, I have a little…situation. We can talk tomorrow, but I'm gonna need the apartment until further notice."

Emma's mouth tightened at the implication of being a *situation*, though she supposed that was as good a word for her as any. The *until further notice* part was awfully ambiguous. She was grateful to have a safe place to go for the night, but she had no idea what would happen after that. She supposed she would need to stay in hiding until all the men involved in her kidnapping were behind bars. And she meant *all* of them.

"Yes, it does. Thanks for understanding, man. Yeah, just let me know. Bye," Beau said before hanging up. Emma watched through narrowed eyes as he placed his phone on the console beside him. Reaching over for the radio dial, he turned the volume up so soft music filled the interior of the car.

Closing her eyes again, Emma heard Beau blow out a big breath. Surely it had been a stressful night for him, too, and he probably wasn't thrilled to have ended up with a stowaway. She'd already been a huge inconvenience in his mission, and now she'd be intruding in his home, too. Everything was beyond screwed up.

The music and gentle motion of the car were soothing enough for her to relax a bit, letting her feet fall to the floor and resting her head against the window. It seemed so surreal that she was finally safe. In fact, the past few days had all felt like a dream—or, more accurately, a nightmare.

A while later, the car began to slow. Only after peeling her eyes open did Emma realize that she'd fallen asleep. She hadn't planned to let her guard down that much, but she was just so exhausted, and the car had grown warm and cozy.

A peek out the window revealed a tree-lined back road dotted with cute little houses. The road was very quiet, but then again, it was very late at night. It seemed like the type of neighborhood where you could scream and there was a possibility of no one hearing you. Emma shivered, not liking where her thoughts were going. She worried that would be her life from now on. Always on high alert, imagining the worst possible situation. Always scared.

They pulled into the parking lot of a complex called *Clear Ridge Apartments*, and her shoulders relaxed. An apartment complex was good. Less space between units meant more of a chance for screams to be heard.

Stop, Emma chastised herself, unwilling to let her life become consumed by fear.

Beau eased the truck into a marked space and turned to face her. "We're here."

He was out and opening her door before she even had the chance to unbuckle her seatbelt. Her strength was low, making her movements slower than usual. Straightening her legs, she swung them out of the car to stand but found herself a bit unsteady on her feet. She took a stumbling step forward, and Beau reached out to grasp her arm for support.

"*Ow*," Emma hissed, instinctively jerking her arm away from his touch.

"Shit. Sorry." He put his hands up as if in surrender.

A blush bloomed on her cheeks. "It's fine," she muttered.

Beau rocked back on his heels. "Uh, we can go right inside here, number thirty-four."

He led Emma to his doorway, which was luckily on the bottom floor and didn't require her to climb any stairs. She walked slowly to make sure she could keep her balance.

Beau slid his key into the lock, and the door swung open. "Come in," he said, gesturing toward the inside of the apartment.

Still standing just outside the door, Emma gave a small shake of her head.

Confusion crossed Beau's expression. "Emma? You okay?"

She nodded sharply toward the doorway. "You first."

His eyes softened. "Okay." He entered his home and quickly scanned the room. "It's safe to come in," he assured her.

With no other choice but to trust him, Emma walked about halfway inside the apartment and let Beau shut the door behind her. The front door opened up into the living room, which was attached to a moderate-sized kitchen. The rooms were furnished with dark wooden furniture with black leather upholstery, giving off a definite masculine vibe. A couch and two lounge chairs framed a fuzzy rug running across the living room floor. Emma couldn't wait to perch herself on one of the cozy-looking seats. It was guaranteed to beat the concrete floor she'd been confined to for days.

She took in the exposed brick throughout the kitchen and stainless-steel appliances gleaming around the perimeter. Four bar stools sat beneath an island counter in the kitchen—another place she couldn't wait to sit, hopefully along with a steaming hot plate of food to fill her empty stomach.

Beau led her through a hallway off the kitchen that contained two bedrooms and a bathroom. He explained that he shared the apartment with his brother, Fletcher, which made sense, given the bachelor-pad vibe. Emma could picture a bunch of guys gathered around the large flat-screen television, watching sports and lounging on the black leather couch and chairs. Everything in the apartment was very masculine, including the man who owned it.

Stripping off his vest, Beau hung it on a hook by the front door, then removed a gun from the holster at his side, a knife from somewhere on his belt, and another from his ankle. He placed the weapons down on the coffee table as if it was the most normal thing in the world to stash deadly weapons in the middle of one's living room.

Emma stood with her arms tucked tightly around herself, grateful she had Beau's jacket to cover her upper half. She didn't have a lot of experience with weapons, but she knew they could do far more damage than bare hands, and those had been enough to knock her around pretty darn good.

"So, I guess the top priorities for you right now are food and rest," Beau said, tenting his fingers on the back of the couch. "Personally, I think you should get some calories in your body before you sleep."

Emma shifted on her feet. "Er, do you think maybe I could take a shower first? It's been a while, and I've been stuck in this nasty dress…"

"Oh, of course." Beau's brows drew together. "Are you… do you think you're steady enough to do it yourself, or do you need help?"

Heat streaked across Emma's cheeks. Sure, she had been walking slowly and perhaps a bit unsteadily around the apartment, but there was *no* way she would allow him to help her in the shower.

"I'll be fine," she said. "And I can sit down if I need to."

Beau nodded. "Okay. You saw where the bathroom is. You can use anything in there. And here, let me grab you some clean clothes." He disappeared into one of the bedrooms and returned with a stack of clothing in hand. "I'm sorry I don't have any women's clothing. These sweatpants are pretty new, so hopefully the elastic hasn't stretched out too much and they'll fit you."

"That's fine," Emma said. Anything would be better than that godawful dress.

"I'll make us some food while you shower," he said.

"Thank you," she replied, genuinely grateful for his kindness. Though she didn't know what kind of man Beau really was yet, he *had* saved her life, and he *was* welcoming her into his home, letting her borrow his clothes, and making her food, so he couldn't be all that bad. No one had done anything that nice for her in a long, long time—or maybe ever.

Emma entered the bathroom and was pleased to find a

lock on the door. As she clicked it into place, an unexpected wave of relief rushed over her. For days, she had longed for a place to hide. A place where she could lock herself up and no one could get to her. And here she was, finally.

Hot, unexpected tears began streaming down her face. She hadn't allowed herself to shed a single one in that place, in front of those awful men, even while they tortured her. She hadn't wanted to give them the satisfaction. They wanted her weak, pliable. They wanted to break her. She'd refused to allow it, but now, alone, she could break.

Quickly turning on the shower to try and drown out the sound of her sobs, she sank to the floor and finally let herself cry. The flood of emotion was cathartic, and she imagined releasing every fear, negative thought, and bad memory as her tears flowed.

After long minutes, the tears subsided, and Emma dragged the repulsive white dress over her head. Tossing it into the corner, she wished it would just get sucked into the ground and be gone forever. Plucking off her filthy bra, she was struck by the realization that she wasn't wearing any panties. She had discarded them as soon as they'd soaked through with blood. She shuddered as she realized that Beau had probably seen everything when he'd carried her out of that building.

Pushing that unwelcome thought from her mind, she carefully stepped into the shower. The piping-hot water rushed over her body in a cleansing deluge. As she lathered up her body with soap, she began to feel somewhat human again. She noted the women's shampoo, razor, and body wash on a shelf in the shower stall. Maybe they belonged to Beau's girlfriend?

Well, too bad for her, Emma thought as she picked up the razor. She had a few days' worth of growth on her legs and under her arms. Cautiously balancing one foot on the edge of the tub, she got to work shaving her legs. The last thing she wanted was to fall over and have Beau come running in to find her sprawled naked in the tub. She shaved slowly and with precision, avoiding a few spots where the skin was broken, including a particularly ugly gash on her thigh.

When she lifted up her right arm to shave her armpit, Emma caught sight of the dark bruises on her side. Some were purple, and some had already started to fade to a grotesque yellow hue. She poked one gently and winced. Shaving under her arm quickly, she let it fall by her side.

Stealing a dollop of body wash, she rubbed it over her newly shaved legs, then washed her hair, which had turned into more of a rat's nest over the past few days than her usual bouncy, blonde curls. She shampooed twice, then used the women's conditioner sitting on the corner of the tub.

After what was probably the longest shower of her life, Emma switched the water off and dried her body with a delightfully fluffy towel. She unfolded the clothes Beau had given her—a pair of gray sweatpants, a large Boston Police Department t-shirt, and a pair of white Calvin Klein boxer briefs. She felt funny wearing his underwear, but after being so exposed for so many days, it felt good to finally be covered up. She rolled up the top of the sweatpants a few times so she wouldn't trip over the bottoms. The t-shirt fit more like a dress, but it was made of such soft, comfy cotton that she didn't mind. The best part was it was loose enough that her breasts weren't visible, which was good because she wasn't putting that dirty bra back on.

In the mirror, she investigated herself a little more. Her face was dotted with ugly bruises, made more pronounced by the paleness of her skin. She'd always had very light coloring —alabaster skin; light-hazel, almost golden eyes; and hair so light blonde that it looked as if she'd bleached it. Running a comb through her hair, she tamed it as best she could, then found a tube of mint toothpaste and squeezed a glob onto her finger, spreading it over her teeth. That would have to do for now.

Once she finally felt clean, Emma reluctantly unlocked the

bathroom door and left her haven of safety. She was greeted with the yummy smell of grease wafting from the kitchen and decided that it was worth leaving the locked room if it meant finally eating some real food.

3

Beau slid two grilled cheese sandwiches onto ceramic plates, feeling like a total schmuck for serving frickin' kid food to a woman who was malnourished, but he didn't have the ingredients for anything else. He *had* found a rogue can of tomato soup in the cabinet that he heated up, thinking the sandwich may be too heavy for Emma in her current state.

He tried to think of anything else she may need. He'd covered food, shelter, clean clothing... *Shit.* He thought back to that once sweet little white dress that had been tainted by large splotches of crimson-red blood. He really needed to look over her injuries. Though he'd only seen bruises so far, that blood had come from somewhere. If Emma had any open wounds, they were at risk of infection.

Standing in front of the refrigerator, Beau watched water stream out of the spout and into the glass he was holding. She would definitely need a good night's rest, too. Maybe he would have her sleep in his room while he took Fletcher's for the night, though he wasn't ready to think about why it felt so right to have her in his bed rather than his brother's.

Pulling away from the refrigerator, Beau placed the grilled

cheeses, waters, and soup on the kitchen island and sat down to wait for Emma. He hadn't even thought to offer her a shower first, but he was glad she'd felt comfortable enough to ask. She was filthy as hell, and while he really didn't mind, it was obvious she had needed the private moment to herself.

The sound of her sobs had torn him up, making it difficult to hold himself back from going out and blowing the heads off of the men who had taken her. The only thing that stopped him was knowing she was in his shower and would soon return.

Emma revved up his protective instincts in a way no one else had in, well…ever. Beau was protective by nature—a fact that had initially led him to become a police officer. The job had seemed perfect for him at first, allowing him to protect and serve his community. But lately, things had become a lot dicier. He saw the news stories the same as everyone else, but he also heard whisperings of even more scandals that didn't reach the public's ears. The wrongdoing had been grating on him for years, but the way the force had let Sofia down was the last straw.

Leaving the force hadn't dulled his inclination to protect. The visceral urge to keep Emma safe pounded through his veins. He'd saved plenty of women in his time—many of them attractive, similarly aged women who were not unlike Emma—and while he'd often appreciated their looks or flirtation, he'd never felt any real attraction to any of them. They were just a job.

But Emma…she was different. Perhaps it was because he hadn't rescued her in an official capacity, but rather a personal one. Or maybe it was because the whole situation hit so close to home because of Sofia. Hell, maybe he was just getting soft. Though he wasn't sure why, Beau knew that he'd never felt like this before.

Not to mention that Emma wasn't his usual type—like, not by a million miles. Beth from the bar, minus all the clinginess, was much more his speed. He liked his women confident, bold, maybe a little outspoken, and definitely overt with their sexuality. Beau's brothers, Fletcher and Jack, had deemed his type the *brassy broad*. He liked a girl who didn't need protecting. If some dude she didn't like started hitting on her at the bar, she could take care of herself. Perhaps it was because he spent all day watching out for people, but Beau appreciated when a woman didn't need him so much. Plus, if she never got too dependent on him, it made it easier to break up with her when he got bored.

So far, Emma seemed to be the polar opposite of just about everything he usually looked for in a woman. Sure, some of it could have been due to the trauma she'd experienced, but something told him that most of it was simply her personality. So, why was she hitting all of his hot buttons?

Beau scrubbed a hand over his face and leaned against the counter, listening to the steady beat of water against the shower walls and trying his hardest not to picture Emma in there. Her blonde hair would be soaked by now, the water flowing down her creamy skin. It would bead in her long eyelashes and trail down her face, washing away her tears, then travel lower, over her defined collarbones and—

"*Fuck*," he muttered to himself. Not only was his attraction to Emma totally perplexing, it was also extremely inappropriate. The last thing she needed was an ass like him lusting over her.

His efforts to remain neutral were tested moments later when she emerged from the bathroom, looking utterly adorable in his sweats and favorite worn-out Boston P.D. t-shirt. Beau's heart stuttered as he took in the sight. Christ, she was beautiful. The only possible flaws were the dark bruises marring her pale skin. And damn, he shouldn't have given her a pair of his boxers, because all he could think about right now was how she was wearing them under those sweats.

Entering the kitchen slowly, Emma crossed her arms over

her chest. Her golden gaze met his, and she tightened her arms around herself a little more. "Thank you for the clothes."

"Don't mention it." Beau gestured to the sandwiches and soup. "I'm sorry, this is all I have for you. I couldn't find much else in the cabinets."

She appeased him with a sweet smile. "This looks great. I could smell it from the bathroom."

Sitting down gingerly, she winced as her body met the island stool. Beau could see a few bruises sprinkled over her arms, but he imagined her clothing covered many more. Once again, he felt the urge to pummel any man who had ever touched her.

Instead, he stuffed his mouth with a large bite of grilled cheese. "You should probably start with the soup," he said once he'd chewed enough that he could speak without offending. "You know, take things slow."

Emma nodded and ladled a bit of soup into her mouth, closing her lips around the spoon to suck it off. She let out a soft moan, and Beau tore his gaze away, forcing himself to look at anything but her lips.

"This is so good," she said. "I haven't…well, I haven't had a proper meal in a few days."

Beau scowled. "I figured. You're welcome to anything in my cabinets, but like I said, it's not much."

Emma brought another spoonful of soup to her mouth, her eyelids drooping as the warm liquid hit her tongue. "S'okay," she murmured after swallowing.

He continued eating his grilled cheese, allowing her to enjoy her meal in silence. While he was eager to start asking her questions and working on his private investigation, Beau could see that Emma was fading quickly. She let out a big yawn before polishing off the last bit of soup. She hadn't taken even a bite of her sandwich, but that was probably for the best. If she'd gone a few days without eating much, something too heavy might shock her system.

"Why don't you try and get some rest? You can take my bed for the night," Beau offered.

Emma glanced at the untouched grilled cheese then back at him. "Okay," she said as she slid off the stool, her easy acquiescence a sign of her fatigue. She followed Beau as he led her to his bedroom.

As they walked, it dawned on him that he'd led many women this same way before but expecting a vastly different outcome. For some reason, the thought made his skin crawl.

"Ta da," he said, gesturing to the freshly made bed. "There are extra blankets in the closet, and I'll be right across the hall, so just yell or knock on the door if you need anything."

Emma was already climbing into bed as she said a faint, "Thank you."

"Sleep well," he replied, watching as she pulled the covers up to her nose. Flicking out the lights on his way out, he couldn't help but grin at the thought of Emma all cozied up in his bed. Hopefully, she would have a restful night, and they could talk in the morning.

He walked across the hall to Fletcher's bedroom, exceptionally grateful that his brother had chosen to sleep at Christa's. It wasn't that Beau didn't want Fletcher to know about Emma; he just didn't want her to have to meet any other men on her first night back in safety. He'd gone through enough training to understand how hard it could be for women who had suffered abuse of any kind to trust men. Emma was probably having a hard enough time relaxing with one man in the house, let alone being outnumbered by two.

Stripping off his t-shirt and pants, Beau began to tug off his boxers, then thought better of it. If Emma awoke in the middle of the night and needed him, he'd better have *some* sort of clothing on. The boxers he wore were identical to the ones he had given her, and he fleetingly imagined that they must look better on her.

Cut it out, McNally, he scolded himself. Emma was a woman he was protecting, not a potential lover. If he made any type of pass at her, it could scare her away or trigger her. He was determined to catch the men who had held her captive, which meant he would need her help. He couldn't have her running off and taking any potentially useful information with her, or risk her being captured again.

Beau crashed onto Fletcher's bed and fell into a light sleep, ensuring that he would wake quickly if Emma needed anything. He almost hoped she would, because it would give him an excuse to help her and gain her trust, but in reality, he knew it would be better if she got a good night's sleep.

He awoke at his usual rising time—eight a.m.—in his usual rising state—hard as stone—and had a driving urge to piss. That was going to be a bitch with this morning wood. He yawned and rolled out of bed, heading for the bathroom. It had been an uneventful night with no wakings, so he'd assumed Emma slept soundly. But as he neared the bathroom, he saw the door was closed, so she must have already woken up.

Beau knocked tentatively on the bathroom door but received no answer. He knocked again, calling out Emma's name this time.

"One second!" came her soft, sleepy voice before she opened the door slightly, peeking out just enough so he could see her face.

"You okay?" he asked, taking in her slight frown.

"Er, yes, just fine," she mumbled.

Beau's bladder was screaming at him to forget the niceties. "Well, can I take a leak in here?"

Emma blinked in surprise. "Oh, um, of course." She opened the door the rest of the way until he could take her all in. There she stood, all pale skin and messy curls, yawning like a sleepy kitten. The sight took his breath away, appreciation momentarily overtaking his biological needs.

Emma did her own once-over of him, her eyes widening as she took in his less-than-presentable state. Beau hadn't bothered to put anything on over his boxers, as he hadn't expected to run into anyone on his walk to the bathroom. There was also an unmistakable bulge beneath them. *Fuck*, he cursed himself, feeling like a prick.

Emma swallowed hard, and he grasped for anything he could say to take her mind off his appearance. Looking beyond her shoulder into the bathroom, he noticed a pillow and blanket laid out inside the bathtub.

"What were you doing in here?" he asked.

Emma's gaze dropped to her feet as her cheeks grew pink with embarrassment. "I, um, well...I sort of slept in here."

"In the bathtub?" Christ, she looked so cute blushing with embarrassment. Beau cleared his throat. "Do you mind if I ask why? Did you not like the bedroom?"

"No, no," she answered quickly. "The bedroom was great. Thank you. It's just that...the bedroom door doesn't have a lock on it. But this one does."

He stared at her as his heart shattered into a million pieces, the shards poking at his ribcage. This poor angel had slept in a bathtub just so she could have the security of a locked door. Of course she would seek to protect herself. Beau made a mental note to buy a lock for his bedroom door A.S.A.P.

"Oh," he said casually. "Well, let me just pee real quick, and then it's all yours."

"No, it's fine. I'm already awake," Emma said, grabbing her bedding and scurrying out of the bathroom. Beau was glad she seemed slightly steadier on her feet this morning, but he was bothered that she was embarrassed. After all, she had the right to act a little erratic in light of recent events.

When Emma disappeared, he entered the bathroom and took care of business, then returned to his bedroom to pull on a pair of gray sweats and a tank top. By the time he made it out to the kitchen to start breakfast, she was already sitting at the kitchen island, wrapped up tight in a blanket like a caterpillar in a cocoon. She was sipping orange juice from a glass and paused when he entered the room.

"I hope you don't mind…" She gestured to the half empty glass.

"Of course not," he said. "I told you; you're welcome to anything."

She rewarded him with a sweet smile, and he cheered internally. He'd do anything to keep that smile on her face.

"You like eggs?" he asked, poking his head into the fridge to see what else he might be able to scrape together for breakfast.

"Love them."

"Good." Beau pulled out an eighteen pack of eggs and a lone fruit cup that must have been Fletcher's. Sliding the fruit cup in front of Emma, he said, "Eat this while I cook the eggs."

She looked down at the small bowl of berries and melon and licked her lips. "Okay."

Beau's nostrils flared as her tongue flicked out over her perfect pink lips—not a fake shade of pink like Beth at the bar, but a light-rose color that he longed to taste.

Forcing himself to turn and face the stove, he whipped up six scrambled eggs and divided them onto two plates, giving himself a slightly bigger serving than Emma. She smacked her lips together as he presented her with the eggs, eagerly spearing some with her fork. She ate them slowly, letting out small moans of pleasure every so often.

On the other side of the island, Beau ate his own breakfast

as he did his best to ignore the sounds she made. He found himself stabbing his eggs a little more violently with each satisfied sound that came out of her mouth. *She's off limits. She's off limits. She's off limits.*

"So," he said, breaking the prolonged silence punctuated only by Emma's moans of pleasure. "I hate to ruin a nice breakfast, but we've got some talking to do."

She frowned and nodded grimly. "I know."

Beau's chest ached at her despondent expression, but she'd slept and eaten, and now he really needed some information from her. He'd been covertly gathering information on this human-trafficking case for weeks now, ever since Sofia's incident, and Emma's first-person testimony could only help bolster his knowledge.

"I have some questions for you," he said. "But I don't want to upset you, so we can take them as slow as we need to. Just let me know if you need a break."

"Alright," Emma said after taking a deep breath. "What do you need to know?"

He pulled out a pad of paper to take notes on. "First off, when were you taken?"

She snagged her lip with her bottom teeth. "Saturday."

Beau nodded. "That was four days ago," he said, glad it had only been a short time but also understanding that there was a lot of damage they could have done in four days. "What did they do to you while you were there?"

"They...beat me," she replied softly. "They kicked and hit me. Spit on me. And taunted me. They called me...a little slut. A whore."

He cringed. Those bastards wouldn't get away with their abuse much longer if he had anything to say about it. "Did they...touch you in any other ways?" he asked, steeling himself for her answer.

"No." Emma shook her head, looking down at her plate.

Oh, thank Jesus. But why would a bunch of men involved in

a human-trafficking ring capture a beautiful young girl for days and *not* use her for their own pleasure? "I'm glad," he said gently. "But I'll admit, that's a little surprising, and it really doesn't keep with the traffickers' usual behavior."

Emma took a big breath before responding. "They were planning to...do other things," she said, her eyes still downcast. She refused to meet his gaze as she explained the rest. "When they first got me, they took me to that room you found me in and said they had to inspect me and report back to 'him.' They lifted up my dress and saw that I was bleeding." She shivered and pulled her blanket tighter around her. "I... um...I had my period," she finally admitted before the rest of the story came spilling out. "The men were so mad. One of them pushed me to the floor and kicked me, called me a little bitch. They kept coming back to check if I was still bleeding, and every time they saw I was, they would beat me. They kept saying that when it stopped, they were going to give me to their boss. Thank God you got me out of there when you did, because if they had come to check on me again, that's what would've happened."

Yeah, thank God. Beau didn't even want to think about what their "boss" would've done to her. Mason was the biggest snake of them all, and he knew all too well the horrible things that could happen when he got his hands on a girl.

An image of the bloody blanket flashed through Beau's mind. He was clenching his teeth so hard he thought he might explode, but he breathed a sigh of relief when he realized that must have been blood from her period, not some horrible injury. It still royally pissed him off that those men stripped Emma's dignity away like that.

She finally lifted her gaze back to his, and he drank in the sight of those two amber pools for a moment before asking his next question. "So, there were multiple men who hurt you?"

"Yes."

"How many were there?"

"Four. The 'boss' and his three lackeys."

"Do you have any names?"

"They called the boss Mason. The other three I'm not so sure about. They all had foreign-sounding names."

Sounded about right. They were probably immigrants Mason hired on the cheap to do his dirty work. Beau wanted anyone who'd ever laid a hand on Emma to pay, but Mason was the main target. If he could cut off the head of the snake, the whole ring would go down in flames.

"That's helpful," he assured her. "Were there any other girls in the abandoned warehouse?"

"I don't know." Emma shrugged helplessly. "I only ever saw the room they kept me in. They never let me out. I never saw any other girls."

That *was* in keeping with Beau's knowledge of the case. The traffickers usually kept their headquarters only for offices and had separate holding facilities for the victims they trafficked. He still couldn't figure out why they'd kept Emma there. Her appearance also didn't fit Mason's M.O. He was known for grabbing good-looking girls from developing countries, where no one would have the resources to look for them. As far as Beau could tell, Emma didn't fit that bill.

"How did those men get you?" he asked.

Emma's eyes grew wide and fearful at the question. She wrapped herself even tighter in her blanket.

"Emma? Are you okay?"

She nodded but seemed to focus all of her attention on breathing. Her breaths were shallow, as if she was about to hyperventilate.

"Hey," he said, almost reaching across the table to place a supportive hand on her arm before remembering she didn't like to be touched. "Don't worry. We don't have to talk any more right now. We can pick this up later."

Emma gulped in a breath and nodded.

"Why don't you rest on the couch for a bit?" he suggested.

Thankfully, she had finished her eggs before getting spooked by his question. She definitely needed a break, and considering she'd practically smothered herself with her blanket already, moving to the couch seemed like a good idea.

Emma nodded again and slid off the stool, catching her balance. "Sure," she said as she headed for the living room without giving him a second glance.

Beau watched her go, wondering what it was she didn't want to tell him.

4

Emma collapsed onto the couch and dropped her head into her hands, biting back a groan. Beau's question was only natural, given her situation, yet she'd clammed up and probably made him suspicious of her. But how could she explain how messed up everything was? How do you tell someone that your entire sordid existence led to this exact moment? That what happened to you was, in so many ways, inevitable?

Banishing those stressful questions from her mind, Emma sank back into the couch, tucking her blanket around herself. Thankfully, she'd had the foresight to grab the TV remote before bundling up and was pleased to find that the signal reached even through the heavy fabric. She flicked through the channels, not really caring what came on, just needing something mindless. Eventually, she landed on a talk show that seemed asinine enough.

She hadn't realized she'd dozed off until the rattling of a doorknob stirred her. The sound, so reminiscent of the door to the concrete room, sent her into a panic. Still partially bound by the haze of sleep, the best plan her muddled brain could come up with was to flee. Shooting upright, she ripped the blanket away from her body as she prepared to run.

"It's okay," Beau called out as he hurried toward the front door. Emma paused, the tangled blanket slowing her retreat. Beau reached the door just as it cracked open and engaged in a hushed conversation with whoever was on the other side. Then, the door closed again, and Beau approached the couch tentatively.

"Hey." He knelt down until he was at eye level with Emma. "My brother is here to swap out some of his stuff, and he brought some supplies I asked for, too. I was hoping he could just sneak in and out while you slept, but since you're awake, would you like to meet him?"

Emma blinked, not quite alert enough to answer questions yet.

"Otherwise, you can hang out in my room or take a shower," Beau offered.

She took a moment to process. A shower *would* be nice, but somehow, she knew she wouldn't be able to fully relax into one knowing a stranger was roaming around the apartment.

"I'd like to meet him," she decided. "And then I'd like to shower afterward."

Beau nodded. "Great. I had Fletch bring me some of his girlfriend's clothes for you, so you can change into those after."

Emma's heart warmed at his thoughtfulness. "Okay, you can let him in now," she said as she extricated herself fully from the blanket.

Trotting back to the door, Beau welcomed his brother inside while Emma made her way into the kitchen and settled on a stool. She studied Fletcher as he walked in, his arms overflowing with bags. He was a bit taller than Beau, but leaner, and he looked to have a good ten or fifteen years on his brother. Fletcher's blond hair contrasted with Beau's dark-brown locks, and the thin, wire-framed glasses perched on his nose gave Fletcher a wise and refined look.

His eyebrows shot up as he took in her appearance, and Emma realized that from everything she'd heard of Beau's phone conversations, he had no idea what was going on except that Beau had a "situation." He probably hadn't expected to find a woman covered in bruises and wearing his brother's pajamas in their kitchen.

"Fletcher," Beau said, taking some of the bags from his grasp and placing them on the counter. "I'd like you to meet Emma. Emma, this is my brother Fletcher."

She immediately flinched when Fletcher stuck his hand out toward her. Upon realizing that he meant only to shake her hand, she hesitantly reached out her own.

"Nice to meet you," she said, shaking Fletcher's hand as limply as a dead fish.

"Good to meet you, too," he said politely as his gaze roved over Emma's bruised arms and face. She pulled her hand away to cross her arms, hoping to hide at least some of her injuries.

"Hey." Beau caught her attention, wielding one of the plastic grocery bags. "Here are those clothes I was talking about. Why don't you grab these and take your shower while Fletcher and I talk?"

Emma nodded, sensing her dismissal. Beau obviously didn't want her around while he explained the situation to his brother, but she was curious about what he had to say. Heading to the bathroom, she left the door slightly ajar and stood with her ear at the opening.

"What the fuck, man?" Beau growled. "I told you she doesn't like to be touched."

Huh. So he had said *something* to his brother about her.

Fletcher's voice came next. "Sorry, man. I didn't know that meant no shaking hands or anything. What's up with her?"

"She's just…a woman," Beau tried. "I bring women home all the time."

"Not women like her. She's covered head to toe in bruises."

"I know." Beau's voice was troubled, either because of Emma's injuries or because of his brother's curiosity.

"What the fuck is going on, Beau?"

Emma shrank back at the menace in Fletcher's voice.

There was a pregnant pause before Beau finally answered. "I did something last night that I probably shouldn't have."

"Okay…"

"I went after Mason."

"What?! Are you fucking kidding me?"

A heavy sigh. "No, I'm not."

"Did you go alone?"

"Yes."

"What the actual fuck, Beau? You could have been killed!" Fletcher roared.

"Quiet down!" Beau snapped. Then, in a lower voice, he added, "You know I had to do it. The police weren't getting anywhere on this case, so I had to take matters into my own hands."

"Why?" Fletcher asked. "Because of Sofia?"

"Yes, because of Sofia."

That was the first Emma was hearing of Sofia, and she tucked the information away in a back corner of her mind.

"But not just for revenge," Beau continued. "Also because I don't want anyone else to have to go through what I saw Diego go through."

Fletcher sighed. "And what you went through. You lost her, too, Beau."

"I know. But she was never mine to lose. I feel like I have to do this for D."

"So what happened? Did you find Mason?"

Another pause. "Not quite. I followed some intel I overheard at the station and went to the place last night, but instead of Mason, I found Emma."

"The woman?"

"Yes," Beau said impatiently. "She was all alone in this room made entirely of concrete, with only one blanket that was covered in blood. They tortured her, Fletch. I couldn't just leave her there."

"I know," Fletcher said. "You did the right thing. But what are you going to do with her now?"

Having the same question herself, Emma listened eagerly for Beau's answer.

"I honestly don't know," he replied. Okay…not the most helpful answer, but at least he wasn't planning to kick her out immediately. "She doesn't exactly seem rearing to go home. I'm just gonna let her stay here until we can get things figured out."

Relief coated Emma like a warm blanket. She had a lot to figure out, and it was so generous of Beau to allow her to stay with him while she did. She'd need to find a place to live, a way to make money, and do some serious rearranging of her life, but none of that could happen until certain people had been locked away forever.

"So, does this mean I'll be sleeping at Christa's for a while?" Fletcher asked.

"Do you mind?"

"No, man, that's fine. As long as it means you're going to catch that bastard Mason."

"Oh, I plan to," Beau said, the threat in his voice enough to convince anyone that he was capable of doing just that.

"When are you gonna tell Diego?"

Another heavy sigh from Beau. "I've been worried about that since the second this all went down. I'll call him soon. I just need to figure out what to say first. I really hope he'll team up with me to finish this thing."

"I have to say, Beau, I respect what you're doing, but I'm

not thrilled at the thought of you doing it without backup," Fletcher said. "You really need to let Diego in—sooner than later. I'd feel a lot better if you weren't working alone."

"Agreed. I'll have him over soon to explain everything," Beau promised.

"Good. Alright, well, I'm gonna grab some stuff and head to work for a few hours. Then I'll crash at Christa's and give you two your space."

"Thanks, dude," Beau said.

Assuming the conversation was over, Emma silently shifted the door shut and took her shower. Beau's conversation with Fletcher had only raised more questions. Who were Sofia and Diego? And what happened to them that would make Beau want revenge?

She obviously wasn't the only one keeping things close to her chest.

Afterward, she dug into the bag of clothes from Fletcher. It contained a couple of t-shirts and V-neck shirts, a pair of jeans, a pair of shorts, a bra that was thankfully close to the correct size, and an unopened pack of cotton panties.

It felt so good to finally have a bra again, and this one was lacier and more feminine than any Emma had ever owned before. She actually felt pretty for a moment as she clasped it behind her back. That was, until her sight set on the bruises dotting the swell of her breasts.

On a sigh, she pulled on a light-blue, cotton V-neck that covered the bulk of the bruises. Ripping open the pack of panties, she slid a pair on before stepping into the provided denim shorts. It probably wasn't really warm enough for them yet, but she didn't expect to be leaving the apartment, and she *had* shaved her legs, after all. Might as well show them off.

The outfit displayed her feminine figure much better than the bulky clothes Beau had given her. Emma twisted side to side in the bathroom mirror, inspecting herself. Ugly bruising was still visible in many spots, but the clothing went a long way toward making her feel more like an ordinary woman. It would be a long while before she truly felt like herself again, but every little bit helped.

5

As Emma entered the kitchen, Beau realized it was the first time he was seeing her as she must usually look. Her clean, light-blonde hair flowed around her head like a halo. The clothing she now wore suited her much better than his had, though he thought she'd looked sexy as hell in his clothes. The shorts showed off shapely legs and lots of smooth, silky-looking skin.

For some ridiculous reason, Beau was glad Fletcher had left and wasn't getting to see Emma the way she was right now. He didn't want another man looking at her, seeing her in this new light—not even his own brother, who was happily in a relationship.

Emma flashed him her sweet smile as she walked toward him. He scanned her body up and down, his gaze still drawn to her exposed legs. He was enjoying the view until he noticed a huge gash on her upper thigh.

"Come here." He motioned for Emma to walk over to him.

Her smile flipped into a frown as she tentatively stepped forward. "What's wrong?"

Beau pointed to the wound on her thigh. "That's what's wrong."

She looked down at the gash as if just noticing it for the first time. "Oh." She shrugged. "I avoided it while shaving last night. It's not bleeding anymore."

"Yeah, but you weren't able to clean it up well when you were in that building. It could get infected."

Her eyes bugged out. "I don't want to go to the hospital."

The raw fear in her expression tugged at Beau's heart. "I can clean it," he said. "Come, sit here, and I'll grab a first-aid kit."

Emma perched herself delicately on a barstool while he ran to the bathroom to grab supplies. When he returned to the kitchen, she was hugging her legs into her body and chewing on her bottom lip.

Placing his supplies on the counter, Beau coaxed Emma to free her legs so he could access the wound. "Relax, angel."

She cautiously straightened her legs, allowing her feet to rest on the ring around the bottom of the stool.

"I'm sorry, but I'm going to have to touch you to do a good job on this. Is that okay?" Beau asked, knowing the importance of consent after Emma's experience.

Still biting her lip, she gave him a quick nod.

"Tell me out loud," he said softly.

She released her lip from between her teeth and whispered, "Yes."

Pouring alcohol onto a gauze pad, he placed a gentle hand on Emma's thigh to hold it steady. She froze, her muscles tightening beneath his hand. He did his best not to squeeze or do anything to panic her, and after a few moments, she seemed to relax.

"This might sting a little," he warned as he pressed the solution-soaked gauze to her skin. Emma sucked in a breath. He could practically hear her teeth grinding together. Though her distress was obvious, she seemed to be doing her best not to outwardly display her pain.

"I'm sorry," Beau soothed as he continued cleaning the gash. As soon as he was satisfied, he removed the gauze pad and his hand from her leg. Emma released the breath she'd been holding, and he wondered if she was more relieved about the absence of the stinging or the absence of his hand.

"Almost done," he promised. After applying a healthy dollop of antibiotic cream, he tore open the bandage and stretched it over the gash, pressing it gently into place. "There," he said.

Emma relaxed her muscles and tucked her legs away under the bar. "Thank you. I didn't realize it was that bad."

"It's okay. I'm just glad I caught it."

Her lips tipped up slightly at the corners. "Me too."

Beau walked around the island to discard his supplies in the trash, trying not to focus on how twisted it was that he was actually a little grateful Emma's cut had given him an excuse to touch her skin, which was just as silky as he'd imagined it would be.

"Are you hungry again?" he asked, glancing at the clock. Her nap and shower had killed a couple of hours, and it was already time for lunch. He gestured to the bags still on the island. "Fletch brought some food for us. When you're feeling up to it, we'll take a trip to the store and get whatever clothes, food, or other things you need. But hopefully this can tide us over."

Emma chewed on her nail, clearly not eager to venture out into public yet. "What did he bring?"

Beau began pawing through the bags. "Come take a look, and we'll see what we want to eat."

She came to his side, peeking around his arm into the bags. "Mac and cheese?" she asked when she spotted a couple boxes of it.

The excited lilt to her voice had Beau chuckling. "You like mac and cheese?"

"I like anything with cheese," she replied, rifling through another bag before pulling out an item with a frown. "What's this?"

Beau glanced over to find the locking doorknob kit he'd requested from Fletcher. "A lock for my bedroom door," he explained. "I want you to be comfortable. You deserve a bed to sleep in."

Emma blinked, a myriad of emotions crossing her features. For a moment, he worried she was about to cry, but then a small smile touched her lips. "Thank you. That was really thoughtful."

He shrugged, as it seemed like such a small thing. "Sure. I'll install it after lunch."

Emma grabbed a box of mac and cheese with a grin that revealed a renewed sense of excitement. "Lunch should definitely come first."

❦

The rest of the day passed quickly with Emma mostly resting and Beau trying and failing to muster up the courage to call Diego. He knew he had to bring his friend up to speed, and soon, if they were going to have any hope of catching Mason. But the threat of the pain he would unearth by doing so held him back.

Installing the lock on his bedroom door had proven to be a good distraction. No matter how easy the box said something was supposed to be, it just never was, and the task chewed up a good couple of hours. Emma eagerly went to bed behind her new locked door at eight p.m. even after taking a couple of catnaps throughout the day. Beau stayed up for a few hours before going to bed himself.

At some point in the middle of the night, he was jolted

awake by a loud noise. He sat up halfway in bed, trying to determine the source. Something wasn't right. Rubbing one eye, he listened for the noise again, but silence reigned for the next few moments. Then, Emma's strained voice rang out.

"No!"

Leaping out of bed, once again only in his boxers, Beau sprinted to his bedroom. The fear in Emma's cry tightened his chest to the point of pain—or maybe that was the adrenaline coursing through his veins as he prepared to annihilate anyone or anything that was scaring her.

Just as he reached the door, she cried out again.

"Please don't! Stop it!"

"Damn it," he growled as he tried to turn the knob and met resistance. The lock. He'd put it there to make Emma feel safe, and now she was stuck in there, and she was terrified of something. *Or someone.*

Had Mason's men somehow found her? It couldn't be possible.

Beau's heart galloped as he took a few steps back, then rammed his entire body against the door. It weakened slightly—the lock he'd bought wasn't exactly state-of-the-art—and he tried again. The wood groaned but stayed intact. His heart was pounding, and sweat began to bead on his brow. He tried once more, putting all of his force into it this time. The door flew open as a blood-curdling scream sounded from his bed.

"Emma!" Beau shouted, bounding into the room. He scanned it quickly, looking for any signs of danger, but found none. There was no one in the room besides him and Emma, and she was in bed, asleep.

Ah. It dawned on him. She was having a nightmare. Some of the tension seeped from his body at the absence of any real danger, but seeing Emma in distress was enough to keep him on edge.

"Emma," Beau said, trying to wake her without startling

her. Sitting on the edge of the bed, he nudged her shoulder with his hand. "Wake up."

"Don't touch me! Please!" Emma pleaded as she tossed and turned.

"Emma!" Beau said, nudging her a little more forcefully. Tears streamed down her beautiful face as she continued to mumble incoherent words. Beau's heart twisted like a knife in his chest, and he shook her shoulder until her eyes popped open.

"Emma, it's okay. You're safe," he tried to reassure her, but she began scooting backward toward the edge of the bed, seeming eager to get out of his reach. Before she could fall over the edge, Beau reached out and wrapped an arm around her body, pulling her in close to him. Though he knew she didn't like to be touched, he just had to hold her, and she *had* tolerated his touch while he cared for her cut.

Planting both of her petite hands on Beau's chest, Emma tried to push him away. Her eyes were wild as she fought him, clearly not yet coherent. He only held onto her tighter.

"It's me," he said, rocking her gently. "It's Beau."

He saw the exact moment the realization dawned on her that she was in his bedroom, not that horrid concrete prison. The pressure of her hands against his chest slackened, and she sagged into him. "It's you," she repeated. "Beau."

"Yes," he replied softly.

She relaxed fully into his arms as her sobs continued.

"Okay, angel. It's alright," he whispered as he rubbed a soothing hand up and down her back. "It was just a nightmare."

Emma blubbered for a moment before finding her voice. "No," she sobbed. "It was real."

Goddamnit. Beau hugged her a little tighter. It was bad enough she'd had to go through that hell once, but now she had to relive it?

Hot tears hit his bare chest, and he ran his thumb gently

across Emma's cheeks to wipe them away. "You're with me. You're safe now," he soothed, continuing to stroke her and talk to her softly until the crying subsided.

Venturing closer toward the invisible line he'd been treading since he met her, Beau pressed a kiss to the top of her head—one so light it was possible she didn't even feel it through her veil of hair. He waited until her breathing evened out before looking down at her face. Her eyes were closed, those golden eyelashes fanning out over the tops of her cheeks, and her lips were parted in sleep. She made a soft noise and nuzzled her face further into his chest.

Though he knew Emma only dared to get so close to him because she was asleep, he longed for the day she would feel comfortable cuddling into him while conscious. He would do anything in his power to keep her from ever feeling uncomfortable, but he couldn't ignore his intrinsic pull toward her.

Looking down at Emma's slumbering figure, he realized he hadn't seen her so comfortable or content since he'd found her, and he only wished he could make her feel that way when she was awake.

6

Hot water sluiced over Emma's skin as she tried to shower away the embarrassment that clung to her like cobwebs. Not only had she woken Beau up with her screaming, but then she'd cried all over him and proceeded to fall asleep atop him, pinning him down so he couldn't even go back to his own bed. How mortifying.

The only upside was that she'd slept better than she had in quite some time. Beau's bed proved to be much more comfortable than the bathtub, but the security of his arms around her was what really did the trick. Beau was a pillar of strength, both in physical muscularity and the way he faced danger head on. When she was in his arms, Emma knew nothing could ever hurt her.

Beau probably thought she was a total wuss for losing it over a nightmare. It was silly that after everything she'd been through in the past few days, a simple dream had caused her to crumble. But it had just seemed *so real* while her mind was deep in slumber.

Little did Beau know that the nightmare had nothing to do with Mason or his men. No, the nightmare had been inspired by events from long ago, when she was just a girl. Her run-in with Mason had just caused old memories to resurface.

She knew she still had to finish that conversation with Beau. He wanted to know how those men had gotten her, and once he found out, he would have a million questions—ones that Emma didn't know if she had the strength to answer.

Dredging up her past was something she never did with anyone. She very rarely talked about her childhood because it was a time in her life that she was infinitely ashamed of. She'd been weak and cowardly, and in the end, that cowardice had led her to those awful men.

Emma prolonged getting ready as long as she could to avoid talking to Beau—shaving her legs again, even though it wasn't really necessary, and even going as far as to clean up her bikini line, which was even *more* unnecessary, considering no one would be seeing it. Once it became evident that the scalding water couldn't wash away her humiliation, she got out of the shower and spent a few long minutes styling her hair.

Once there was literally nothing else she could do to waste time in the bathroom, Emma dressed and headed for the kitchen. Beau was sitting at the island in gray sweatpants and a tank top that showed off his powerfully built arms. His big, bare feet rested on the ring around the bottom of the stool. A bowl of cereal and a newspaper were laid out in front of him.

Emma watched Beau silently for a moment, the small muscles in his arm flexing as he raised the spoon to his mouth and slurped up a spoonful of cereal and milk. Keeping her arms crossed tightly over her chest, she walked into the room and greeted him quietly.

"Hey."

Beau looked over and wiped away the milk mustache forming on his upper lip. His eyes were soft with a hint of pity that she despised.

"I'm really sorry about last night," she murmured. "I don't know what came over me."

His lips curved into a frown as he turned on his stool to face her. "You have nothing to apologize for."

Rubbing her hands over her upper arms, Emma shrugged. "I feel bad that I woke you up and cried all over you." She winced at the memory.

Beau shook it off easily, waving his hand through the air. "It's no big deal. Honestly, I feel bad that I broke your door."

Emma couldn't help the narrow grin that touched her lips. She'd woken up to find Beau's room absolutely destroyed, with the door kicked in and things strewn all over the place as a result of her thrashing and flailing.

"I appreciate your understanding," she said, then busied herself with pouring a bowl of cereal. His kindness was appreciated, but it didn't make her feel any less embarrassed. Walking carefully to the island with her bowl of cereal, she perched herself on a stool beside Beau. "Thank you for everything, actually. You've gone above and beyond for me."

Beau smiled over at her, baring a set of perfect pearly whites. "I'm just glad you're comfortable." His gaze roamed down to her leg resting right beside his own. He visually inspected the bandaged area, then caught her eye as if asking permission to touch it. She gave him a short nod of approval.

"Let's take this bandage off and see how that gash is doing," he said. Reaching over for the first-aid kit on the counter, he pulled out some supplies, then surprised Emma by gently lifting her leg into his lap.

She tensed momentarily—startled but not fearful. Beau had been so careful with her, but after holding her all night, of course he felt more relaxed about touching her. And honestly, it didn't bother her the way she would have expected it to.

He ran a big hand over the bandaged area, and Emma found herself exceedingly grateful that she'd shaved. Her legs may have been pale and bruised, but at least they weren't hairy.

Gently peeling the bandage off, Beau apologized when it pulled at her raw skin. "No excess swelling or redness, so it's probably not infected," he said after a thorough inspection.

Emma sighed with relief. "Thank God."

"Yes," Beau agreed. "I'll just put a new bandage on. Once it's a little less raw, we can expose it to the air so it'll scab over, but I don't want to risk anything getting into it while it's still open." Expertly applying antibacterial ointment to the bandage, he smoothed it over the wound. "All set." He ran his hand over her creamy skin one last time before placing her leg back down.

Hooking her feet over the rim of the stool, Emma was proud that she didn't so much as flinch or tense at the contact. "Thank you for taking such good care of me," she said.

Beau smiled warmly at her. "It's my pleasure," he said as he got up to discard the used bandage.

She continued eating her cereal and glanced at the newspaper Beau had been reading before she joined him. "Anything exciting going on in the world?"

He returned to his seat and ran a hand over his short hair. "Not really."

Emma swallowed her current bite. "Nothing more exciting than what's going on in my world, huh?"

His eyebrows rose slightly before he let out a surprised chuckle. "Yeah, I guess so."

She nodded and took another bite of her cereal.

"Seriously, though," Beau said. "You can't tell me this isn't the wildest thing that's ever happened in your life."

"I guess so." Emma shrugged. "Being taken by human traffickers, then rescued by a vigilante ex-cop isn't quite my run-of-the-mill week."

"I wouldn't think so."

Fortifying herself with a deep breath, Emma decided it

was as good a time as ever to continue their unfinished conversation. "My life hasn't exactly been normal up until now, though."

Beau's eyebrows quirked up. "No?"

His surprise wasn't shocking. Emma was sure that, to him, she looked like the innocent girl next door. Most people who met her assumed she was. "No. Yesterday, you asked me how those men got me. The truth is that they didn't abduct me. I was given to them."

Beau's eyes widened, a spoonful of milk and cereal frozen halfway to his mouth like something out of a comic strip. "What?"

"I was *given* to those men," Emma repeated. "Well, sold to them." Then, she dropped the real bomb. "By my father."

Beau's spoon clattered into the bowl, splashing milk onto the counter between them. "Your father?"

She nodded solemnly. "Yes. One day last week, Earl said he was taking me out to lunch, but instead of driving me to a restaurant, he drove me to that abandoned warehouse."

"But…why?" Beau asked. His bewilderment was the only natural feeling to follow a confession like that, but to Emma, it was hardly a surprise that her father had sold her to human traffickers.

"How do I explain?" she mused, a sad smile shaping her lips. "My father has been an addict for as long as I can remember. The drug addiction came first. Then the gambling one. He had to pay for the drugs somehow, right? He spent all day getting high and all night gambling to get the money for his next fix. He's a good gambler—if you can consider a cheater good." Emma couldn't help but roll her eyes. "Only, every once in a while, his strategies didn't quite work out. Those nights, he would come home upset. And by upset, I mean drunk and boisterous." She shivered involuntarily, thinking back to those godawful nights when her father came home wasted. Revulsion crawled over her like a line of ants marching down her spine. "He would be so mad—swearing and throwing things. And if I accidentally found myself in his warpath, there was no telling what he might do. He hit me more times than I can count."

Beau's hand tightened around the glass he was holding, his knuckles turning white with the effort. A muscle in his jaw ticked as Emma went on.

"He was unpredictable. On a good night, he was done after a single slap. On a bad one… I might walk away looking like this." She gestured to the bruises dotting her arm. "I missed so many days of school because I couldn't go looking like I'd been beaten up. But no one ever questioned it."

"How long?" Beau snarled.

Her gaze snapped to his. "What?"

"How long did this go on for?"

Her eyes turned toward the ceiling. "As long as I can remember."

The glass in Beau's hand shattered, and Emma jumped back as shards flew across the kitchen island. She watched with wide eyes as Beau took a deep breath before rising from his stool to grab a dish towel.

"Fuck," he ground out as he started sweeping up the shards.

"I can hel—"

"Go sit in the living room," he said sharply.

Emma shrank back at the malice in his tone, though she knew it wasn't directed toward her.

Beau seemed to notice, and his voice softened as he added, "Please. I'll be right in."

She turned and retreated to the living room, propping herself on the couch as she waited for Beau to join her. When he entered the room, his chocolaty brown eyes were full of pity for the second time that morning. God, she hated that look. She'd known it was coming, but that didn't make it any less unwelcome.

A New Beau

He sat on the couch a few feet down from her, opening his mouth then snapping it shut before resting his chin on his fists. Since he didn't seem to be able to speak, she swallowed her own discomfort and did the talking.

"I was a coward," she said softly. "I never told anyone he was hurting me, and I didn't know how to make it stop. Earl fully supported me. He paid for everything for my entire life, and he was so controlling. He never let me get a job or keep money of my own. He didn't let me go to college. He made me entirely reliant on him so he could control my every move, and he hurt me if I ever stepped out of line. So, I just let it go on." Emma stared down at her feet, head bowing under the weight of her shame. She had spent so many years allowing her father to control her life and abuse her without ever fighting back.

"I was starting to come up with a plan to try and get away," she said, talking toward the ground. "I was going to get a job at the local library. I already spent so much time there that I figured Earl wouldn't notice if I started working there a few hours a week. I was going to save every penny, and when I had enough, I was going to run away. But I was so scared to apply for the library job because I knew if Earl found out, he'd be pissed and take it out on me. So, I never got very far with that plan." She heaved a sigh, wishing with all her might that she'd had the courage to go forward with that idea, despite the potential consequences. "No, I just let him continue to use me and control me like some sort of spineless rag doll."

Beau raised two fingers to Emma's chin and tipped her head up, forcing her to hold his gaze. "Do not for one second blame yourself, Emma. You were a victim. And now you're a survivor. You were so brave, angel."

She mashed her lips together, trying to contain the deluge of oncoming tears. "But I let things go on for so long. The human traffickers…it was all my fault, Beau. I've been letting him hurt me my whole life. When he asked me to go to lunch with him last week, I should have known better. But I knew he would get mad if I turned him down, and I didn't want him to be mad at me. He's responsible for my livelihood. So, I went with him. It was my fault I ended up there."

"It was not your fault." Beau released her chin and placed one big palm on her cheek. Emma sniffled, and he swiped away a stray tear with his thumb. "You didn't like what was happening to you, and you were trying your best to find a safe way to stop it. You did what you had to do to survive."

"Thank you," Emma whispered, closing her eyes briefly and settling her cheek into his touch. Now he knew the whole story, and he *still* insisted she was strong. Some of the heaviness in her chest floated away like a cloud. When she opened her eyes, Beau tucked an errant lock of hair behind her ear. "Thank you for listening."

He ran a thumb over her cheek, then dropped his hand. "Of course, angel."

"Does that help your case at all?" she asked hopefully.

He nodded. "It actually explains some of the missing pieces. I couldn't figure out why the men were keeping you in their headquarters. They usually keep women in a separate building. They don't like to mix work and play, as they say. But since you were sold to them by your dad, not abducted and shipped here, they probably didn't have anywhere else to put you yet. And they've definitely moved their headquarters by now, but it shouldn't be too hard to find the new one. They tend to follow certain patterns in their behavior—abandoned warehouses and office buildings are their style." He scratched his chin. "I really need to talk all this through with my partner…uh, former partner, Diego. I've been meaning to call him, but I haven't gotten around to it."

Emma released a self-deprecating laugh. "Sorry, I've been taking up so much of your time."

"No, it's not that." Beau rubbed the back of his neck. "I've kind of been avoiding it. But I'll give him a call this week and see if he can come over to work on the case, if you're okay with that?"

Emma nodded. If Beau trusted Diego, then she ought to as well. And if he could help catch the horrible men who'd held her captive, then any discomfort she might feel about having another man in the apartment would be well worth it.

7

Heading into the privacy of his bedroom, Beau knocked the door shut with his foot. Emma was exhausted after a short outing to the local grocery store to pick up more food. She'd spent most of the time glued to his side, peeking behind them to make sure no one was following. A few times, Beau questioned if he should have pushed her to get out of the apartment, but the whole trip had been worth it to see her eyes light up in the snack aisle.

She'd plucked fudge-striped cookies, pretzel rods, and microwave popcorn off the shelves, filling her arms before turning to him with a guilty grin. "Mind if we get a few snacks?" she'd asked.

Without hesitation, he had taken the food from her arms, placed it in the cart, and grabbed a second box of each item she'd picked. "Always get two of your favorites," he said, his heart giving a little kick at her resulting smile.

Emma had crashed as soon as they returned home, and he'd left her resting on the couch so he could finally do what he'd been putting off for days. Taking a seat on the edge of his bed, he hit Diego's number in his phone.

"Hello?" his friend said after the second ring.

Beau couldn't help but smile at the familiar rasp of his voice. "Hey, D. Good to hear your voice."

"You too, man," Diego replied, and Beau was grateful for his warmth. After what went down with Sofia, Diego easily could have turned on him.

"How's Isabella?" Beau asked about his wife to ease into the conversation. They were so madly in love there was no way talking about her wouldn't lighten things up.

"She's great." Diego sighed. "But she worries about me too much. And she works too hard taking care of me."

"She's a good woman."

"Yes," Diego replied fondly, and for a fleeting moment, Beau imagined what it would be like to be that in love. It would be nice—having a woman to come home to, to care for, and to have take care of you. A shiver pricked at his skin. *Nah.* He didn't need anyone to care for him.

"Listen, D, we've gotta talk."

"*Si, hermano,* we do. You had your last shift, right?"

"Yeah," Beau replied. "But I still have one more case to finish."

There was a short pause. "What are you talking about?"

Beau's foot tapped rhythmically against the floor. "I'm working on the human-trafficking case myself. The precinct is doing jack shit, so I've decided to take things into my own hands. I collected as much information as I could before I left."

"Hang on a second, you're chasing the traffickers yourself?" Diego said, his voice rising. "Without backup? Are you shitting me?"

"That's why I called you," Beau explained patiently. "I've taken this as far as I can alone, and I'm going to need your help."

"Have you made any progress?"

Taking Diego's curiosity as a good sign, he rose from the bed and began pacing around the small room. "Yeah, actually.

A few nights ago, I raided this abandoned warehouse that was rumored to be the ring's headquarters. Turned out it was, but before I could find Mason, I found a victim. A woman—all bruised and beaten."

"A woman? In the headquarters?" Diego's disbelief mirrored his own.

"Yeah. I'll explain, but…I brought her home with me."

Another pause. Diego was sharp and typically quick on the uptake, but Beau *was* throwing a lot at him.

"She's there with you now?" Diego asked.

"Yeah. She's been staying with me and healing for the past few days."

There was a heavy pause. "How is she?"

Beau chose his next words carefully, knowing Diego would associate Emma with Sofia, and that would make hearing about her condition all the more difficult.

"She's…hanging in there. She's covered in bruises and pretty panicky at any physical touch or sign of violence, but she's so strong, D, and she's getting better every day."

"Fuck," Diego muttered. "Have you been able to talk to her about what happened? Get any information?"

Beau let loose a sigh. "Yeah, and it's really fucked up. Her *father* sold her to the traffickers. That's why they were keeping her at their headquarters and not in their usual separate area."

Diego sucked in a breath but didn't speak. Beau forged on.

"She was held captive for four days by Mason and three of his men. They didn't give her any place to sleep or much food. They beat her up and verbally abused her. They would have done worse, but she had her period, and that pissed them off." He paused as he heard the telltale shallow breaths that indicated Diego was beginning to cry. "I'm so sorry," Beau said softly into the phone.

"Don't apologize for telling me the truth," Diego said

through his tears. "I need to hear this. It just fires me right back up about destroying these men."

Beau grinned slightly at his friend's ferocity. "I'm glad to hear that, because I'm going to need your help. Can you come over tomorrow to help me put the case together?"

Diego agreed, and after a few more minutes of discussing logistics, the two men hung up.

Flopping down on the bed, Beau ran a hand wearily over his face. The past few days had been nothing short of bizarre. Although, things *had* been feeling off ever since Diego went on leave.

Diego had been his partner ever since they graduated from the academy together, and Beau had hated working without him. Roger had been only tolerable as his partner. He was too chatty, and Beau had spent a good deal of time trying to avoid him by hiding in different places throughout the precinct. That avoidance, though, was what had led him to be in the right place at the right time to overhear some detectives talking. Okay, and maybe he'd been eavesdropping a little bit, too.

Detectives Isaac Williams and Sean Reed were cagey bastards, always whispering in dark corners, and the only way Beau was going to overhear anything they said was to snoop a little. They both worked in the precinct's Special Victim's Unit, which had been partnered with the FBI for months trying to catch Mason and his disgusting human-trafficking ring. Beau himself hadn't had much interest in the case until six weeks ago when everything changed.

Heaving a sigh, he forced himself up off the bed. Just as he'd had to prepare Diego to meet Emma, he had to prepare Emma to meet Diego. She'd been so honest with him that morning; it was time for him to be honest with her, too.

Heading to the living room, he found Emma huddled in one corner of the couch, all wrapped up in a fuzzy blanket. It seemed like she was always wrapping herself up and making herself as small as possible, as if maybe she could just disappear altogether in a puff of smoke.

Glancing at the TV, he noted the outrageous reality show she'd been watching. "*The Kardashians?* Really?" he asked.

Emma giggled—a light, tinkling sound. "You know about this show?"

"Of course I know about it. Everyone knows the Kardashians."

"Oh." Emma frowned, and Beau immediately regretted his cavalier comment. "I'd never heard of them before."

Feeling like a total dick, he tried to walk things back. "Don't watch much TV? That's nice. I watch way too much."

With a shrug, Emma pulled the blanket tighter around herself. "My dad didn't pay for anything beyond basic cable. I don't know a lot about pop culture."

Beau took a seat beside her on the couch. "Well, I pay for way more trash channels than I should, so feel free to catch up while you're here."

She treated him to a heartbreaking grin that only made him feel worse about the harrowing story he was about to tell her.

"Listen," he began gently. "Diego is going to come over tomorrow to help me with the case, but I need you to know some things before you meet him."

"Okay…" Emma said, and Beau could practically see the little wheels in her head turning.

He cleared his throat before explaining. "As I told you, Diego was my partner on the force. He's currently on an extended leave because his sister, Sofia, was taken by Mason's men, too…except, she didn't make it out."

Emma gasped. "What?"

Beau inhaled deeply in an attempt to stay calm as he said the next part. "Six weeks ago, Sofia was visiting family in Mexico when Mason's men grabbed her. They shipped her, along with eleven other women, to the States, where they were to be sold off. Unfortunately, the shipping container was sealed tight and took longer than expected to arrive. All twelve women suffocated to death on the journey."

Emma let out another strangled gasp, and her eyes glossed over with unshed tears. Beau longed to reach out and comfort her, but he knew that touching her might inadvertently make it worse. Waiting until reality sunk in, he watched a wave of emotions wash over her features before settling into grief.

After a moment, she wiped her face with the back of her hand and said in her sweet voice, "That's awful. They must have been so scared."

Beau shook his head. "I can only imagine. I'm sorry. I know this must be upsetting for you to hear, but I wanted you to know before you met Diego. He's obviously been wrecked by this whole thing, and it's going to be hard for him to see you…especially looking like"—he gestured to the bruises on the arm peeking out from beneath her blanket—"that."

Emma frowned down at her arm, studying the dark spots. "You think I'll remind him of his sister."

"I *know* you will," Beau corrected. "Diego saw her and the other women in the shipping container when it arrived here. He wasn't allowed on the case, but he nosed his way in anyway." He swallowed the lump clogging his throat. "When they opened up that container, the women were…well, they didn't look good."

Emma's face turned sheet white as she gripped the edge of the couch. "Oh."

Beau leaned toward her, ready to stabilize her if she keeled over. "You okay?"

"Yeah," Emma said faintly. "I just…I just realized how close I came to meeting the same fate."

His stomach turned at the thought, and he scrubbed a hand over his face. "I'm glad as fuck that you didn't."

She peeked up at him through long, golden eyelashes. "Me too."

"I'm going to do everything I can to catch those bastards, Emma," he promised, physically restraining himself from touching her by clasping his hands together. "And I'm not going to let anything happen to you in the meantime. You can trust me. I'll protect you."

Emma met his gaze, nodding silently. He waited a few moments as she regained color in her face.

"Diego feels like it's his fault Sofia died," Beau added. "He thinks he should have been able to track the shipping container sooner, or stop her from going to Mexico in the first place, or he should have somehow prevented her capture. But really, no one would have done anything differently from him."

Plus, Beau knew Diego definitely wasn't to blame, because it was *his* fault Sofia had died.

"Diego shouldn't feel that way," Emma said, her voice tinged with indignation. "He did everything he could."

"Yes, he did," Beau said, smiling faintly at her fervor. Tiny as she was and wrapped up in a blanket like a burrito, Emma hardly constituted a threat. She was like a Chihuahua baring its sharp little teeth and barking at all the bigger dogs. "I'm really glad that I've looped him in, and he'll be able to help me now."

"You're a really great friend," Emma said, and her compliment warmed Beau more than it should have.

"Not that great," he muttered. "Anyway, I wanted you to know all this before he comes over. Over the next few days, we'll be going over all the information I've collected so far and potentially going out to get more. We'll do it like a real investigation, only without all the red tape."

"I'll do anything I can to help you," Emma said. "For myself, Sofia, Diego, and you, Beau. You saved my life. You and Diego are both heroes already. But God, would I love for Mason to be behind bars. I don't want any other women to have to go through what I did—or worse."

Beau shook his head, in awe of Emma's strength. He'd been picturing her as this fragile little flower, and yet here she was, so ready to fight.

"That's exactly what I want, too," he agreed. Mason behind bars would be the best thing to happen to this planet in a long, long time. "We're going to get him, Emma. I promise."

8

Diego Sanchez was a handsome, thirty-something, Latino man. His charming accent was somewhat thick, but he was easy enough to understand. His short, dark-brown hair matched his very dark, very sad brown eyes. Emma had been nervous to meet him—worried about upsetting him or bringing up bad memories—but while Diego had obviously been troubled by her appearance, he also seemed to find a sense of hope in her survival.

"*Dios mio.*" Diego blessed himself with one hand after Emma finished telling him about her time in captivity. "Thank God you got out."

"Yes, thank God for Beau," Emma said. He shifted in his seat beside her and placed a hand on the back of her chair.

"We've got to catch this bastard," Diego muttered as he wiped away a few stray tears.

"Yes," Beau agreed. "I'm glad you're in, because I don't think I can do this without you."

Diego shook his head fervently. "You don't have to. I'm in this fight with you. And I'm *ready* to fight," he said.

Beau stuck out his hand, and the two engaged in some sort of complicated bro-handshake. Beau had told Emma that he and Diego had been partners and friends ever since graduating from the academy together. From what she could see, they were even more like brothers.

Diego turned to her after the last fist-bump-high-five combo of the handshake. "Thank you for helping us, Emma. I know you've been through a lot, and you are invaluable to this investigation."

"I'm happy to help," she said. "No one should have to go through what I went through, and especially not what Sofia went through."

Diego closed his eyes for a long moment. "Is there anything else you can remember? Anything at all that might help us find Mason again? I'm sure he's long gone from that building now that he knows someone was onto him."

"I'm sorry. I never really heard anything important. The men who came into my room mostly talked about women. Me, and I guess other ones they've had."

"Did they say anything about new women?" Beau asked. "Ones they had gotten recently or ones who were coming in soon?"

"Hmm…" Emma tried to think back to every detail of the conversations she'd overheard. "They did say something about new girls coming in. They said even if I turned out to be a dud, it would be okay because they had new girls on the way."

"Assholes," Beau snarled.

"Any idea when they were coming in?" Diego asked.

"Not sure…but definitely in the near future. The men said they were clearing out some old rooms for them."

Beau looked toward Diego. "We've got to sort through the paperwork I've collected A.S.A.P. If the police weren't able to catch the last shipment in time, there's no way they'll catch this one."

Diego hung his head. "I know. What the hell is wrong with them? They drag their feet on every lead!"

"That's why I had to take matters into my own hands,"

Beau said, motioning to the three of them as they sat at the table. "No one else has the motivation that we do. If the police aren't going to give this case their all, then we'll have to."

"When do we start?" Diego asked.

"I have all the stuff I've collected so far right here." Beau pointed to a bulging backpack. "But I'd like to take one more quick spin around the station to gather any updated information, and then we can put it all together."

"Won't that look a little suspicious—you snooping around the station just days after you quit your job?" Diego asked.

Beau shrugged nonchalantly. "I'll tell them I forgot something in my locker." His confidence bordered on cocky, but somehow, Emma knew that he'd be able to get away with it.

As the men planned their next get-together to sort through all the evidence, her stomach let out a distinctly unladylike growl. She quickly covered it with her hand, not that it did anything to quell the sound.

Beau's eyebrows rose. "Hungry?"

She shrugged. "A little," she lied. Really, she was starving, but she knew if she said that to Beau, he would feel bad for forgetting to feed her for so long.

"How about we order some takeout. You in, Sanchez?"

"Sure," Diego said. "Just let me tell Isabella I'm eating here."

"His wife," Beau explained as he rifled through a drawer of menus. "What do you think about Chinese?"

"I don't know." Emma shrugged noncommittally. "I've never had it."

"What?" came the two men's voices in unison. They both stopped what they were doing and turned to look at her. Beau's hand remained deep in a pile of paper menus while Diego's finger hovered above the button to call his wife.

Emma's cheeks blushed bright red. "I'm not very...worldly," she admitted. Beau knew all about her unique childhood, while they had only told Diego the basics.

"Well, you haven't lived until you've experienced Chef Chang's," Beau said seriously. "Best egg rolls in Boston."

"Put me down for some of those, then. I'll have whatever you're having."

The men went back to what they'd been doing, and Beau ordered them a veritable feast of egg rolls, lo mein, pork fried rice, sweet and sour chicken, dumplings, crab rangoons, and fried wontons.

They all laughed as they attempted to eat their meals solely with chopsticks. When Emma failed to wrangle a dumpling for the third time, Beau offered to help show her how to use the chopsticks. She agreed, her heart thudding as his warm palm covered her hand.

"Like this," he said as he showed her how to pinch her fingers together over the chopsticks and pick up her food. "There you go!" he exclaimed as she shoved a dumpling into her mouth.

Emma giggled as she chewed, and Beau and Diego both clapped politely at her accomplishment. The delicious meal was topped off with fortune cookies that had little quotes in them. The whole meal was so fun, and Emma couldn't believe she'd never experienced it before.

"*Something wonderful is about to happen,*" Beau said, reading his fortune-cookie quote. "I hope that's a good omen about catching Mason."

Emma snorted as she read hers. "*There is love in your near future.* I don't know, Beau. These don't seem very accurate."

"Why not? You could have love in your near future."

"You think I'm gonna be dating anytime in my near future?"

"Maybe not, but love can show up in even the most unexpected ways. Just ask Diego." Beau chuckled, and Diego joined him, his hearty laughter warming Emma's heart after he'd been so somber during their earlier conversation.

She was unable to help her smile at their contagious laughter. "What is it?"

"I met my wife at a strip club," Diego admitted. "I never go to those kinds of places, but I was working an undercover case. Isabella was tending bar. She was still illegal at the time, and it was the only place that would hire her. We ended up talking all night and bonding over our mutual disgust of the place. The rest is history. We've been married for five years now."

"Good for you. Congratulations," Emma said with a warm smile, glad that Diego had someone special to him to support him through such difficult times.

"Speaking of my wife, I'd better get going. She likes to get to bed early, but she won't fall asleep without a goodnight kiss," Diego said with a wink.

"Pussy," Beau said, disguising the word as a cough.

Diego slapped Beau's chest. "Call me what you want, but at least I have a woman to keep me warm at night."

"Touché." Beau laughed.

The men did their special handshake again, and Emma said goodbye to Diego, actually surprising herself by wrapping him up in a big hug before he left. Despite being a large, muscular, and potentially lethal man, she intuitively knew he would never do anything to hurt her. They were connected by something bigger than themselves—something that most people could never even imagine. Something so horrible and heartbreaking that it should have broken them, but it didn't tear them down, because they wouldn't let it. They had vowed to fight back, and that was exactly what they were going to do.

As Emma headed off to bed, it dawned on her that she had just experienced one of the most fun nights she'd had in a long time—possibly ever—mere days after being rescued from a human-trafficking ring. She had been able to actually laugh, enjoy her meal, and even make a new friend, and she owed it all to Beau. He had saved her and continued to save her in even the littlest ways, from paying for her new clothes to teaching her how to use chopsticks. He'd even put that lock on the bedroom door.

Despite the abhorrent circumstances that had led to their meeting, Beau coming into her life had been nothing short of a blessing.

9

"Plain or chocolate chip?" Beau asked as he held up two bags of frozen bagels.

"Definitely chocolate chip," Emma replied.

He quirked a brow. "Why is that a definite?"

"Because," she said, plucking a bagel from the chocolate chip bag and bypassing Beau's massive body to pop it in the toaster. "Chocolate makes everything better."

"Chocolate and cheese, huh?" he asked, his lips lifting in a wry grin.

Emma grinned. "*Anything* sweet and cheese," she corrected. She was feeling lighter after a few good nights of sleep. Despite having her usual nightmares, they had been far less intense, and she'd woken herself up before becoming agitated enough to awaken Beau.

"Ah, I see." He chose a plain bagel, placing it on the counter before putting the rest away in the freezer. Then, he leaned against the fridge, his arms crossed. "So, I was thinking I would go into the station today. Diego and I have exhausted all the information I've gotten so far, and I want to collect data on all the abandoned buildings in a ten-mile radius. Mason and his men probably won't be going too far."

Emma shot him a quizzical look. "You can do that?"

"Absolutely," he boasted in that arrogant yet endearing way of his. Beau's self-confidence was actually kind of sexy.

The thought surprised Emma as it poked through her carefully constructed walls. She hadn't had legitimate sexual feelings for a real man in, well, forever. Her father had given her a pretty skewed idea of what relationships were like, and she'd never had a model of what love was supposed to look like. Her mother had never been in the picture.

Emma's only exposure to healthy relationships came exclusively in the form of her beloved romance novels. She loved all sorts of books, from the classics to the occasional thriller, but romance had always been her genre of choice. Her room was full of beat-up mass-market paperbacks she'd thrifted and read multiple times over. They may have been fictional, but they satisfied that primal craving she'd never been able to allow herself to explore with another human. Sure, she found ways to pleasure herself in the comfort of her own bed at night, alone, but the thought of an actual man touching her usually made her feel like her throat was closing up.

Beau had touched her many times now, and it had always been pleasant enough—actually, *more* than pleasant. His hands had become a source of safety and healing, and she was beginning to enjoy the feeling of his hands on her. Crave it, even.

His voice pulled her from her straying thoughts. "Hopefully I'll be able to get a lead on where the headquarters may be, or when a new shipment of women may be coming in."

Emma's brows rose. "You think you'll be able to get information without being caught?"

Beau removed her bagel from the toaster, replacing it with his own. Grabbing a plate from the cabinet, he placed the perfectly toasted chocolate chip bagel on a plate and handed it to Emma along with the butter container. Something in her heart tugged at the notion that he knew how she liked her bagels.

"I should be able to," he said. "I asked a buddy of mine to take me in as his guest, claiming I had a couple people that I still needed to say goodbye to. So, no one should question it if I'm wandering around a bit, and there's always so much going on that I don't think anyone will notice me printing out a few documents."

Emma spread butter over her bagel, thinking about how difficult it would be for him to gain access to the station again if he didn't find anything helpful today. "I hope you're able to get a lead on something."

"Me too," Beau said, his emphatic declaration emphasized by his bagel popping up in the toaster. "Because I'm not leaving there without one."

They moved to the kitchen island to enjoy their breakfasts, eating in comfortable silence. Beau scarfed his entire bagel down in the time it took Emma to get a quarter of the way through hers.

"I'll leave around noon," he said, glancing toward the clock on the oven. "I asked Fletcher to come stay with you. He's a teacher, but the kids have a half day today, so he said he could stay for the afternoon."

Inside, Emma was relieved that she wasn't going to be left alone, but aloud she said, "You don't have to wait for him to come home. You can leave whenever you want to."

Beau looked over at her with a frown. "I'm not going to leave you here alone."

"It's not like Mason's men are going to be able to find me, right?" she asked, hoping like hell that was true. "They have no way of knowing where I am."

"No, probably not. But I'm not taking any chances," Beau insisted. "Besides, I don't want you to be alone. You've been through a traumatic experience."

Emma looked down at her fingernails. When she looked back up at Beau, he cocked an eyebrow.

"Do you want to be left alone?"

"Not really." She laughed nervously. "I just don't want to be a burden."

"Oh, Emma." Beau sighed. "You are not a burden. And you have to be honest with me about what you need. Don't lie just because you think you have to."

She was so used to backing into the shadows and saying whatever it took to be the least burdensome. It was difficult to ignore that instinct. "Okay," she conceded.

"I'm serious. I want to give you what you need, but you have to tell me what that is. Never lie to me."

"Okay," she agreed once again.

"Good." Beau slapped his hand on the table as if he was striking a gavel. "Now I have to shower and get ready so I can go down to the station and kick some ass."

"Kick some ass…covertly," she reminded him.

"Right." Beau winked, and Emma's heart did a funny fluttering that she'd never felt before—at least, not outside of a romance novel.

※

Fletcher showed up at noon as expected. Emma had curled herself up on an armchair and was reading a book she'd found on the bookshelf—*To Kill a Mockingbird*. Not one of her beloved romances, but she'd read it before and always loved it. Coming back to it felt like wrapping herself in a warm, cozy blanket, which she had also done literally.

Beau welcomed Fletcher, and they spoke quietly in the doorway for a few moments before Fletcher came fully inside. He headed straight to his bedroom with a bag, probably dropping off or picking up more stuff.

Beau came over to where Emma was sitting and knelt down beside her. "I've gotta go," he said. "Fletch is gonna hang out with you for a few hours, and I'll be back as soon as I can."

"Okay." Emma smiled as he gave her a gentle pat on the arm, then headed out the door.

Fletcher reemerged after a few moments and took a seat on the couch. He crossed his legs, then uncrossed them, rubbing his hands down his thighs. He looked around the room once, then twice, before settling his gaze on the television that wasn't even on.

Noting his discomfort, Emma placed her book on the end table and said, "I'm sorry about this. I know babysitting me is probably the last thing you want to be doing."

Fletcher sighed and relaxed his rigid body. "I really don't mind," he said. "I just don't quite know what to say to you. Beau told me a little about what happened, and I don't want to offend you or scare you or anything."

"It's okay, Fletcher. Just treat me like any other woman your brother would bring home."

Fletcher smirked. "Any other woman my brother would bring home wouldn't be reading Harper Lee in her spare time."

Emma glanced at the book beside her. Reading had always been a favorite pastime of hers. It provided a much-needed escape and allowed her to experience the world in some capacity. The women Beau brought home were likely the type that had no trouble experiencing the world for themselves. A man as virile as him would probably go for women who were just as bold—in other words, nothing like her.

"I love the classics," she remarked.

"Ah, a woman after my own heart." Fletcher grinned. "I can never quite choose a favorite, though. Gatsby's exciting and mysterious, but I really have a soft spot for Holden

Caulfield. He's the quintessential teenager, with all the angst and the rebellion. Salinger's brilliant."

Emma stared at Fletcher, impressed by his knowledge of literature. She'd spent a lot of time reading growing up but had never had anyone to discuss books with. Kids her age were more interested in going to the movies, shopping at the mall, and drinking at parties. All things she couldn't do because her father wouldn't let her leave the house, except to go to school.

She relaxed a bit more into the couch. "I'm in a similar predicament. *To Kill a Mockingbird* was my number one until they released *Go Set a Watchman*. Part of my love for the original was that it was her only published work. It made it that much more magical. Plus, the Atticus Finch in *Watchman* is *not* the Atticus Finch I grew up loving. So, now I'm leaning toward *Pride and Prejudice*. It's a tried-and-true classic. You can't go wrong."

"Come *on*." Fletcher groaned comically. "Don't tell me you fell for that Mr. Darcy crap. He was such a douchebag."

"But he shows that people can change! He's such a good guy by the end."

"But at the beginning? *Ugh*. He was insufferable."

Emma giggled. "Okay. You're right." She pulled her legs up onto the couch, tucking her feet beneath herself. "How did you come to love books so much? I'm getting the feeling that Beau doesn't share that trait with you."

"Not so much," Fletcher agreed. "My father was a huge reader. When I was a kid, he read to me every night, and when I got old enough, we would read the same books and discuss them. That's where I got my love of literature." His gaze dipped to the floor. "He passed away when I was fourteen. Beau was only two, so he never got to experience books the way I did."

She sucked in small gasp. "Wow. I'm so sorry, Fletcher. That must have been tough."

"It was. But I'm grateful I got to know him for fourteen years, even though it wasn't nearly long enough. I feel sorry for my younger brothers that they never really got to know him."

"And they never learned to love to read."

"Exactly." Fletcher's melancholy expression dissolved, a small grin taking its place. "That's why I became a teacher. I want to teach kids to love books."

"That's so cool. I loved school as a kid." It was the only time she ever spent away from her father. The only place she felt somewhat safe. "Your students are very lucky to have you."

"Thanks." Fletcher shrugged off the praise. "I really love it. What do you do?"

Emma hesitated. She'd never had a job. It was unusual, at twenty-four years old, but her father had never allowed her to hold a job because he didn't want her to have money of her own. He'd known that would lead to her being independent and ultimately leaving him. "I'm, um…in between jobs right now," she finally said. "Which is probably good because I'd have missed a lot of work by now."

"True," Fletcher agreed. "I'm so sorry about what happened to you."

Emma shrugged. "It wasn't your fault."

Fletcher's gaze bore into hers. "It wasn't yours either."

She had to look away to hide the tears that threatened. Fletcher couldn't know how much those words meant to her. She'd admitted to Beau that she felt she was to blame for becoming one of Mason's hostages, but Fletcher didn't know about that. He was saying it simply because it was the truth.

10

Beau sat in his car for a moment to decompress before entering the apartment. After getting into the station, he'd spent far more time than he would have liked to chatting with old coworkers to legitimize his guise of saying some final goodbyes. Then, when he'd finally gotten a chance to snoop a bit, all he'd found were preliminary leads that hadn't received an ounce of investigation, making it difficult to know where to start.

Despite the less-than-stellar results, having a place to start was better than nothing. It just meant more time spent following leads that may or may not pan out and potentially pursuing a lot of dead ends before finding anything useful.

Rounding up all the documents he'd managed to stuff into his backpack, Beau headed into the apartment. Laughter greeted him as he stepped inside—both the gentle, tinkling giggle that was exclusive to Emma, and Fletcher's deep, throaty chuckle he'd heard millions of times growing up.

"What's going on in here?" Beau asked as he placed his backpack on a kitchen chair.

"Oh." Emma quickly rose from her chair. "Hey, Beau. You're back."

"I am," he said, one eyebrow cocked up in suspicion. The guilty expression on her face was adorable, but he wasn't sure he liked her conniving with his brother.

Fletcher shielded his eyes with one hand and glanced out the window. "Tut tut, it looks like rain," he said, imitating the *Winnie the Pooh* line Beau used to chant on cloudy days as a child.

Beau groaned and hung his head. "You did not tell her about my *Winnie the Pooh* phase."

"I sure did," Fletcher said with a wide grin. "It was my favorite of your embarrassing phases. You used to run around in a red t-shirt and refuse to put pants on because Winnie didn't wear them. Mom couldn't take you out in public for three months because you'd be breaking public nudity laws."

"Fuck you, dude." Beau smacked Fletcher on the chest. Emma giggled, making his heart swell, and suddenly, he didn't care that his older brother was embarrassing him, because Emma was laughing.

"I do love A.A. Milne," she said between giggles. Fletcher nodded his agreement, though Beau didn't understand the reference.

"I've got ten times more blackmail that I'd be happy to share with you," Fletcher said, turning to Emma, "but I'm afraid you'd never be able to look him in the eye again if I do." He turned back to Beau. "Don't forget that I practically raised you. That gives me the right to share as many embarrassing stories as I want."

Beau scowled at his brother, then sobered. "I know." He would never forget everything Fletcher had done for him. He'd been the father Beau had never had, and he would always be grateful for him.

"I'd better go before I think of another story Emma might be interested in," Fletcher said with a wink that made her smile. "It was lovely to spend the afternoon with you."

"I had a great time," Emma replied, standing to give

Fletcher a hug and once again pleasantly surprising Beau with her trust in the men in his life.

"Get out of here," Beau said good-naturedly as he ushered Fletcher to the door. "And whatever you did to make her so comfortable, thank you," he whispered to his brother before they shared a wave goodbye. Fletcher gave him an understanding nod on his way out.

Beau shut the door and turned his full attention to Emma. "Well, you two sure hit it off."

Emma shrugged. "You were right. He's a nice guy."

"So, what did you do? Other than shit on me, of course." Beau grimaced.

Emma's eyes widened slightly at his profanity. "Well, we talked a lot about literature. It turns out we have a lot of favorite books in common." She shrugged. "We had a really nice conversation."

A pang of jealousy tore through Beau's chest. He could never talk to her about something like literature. Most of that stuff went right over his head. And she'd seemed to have such a good time with Fletcher. He wanted Emma to have that good of a time with him.

He cleared his throat. "That's good. I'm glad."

"How was your afternoon?" she asked. "Did you get anything good?"

He sighed. "Nothing amazing, but I did manage to snag a few promising leads. They'll need a lot of research, but Diego will help me with that. He's excited to have a bit of a distraction."

"That's good." Emma seemed encouraged by the information. "Is there anything I can help with?"

Beau smiled at her eagerness. "Not right now. My work is done for today. Diego will come over tomorrow to sift through these files with me. You can help us if you'd like. Right now, though, all I want to do is put my feet up and relax."

"Sounds nice. Your couch is very comfortable." She

followed him into the living room and perched herself on one end of the couch.

"Glad you like it." Beau dropped down onto the other end and, as promised, kicked his feet up on the coffee table. He shifted until his body sank into the cushions at the ideal angle. He had just reached peak comfort when his stomach grumbled. "Shit, I'm hungry. Should we order in again?"

"Actually, would you mind if I cooked something?" Emma asked.

His eyebrows shot up. "You don't have to do that."

"I want to," she said, her cheeks tinting a tantalizing shade of pink.

"Well, if you really want to...then sure," he said, hoping she didn't feel like he expected her to wait on him. She'd made a few comments about not wanting to be a burden, and perhaps she felt the need to repay him somehow. In Beau's mind, there were no debts to be repaid.

"I want to," Emma assured him. "You relax; you've had a long day. I'll make us something yummy."

"Okay. Thanks, Emma." He gave her a warm smile as she walked out to the kitchen. In the short time he'd known her, Emma had never failed to surprise him—from the depths of her strength to the height of her sweetness.

Doing as instructed, he relaxed and grabbed the TV remote. There wasn't anything too interesting on, so he stuck on an old ball game—something mindless to distract him from his long day. Emma's gentle footsteps padded around the kitchen, and the domestic sound brought an unexpected grin to Beau's face.

He couldn't remember the last time he'd eaten a homemade meal. Fletcher usually ate at Christa's, and Beau either ordered in or went out to the pub with his fellow officers after shift. After a few minutes, the enticing aroma of garlic filled his nostrils. *Mmm.* He couldn't wait to see what she was making.

A couple of innings had passed before Emma came and tapped Beau on the shoulder, alerting him that dinner was ready. She'd set up two place settings on the kitchen island, and there was a big bowl of spaghetti in the center. The pasta was shiny—olive oil, maybe?—and scattered with bright-red tomatoes. It smelled divine.

"Emma, this looks fantastic," Beau said as he slid onto a stool.

"Thanks." She smiled sweetly. "It was really simple. I just tossed the spaghetti with olive oil, salt, and pepper, and sautéed the tomatoes with garlic for a few minutes so they'd be warm."

"Simple," Beau scoffed. "I can handle grilled cheese, but that's about it."

"That may be so, but your grilled cheeses are the bomb. You should be proud."

"If you say so," Beau replied, secretly thrilled that Emma liked his cooking. He served the spaghetti onto two plates, and they both dug in. The dish was so tasty he couldn't help but release a groan. "Damn, woman. You can cook me dinner anytime."

Emma beamed at his praise. "Glad to hear it. But I did enjoy the Chinese food the other night. Maybe we could order another kind of food sometime?"

"Of course." He would give her anything she wanted.

"I've been wanting to try Mexican. Do you know a good place?"

"Hell yeah!" he said. "There's a taqueria not far from here that delivers. It's Diego-approved, and he's a real Mexican."

Emma giggled. "That's quite the seal of approval. I'd love to try that sometime."

"So, you've never tried Chinese or Mexican food. Never

heard of the Kardashians. What else do I need to educate you about?"

Immediately after the words exited Beau's mouth, he regretted them. Not because he thought she'd take them the wrong way, but because they made *his* mind wander to sex. He'd sure like to educate her about that.

Cut it out, he chastised himself for going there. Sure, he would like to show Emma how a real man treated a woman. But even if she were open to it, he would have to take things slowly.

"Hmm..." Emma mused. "Well, like I said, I don't watch much TV. I only get three or four channels, so my options are very limited. I mostly just watch the news. I don't like sports. One thing I never get to do is watch movies. I don't get any of those channels, and I very rarely go to the theater. I haven't seen a movie in…let's see…probably three years," she said, tapping her chin.

"No kidding?" That surprised Beau. Every few months, a movie would come out that he was interested in, and he had no shortage of friends who would go with him.

Emma scratched her temple. "Well, you know that my father didn't let me get any movie channels on my TV, and he wouldn't let me have my own car, so he had to drive me everywhere."

The life Emma described was barely a life at all. Every new detail he uncovered about the way she'd been living made him long to show her what life was really supposed to be like. At that moment, Beau decided to make it his mission to show Emma everything she'd been missing, from food, to movies, to—if he was lucky—intimacy. His attraction to her was undeniable, and he refused to believe that it was one-sided. He'd seen the looks Emma gave him and the way she reacted to his touch. She was shy and, of course, cautious, but Beau believed that, given time, she would open up completely with him. He couldn't wait for that to happen.

"Well, I think we can remedy the lack of movies tonight," he said. "We've got Netflix on our TV. It's got tons of good movies to choose from. What kind are you into?"

"I, er…I'm not sure," Emma confessed. "What's your favorite movie?"

Beau thought for a moment. "I think I'd have to say *Good Will Hunting.*"

"I've never seen it. Let's watch that."

"You sure? It's no chick-flick," he warned.

Emma gasped playfully. "Beau McNally. I am not that shallow. If my brain can handle classic literature, I think it can handle a movie with some substance."

"I'm sorry." He chuckled. "I didn't mean to insult you. I just thought you might want something a little more mindless. You know, a nice little distraction." Plus, all the women he'd dated before had wanted to watch chick-flicks. But Emma was different, and she kept reminding him of that.

"I think *Good Will Hunting* will make a fine distraction."

"Great," Beau said, standing up to clear the dishes.

"Oh, I can take care of that."

"No way. You cooked. I clean. You go get settled on the couch, and I'll be right over."

Beau loaded up the dishwasher and gave the island a cursory cleaning, then joined Emma on the couch. Once again, she'd gotten herself all bundled up in one corner. He sat on the other, giving her plenty of space. All he wanted to do was pull her into him and hold her while they watched the movie, but she wasn't ready for that. Not yet.

"Let's see." He clicked through the options on Netflix and located *Good Will Hunting,* setting it to start before getting up to dim the lights for prime movie-watching conditions.

Emma sat very still, her gaze transfixed on the screen as if she was determined not to miss a single second of the movie.

They watched together, rarely speaking but simply enjoying one another's company and a great movie. About halfway through, Beau paused it. Emma blinked twice and looked over at him.

"I think it's just about time for some popcorn," he explained.

"Oh, yum! I think I'll take a little bathroom break, too."

"I'll get the popcorn started," Beau offered. By the time Emma returned from the bathroom, he had one large bowl filled with buttery popcorn.

"Mmm, that smells amazing!"

"It's only fair. You made dinner. I made dessert."

He brought the popcorn back to where they'd been sitting on the couch. Realizing too late that he should have split the popcorn into two bowls, he sat down on his end. Emma eyed the bowl and sat beside him on the middle cushion without complaint. He happily took the small win.

Turning the movie back on, Beau grabbed a fistful of popcorn. Emma did the same, their hands lightly touching in the bowl. She froze momentarily before continuing to eat. When the popcorn was all gone, Beau pushed the bowl away from them on the coffee table. Despite the fact that she no longer needed to be right next to him, Emma didn't move over, which made Beau smile to himself.

It wasn't the shortest movie, and he noticed as Emma began to tire halfway through. She started nodding off before her head lolled to one side and her eyes closed, her long eyelashes feathering down toward her cheeks. Beau reached over and tentatively brushed a stray hair away from her forehead.

Emma let out a soft humming sound and shifted so her head rested on his shoulder. Carefully wrapping an arm around her, Beau held her to his chest. She responded by nuzzling her cute little button nose into his t-shirt.

Ahh. Beau's heart ached. He loved the feeling of her

warm, soft little body resting against his. He loved that she let him touch her and that she felt safe with him. Juxtaposed with all those warm and fuzzy feelings was a profound sense of hatred for every man who had ever mistreated her.

Her damn father had controlled every move she'd ever made. She'd never been able to experience a normal childhood, never did normal teenage things. On the contrary, her teenage years were spent in fear of the next time her father would miss big at the casino and wind up hurting her. And then, to top it all off, he'd sold her to human traffickers. *The fucking bastard*. He'd willingly given his own daughter over to people he very well knew would hurt her in unimaginable ways. The bruises that still marked Emma's beautiful skin were constant reminders of her mistreatment, and Beau still felt a driving urge to bury the men who had put them there.

Not only was he going to give Emma back her life, he was going to end the lives of everyone who had hurt her. Whether it meant putting them in jail or killing them, Beau didn't care. He just cared that they were gone for good.

11

Emma's eyes scrunched against the soft morning light peeking through the blinds. She wasn't ready to get up quite yet, so snug and warm in her bed.

Letting out a small yawn, she shifted, sinking into her pillow…only to realize that it wasn't a pillow at all. It was Beau's hard chest, cushioned by a fuzzy blanket. She was still on the couch and, by the looks of things, had been there all night.

She froze. Trying not to make any sudden movements, she shifted her gaze slowly toward Beau and was surprised to find him peering down at her.

"Hi," she chirped, her cheeks warming.

"Good morning," he said, a slow smile spreading across his lips. "You slept well."

"Umm…" Emma sat up and smoothed out her clothes. Interestingly, she *had* slept quite well. No nightmares whatsoever. "I'm sorry I fell asleep on you again."

"S'okay." Beau shrugged. "I slept just fine." He reached both arms above his head and took a big stretch. The movement tugged his t-shirt up, revealing the bottom of a six-pack and a very intriguing smattering of hair below it.

Emma stared for a moment at the exposed skin before coming to her senses. "I just feel bad that you had to sleep out here on the couch." She shook her head. "Ever since I came here, I've been putting you out."

"I really don't mind," Beau said. "I'm just glad you're comfortable here."

"Thank you," she said, picking invisible dirt from beneath her fingernails. She truly *was* comfortable there, despite every reason she had not to be.

He dipped his head toward her, catching her attention. "I'd like to do a workout this morning. I was thinking of going for a run. Would you be okay with that?"

Pursing her lips, Emma looked up from her hands. "Will you be going far?"

"I usually do a three-mile loop, so I'm never very far—not like when I had to go to the station. But if it makes you uncomfortable, I don't have to do it."

"Um..." she hedged. The truth was, she really didn't want to be left alone. Although she was fairly certain Mason's men wouldn't find her at Beau's apartment, the thought of being left there defenseless scared the snot out of her. On the other hand, she didn't want to be a bother by keeping Beau from his usual routine.

Reaching out slowly, he wrapped one of her hands in his. "Be honest with me, angel. Remember, you've got to tell me what you need."

Swallowing her pride, she admitted, "I would rather not be alone."

"Of course." His eyes softened as he gave her hand a quick squeeze. "I can work out right here in the living room today."

Emma nodded, resisting the urge to ask if he was *sure* he didn't mind skipping his run. Instead, she replied with a simple, "Thank you. I guess I'll take a shower while you exercise."

"Go for it. You know where the clean towels are?"

"Yes, I think so." She began heading toward the bathroom. "Enjoy your workout." She'd just shut the bathroom door when hard-rock music began to play in the other room. Or maybe it was heavy metal? She honestly wasn't sure, but the music suited him—loud, powerful, and *very* Beau.

The music dimmed to a faint pounding as Emma stepped beneath the cascading water. Closing her eyes, she let the steady stream of hot water pour over her body. She'd always found showers rejuvenating, but ever since being held captive for days without the luxury of one, she appreciated them more than ever.

As she gently scrubbed each part of her body, she reclaimed her power over it. Thinking back to those nights when her father would come home drunk, intent on taking his anger out on her, she scrubbed a bit harder. He had always made her feel as if her body wasn't her own. Then, Mason's men had done the same in that abandoned warehouse. For so long, her body had felt more like a punching bag than a vessel she had control over.

Ever since Beau had saved her, that was beginning to change. When he touched her, it was only to help and never to hurt. Even after falling asleep on him twice—leaving herself totally vulnerable—he hadn't taken advantage of her. Not once had he touched her out of turn or in a sexual way. The wild thing, though, was that she was starting to think that maybe she wouldn't mind if he did.

Beau brought out feelings in her that she hadn't felt in… well…ever. Butterflies took flight in her stomach when he smiled, and her skin tingled where he touched. He was handsome by any standard, but it was more than that. Beau was *good*. He'd risked his life to save her and shown her nothing but compassion since. He was understanding, and thoughtful, and sweet alongside his protectiveness and power.

And then there was his body.

A New Beau

Strong, bulky, capable—those were just a few of the words that came to mind. His hands were so big Emma could only imagine the things they could do. Her initial worries of him snapping her neck with his bare hands had turned to fantasies of him touching her in ways she'd only read about in books.

Running her soapy hands down her arms, she imagined Beau's doing the same. The thought had her shivering despite the hot water raining down on her. Tipping her head back, she brushed her fingertips over her neck, then lower to her breasts. Her nipples perked up at the attention, and she treated each of them to a little squeeze.

Drifting lower, her hands roamed over her stomach and down to the tops of her thighs. She caressed herself with the lightest pressure, but it was enough to get heat swirling low in her belly. One hand skimmed between her inner thighs, and her eyes popped open when her body bucked in response.

Pulling her hand away quickly, Emma realized what she'd been doing.

When was the last time she had been *this* turned on? And good Lord, how long had she been in the shower? What if Beau got suspicious? What if he somehow realized she was imagining him and touching herself? Smacking herself on the forehead, she quickly rinsed her hair and finished her shower.

To her relief, when she turned the water off, Beau's pump-up music was still blaring. Towel-drying her body, she combed her hair and dressed. When she made her way out to the living room, she found Beau on the floor in a push-up position. He was facing away from her and didn't realize she'd walked in, so she took the opportunity to watch him silently for a few moments. He bent his elbows and straightened them, propelling his body up and down, again and again, moving like a machine.

He was shirtless but wearing a black vest of some sort. It looked similar to the bulletproof one he'd been wearing when he'd saved her, but she didn't understand why he would wear that to workout. His muscles contracted with each push-up, his broad shoulder blades clenching and releasing. The tattoo that wrapped around his bicep moved in intriguing ways as his muscles bulged.

After ten or twelve pushups—Emma lost count amidst her gawking—Beau hopped onto his feet and grabbed a water bottle from the end table, chugging half of it in a single swallow. Placing the bottle back down, he stretched his arms over his head, revealing that swath of skin beneath the vest again. Finally, he turned and noticed her. She tore her gaze away in a pathetic attempt to look as if she hadn't been mesmerized.

Beau quickly lowered his arms and moved across the room to lower the music. "Hi," he said once the volume was turned down.

"Hey," Emma replied, grasping for something to say that wouldn't make her sound like some sort of voyeur. "Why are you wearing your bulletproof vest?"

"Oh." He chuckled. "This isn't my Kevlar. This is a weighted vest to workout in."

"Ah." She eyed the vest again. "That makes more sense. Is it heavy?"

"Ten pounds." He shrugged as if it were nothing. "You want to try it on?"

She nodded. "Sure, why not?"

Beau undid the Velcro and removed the vest, revealing his bare torso. Emma's eyes slid over his chiseled chest and abdomen in appreciation.

"Here," he said, holding the vest open for her to put on. Though he placed it gently on her shoulders, she still swayed under the weight.

"Whoa, you okay?" he asked, grabbing her arm to steady her. His fingertips singed where they gripped her—not hurting her but making her skin feel as if it was buzzing with electricity.

"I'm fine," she muttered, annoyed at both her troublesome

reaction to Beau's touch and her weakness under the weight of the vest.

He helped her take it off and dropped it to the floor with a loud *thunk*. "It takes time to work up to using one of these. You have to be able to perform the exercises well on your own before adding extra weight."

Emma nodded, even more impressed by Beau's strength now that she knew he was doing all those strenuous exercises with the added weight. "Do you think maybe…you could teach me some exercises sometime?" she asked.

Beau's eyebrows furrowed, but he agreed with an easy, "Of course."

Her gaze roamed over his defined muscles. "I just…I want to be stronger. Like, maybe be able to defend myself?"

"That makes sense," he replied with a kind smile. "We can definitely go over some strengthening exercises as well as some self-defense moves."

"Awesome," Emma said, chewing on her lip as she thought about how challenging it would be. "I'm just so sick of being weak."

"Hey," Beau countered, using his fingers to tilt her chin up. "You are not weak. Sure, maybe you can't handle a weighted vest yet, but with everything you've survived in your life—hell, everything you've survived this *month*—you're the strongest woman I've ever met."

Emma blinked up at his serious face. "Really?"

"Absolutely," he said, his finger drifting up over her cheek. "Emma, I'm in awe of you. You're so strong." His finger traced her jawline. "Brave." The tip of his thumb brushed her bottom lip. "Beautiful."

His voice softened on the last word, and Emma's heart melted right with it. Beau had a knack for building her up and making her see herself in a different light. With him, she didn't feel weak or worthless. She felt like someone who mattered. Someone whose life held possibility.

And perhaps that was what gave her the courage to lift up onto her tiptoes and press a kiss to his mouth.

Beau's hand froze on her face when their lips met, but after a beat, he cupped her cheek and softly returned her kiss. Emma delighted in the feeling of his firm lips molding to hers. He was gentle and refrained from using his tongue but guided her lips with a definite expertise.

He tasted a little salty from all the sweat, and she couldn't get enough of it. Kissing Beau was unlike anything she'd ever felt before. The fact that she'd made the first move was empowering, and the fact that he'd so eagerly reciprocated made her feel desired like never before.

Wanting to deepen the kiss, she brought a hand to Beau's arm but quickly removed it when she registered his slick skin.

He pulled back and dropped his hand from her face as if it were a hot potato. "Sorry," he apologized. "I'm all sweaty."

She couldn't help but giggle at the least romantic ending to any kiss ever. When she looked up and saw that Beau was barely containing his own laughter, she broke out in full-on hysterics. She was probably just delirious from having the best kiss of her life, but something about it struck her funny bone. Biting her bottom lip, she tried and failed to hold back more laughter.

"God, I love that sound," Beau breathed as he tucked her hair behind her ear.

"What sound?" she asked once she'd caught her breath.

"Your laugh," he said, his gaze lingering on her lips. "It's the most beautiful sound in the world."

Stunned by that declaration, she stood silently, studying him as he studied her.

"I should probably shower," Beau said, though he didn't seem in any hurry to move on.

"You probably should," she agreed, equally hesitant to break out of the moment.

Running his hand over her shoulder, Beau seemed to be

working hard to compose himself. Emma was secretly thrilled the kiss had rattled him as much as it had her.

Stepping away, Beau skimmed his hand over his jaw. "Would you be okay with going over to Diego's today? We want to work on our case, and I was thinking you could hang out with his wife, Isabella. I think you'd really like her."

"Oh, sure," Emma replied, not really caring where she was as long as Beau was with her. "But I really wanted to help you guys. Maybe there'll be information that would be familiar to me somehow."

"Of course you'll get to help us," Beau assured her with a light squeeze on the shoulder. "We couldn't do it without you. But sorting through files is boring work. We'll do the nitty-gritty stuff and put together an evidence board. Then, you can come in and look it over."

"Okay," she replied with a nod. "That sounds good." She really didn't know anything about the process of going through evidence, so it made sense to leave that to the guys. She could only hope that something she saw would trigger a memory that would help the case. She wanted so badly to be useful in catching Mason and his men. Getting them locked away for life would be a relief. But as much as she wanted the men who had held her captive to rot in prison, she had a much bigger monster in mind. The one who'd been torturing her her entire life. *Her father.*

12

To Beau's relief, Emma seemed to like Isabella. He secretly hoped they would become friends and that Emma could do all the girly things that women normally did with her. Today, the ladies had gone off to do God knows what—he thought he'd heard Isabella mention something about buying make-up—and he had worried that Emma would be nervous about going out in public again, especially without him.

As it turned out, Emma was eager to get herself some new personal care products, and Isabella was only taking her to the drugstore down the street. Still, Beau was pleased that Emma was game for the outing. To his satisfaction, she was growing bolder by the day.

He and Diego had been busy sorting through all the evidence they had so far. It was a tedious job to sift through the photos and documents, but there seemed to be some valuable stuff.

"Is this the old mill building on Mullen Street?" Diego pointed to a large structure in one of the photos.

"Yeah," Beau replied. "It looks like that was the headquarters a couple months back," he added, pulling a document out of a stack of papers that contained a recorded conversation between Detective Williams and one of Mason's old men. "This suspect confirmed it. He squealed as soon as they got him in the interrogation room." Beau snorted. "Pussy."

Diego snickered. "Well, we can't all have your steely resolve."

"I'm just saying, these guys are pathetic. While Mason's got them under his spell, they'll do anything he says, but as soon as the cops get them, they're willing to give up everything."

Diego shook his head. "They have no loyalty to Mason. As soon as he's not providing them with a cash flow, they don't care what happens to him. And they'll say anything to get themselves a lighter sentence."

Beau grunted in response, sticking the picture of the mill building up on their evidence board with a tack. They were trying to create a timeline with all the locations Mason and his men had ever set up a headquarters. If they could pick up on a pattern, it would help them scout out where the new one might be.

"You'd think they'd have run out of empty buildings by now," Beau mused, staring at the long line of photos.

"You'd be surprised how many places there are in and around the city to hide," Diego muttered. Sighing, he ran a hand over his weary face.

"Say the word, and we'll take a break," Beau offered.

"No, no," Diego insisted. "There are only a couple more files to go through in this stack. These ones have information on buildings the police are watching, right?"

"Right."

After studying the rest of the files, the men had come up with a list of six areas they wanted to check out to see if there was any action. Each area housed various abandoned or otherwise empty buildings. They decided to check them out under the cover of night to lessen their chances of being seen.

It wouldn't be an infiltration like Beau had done when he'd found Emma, just a stakeout to get a feel for the locations to determine whether or not any of them were worth looking into further.

As the front door opened, two feminine voices floated into the kitchen. The distinct sound of Emma's tinkling laughter immediately brought a grin to Beau's face. When Diego shot him a funny look, he forced himself to cough into his fist to hide his goofy smile.

The two women entered the kitchen and placed two shopping bags each on the table.

"Well, it looks like you two had a successful shopping trip," Diego said as he got up to give his wife a peck on the cheek.

"We sure did." Isabella sported a Cheshire cat smile that said she'd spent a good deal of her husband's money. "We decided that Emma needed some new hair and skin products, nail polish, and make-up to help her feel a little more like herself. Not that she needs anything extra to be drop-dead gorgeous."

Beau shot Emma a smile. "I couldn't agree more."

A soft blush rose in her cheeks as she averted her eyes to the ground.

"Are you boys working too hard, as usual?" Isabella asked, coming up behind Diego to rub his shoulders. A twinge of jealousy snagged in Beau's chest at the casual display of affection until Emma came to his side and brushed her fingers lightly over his bicep in greeting. Though it was far less contact than Bella was giving Diego, it meant infinitely much more.

"We're working just hard enough," Diego said. "The information Beau gathered at the station the other day has proven very useful."

"Good," Isabella said. "It looks like you've gotten a lot done."

Emma walked toward the evidence board. "This is wild," she said as she took in the array of photos and notes with arrows drawn between them. She studied the display intently, no doubt looking for the building she'd been kept in.

Standing behind her, Beau placed one hand gently on her arm. "This is where I found you," he said, pointing to one particularly dilapidated brick building.

She stared at the photo for a long moment. "I recognize it."

Beau was about to ask how, as the victims were usually blindfolded, but then remembered that her father had driven her to Mason that day, so she would have seen the outside of the building. He stepped to her side and gave her arm a comforting squeeze.

Emma glanced around the board once more until her gaze landed on a photo in the top left corner. All the color drained from her face, leaving her pale white, her eyes wide.

Beau's chest tightened at the fear in her expression. "Emma? What's wrong?"

"Why is he on here?" she asked, one slim, shaky finger pointing to a picture of Detective Isaac Williams.

"He's the lead detective on the case," Beau said, puzzled.

Emma seemed to grow even paler at his explanation. Slapping a hand over her mouth, she struggled out of his hold.

"Emma?" he asked, at a complete loss as she ran toward the bathroom. Dropping to her knees, she vomited violently into the toilet.

"Shit," Beau muttered, rushing to kneel beside her and collecting her silky blonde hair into his hands to hold it back from her face. She continued to heave until her stomach was surely empty. He rubbed her back soothingly until she rocked back on her heels.

Sticking her head in the doorway, Isabella wore a look of

grave concern as she silently handed Beau a cold washcloth. He nodded in thanks before handing it to Emma.

"Here," he said as he continued to stroke her back. Closing her eyes, she pressed the cloth to her forehead and sighed. He released her hair, letting it fall over her shoulders and marveling at how silky and soft it was. How Emma managed to still look beautiful after puking was beyond him.

Isabella showed up in the doorway once more with a toothbrush still enclosed in its plastic packaging. Beau quietly thanked her and placed it on the bathroom counter. Emma had moved into a sitting position with her back against the tub.

"You okay?" He eased down to sit next to her on the floor. She nodded, eyes still closed, before removing the cloth and draping it over the side of the tub. "What was that all about?" he asked gently.

"That man…" she began. When she trailed off into silence, Beau sat and waited for her to be ready to continue. "I recognized him."

He froze. "From where?"

Emma fidgeted absentmindedly with the cloth. "He was friends with my father. I remember him coming around the house when I was younger."

"They were friends?" Beau asked, his brow creasing with confusion.

Emma nodded. "One time…one time he was with my father when he came home drunk. My father was picking on me, and he slapped me around a little, and then that man…he *punched* me. I guess he took my father's abuse as permission to abuse me himself. He hit me harder than my father ever had. It knocked me out. When I came to, they were both standing there, just laughing at me."

Beau dropped his head into his hands. The thought of Isaac Williams, a freaking detective, hurting Emma made him want to throw up himself. He'd always wondered why the police weren't doing more on this case, why they hadn't followed any leads more aggressively. Now, he knew. The team on the case was corrupt—or at least one member of it was. Fucking Isaac Williams was an abusive asshole. Of course he wouldn't care about girls being bought and sold.

"You're sure that's the same guy?"

"Positive," Emma murmured. "I've never forgotten his face."

"I'm so sorry." Beau rubbed her knee in gentle circles. "What can I do to help?"

"Nothing." She sighed. "It helps just having you here," she added, placing her hand over his.

Beau turned his palm up and intertwined their fingers. "I wish I could take away every bad memory," he told her, squeezing her hand lightly. "But since I can't, I plan to catch every single person that's ever hurt you and make sure they never see the light of day again."

Emma shivered at his harsh words. "Even if it's a police officer?"

"*Especially* if it's a police officer."

She pursed her lips at his venomous tone, and he rubbed his thumb over her hand.

"I should really clean myself up," Emma said, no doubt becoming self-conscious of her flushed skin and filthy mouth.

"Okay." Beau brought her hand up to his mouth and placed a kiss on the back of it before letting her go. "Bella left a toothbrush here for you." He gestured in the direction of the sink. "Take your time."

Exiting the bathroom, he quietly shut the door behind him. Diego and Isabella both pounced on him as soon as he reentered the kitchen.

"Is she okay?" Isabella asked at the same time Diego said, "Is she sick?"

"She's fine," Beau assured them. "Let's sit." He gestured toward the kitchen table. Diego and Isabella knew that Emma had been held by Mason and his men, but they still didn't know that her father was involved.

Though he hated to violate Emma's privacy, Diego had to know about her father's involvement and how that was tied in with Detective Williams. Beau explained the whole story as quickly as possible before Emma came out to join them.

A few minutes later, she exited the bathroom with slightly more color than she'd entered it with. "Sorry about that," she said softly as she pulled out an empty chair.

"Don't you worry about it for one more second," Isabella insisted, grabbing a pitcher of iced tea from the fridge and pouring glasses for everyone. She placed the first in front of Emma, who gratefully accepted it, taking a big gulp.

Beau placed a comforting hand around her forearm. "I hope you don't mind that I caught them up on what's going on."

"No." Emma shook her head. "I'd rather not relive it, so I'm glad you told them."

He wanted so badly to comfort her, to kiss her and tell her how strong she was again, but he settled for a quick pat on her arm.

"Isaac Williams is an asshole," Isabella growled over the rim of her glass. Knowing that she was also a survivor of various types of abuse, Beau appreciated her rage toward Williams.

"He's also a criminal," Diego added.

Beau nodded his agreement. "If he was friends with Emma's father, chances are he's involved in the illegal card games, the drugs, and possibly even worse. He might even be involved with the traffickers."

Diego sucked in a breath as Isabella slammed her fist on the table. Beau didn't miss the way Emma jumped at the noise, and he slid his hand down her arm to grasp her hand in reassurance.

"That *fucking* bastard," Isabella growled.

Emma looked a little green, and Beau worried she might be sick again. He tried to loosen his grip on her hand, but she just held on tighter.

Diego grasped his wife's fist, speaking in a tone he'd obviously had to use with her before. "*Mi amor*, I think it's safe to say we all agree, but let's try to stay calm, yes?"

Isabella continued fuming. "I want him kicked off the force. He should never be allowed to work as a cop again. I want him arrested. I hope his wife leaves him. And I hope he falls on top of a sharp knife."

Beau heard a small chuckle from beside him, and he was delighted that Emma was able to find humor in Isabella's tirade. He gave her hand a quick squeeze.

"Do you really think there's a police officer involved with the traffickers?" Emma asked.

"I do," Beau said. "I'd be willing to bet he was your father's connection to the traffickers. Your dad needed some quick cash, and he turned to his old pal for an idea. Williams obviously has no problem abusing women, and if he was working with the traffickers, it would explain why the case never went anywhere. Williams got the best of both worlds—an influx of cash for trafficking girls and a job where he can control all the evidence that comes in about it."

"That fucking jackass!" Isabella threw her hands up and jumped out of her chair to pace the floor.

Diego got up to soothe his wife, pulling her into his chest. "Don't worry, *Bella*," he crooned. "We'll make sure he gets what he deserves. We'll tell my sergeant everything and have him fired right away."

"I don't think we should turn him in just yet," Beau cautioned.

"What?!" came a chorus of three voices.

"Emma's in hiding right now. She can't make a statement, and they won't make any moves until she does. Plus, if Williams is involved with the traffickers, who's to say that other police officers aren't in their pocket as well? I think we're on our own here."

Emma leaned back a bit in her chair. "How could he not have gotten caught?"

"He's in the perfect position. No one would ever suspect that the cop on the case was also one of the criminals."

Diego nodded. "That makes perfect sense. Man, I can't believe there's a fucking cop involved in this shit."

"We definitely can't report Williams until we catch Mason ourselves. If we do, he could start destroying evidence or do something else to sabotage the case," Beau said.

"Good point," Diego said. "We have to keep this to ourselves for now."

Isabella finally sat down again with a dramatic thud. "I don't like it," she said bluntly. "I don't like that Williams will get to keep walking the streets like he's a respectable guy who wants to serve and protect his community when we all know he's really a scummy little prick. But I know you guys are right, and I really want him behind bars for life, so I'll wait."

Diego smiled fondly at his wife. "You say that as if you're the one who'd be turning him in."

"Oh, trust me. If I didn't agree with your plan, I'd sure as hell be on my way to the station right now. But I want justice for Emma and Sofia, and I don't want to screw that up by acting rashly."

"Glad you agree." Diego pressed a kiss to her forehead and turned his gaze to Beau. "We've got a lot of work to do."

"We sure do," Beau said. A familiar sense of satisfaction surged through his veins as the puzzle pieces began to fit together. Discovering that Detective Williams was probably connected to the human-trafficking ring was a huge step forward and changed the entire trajectory of the case.

He turned to Emma and explained, "Now that we've got a good lead, we have to go through all of Williams' files again with a fine-tooth comb. It's going to take us a bit. Why don't you and Isabella go hang out for a while?"

"Are you sure you don't want me to stay and help?"

"No, angel, it'll just be boring stuff. Looking for discrepancies and all that. You've already been a huge help today."

She smiled at that, sporting a playful twinkle in her eye that Beau hadn't yet seen. "Except when I was puking."

A grin touched his lips. "Hell, I'll take a little vomit any day if it means cracking a case."

"Come on." Isabella grabbed Emma's hand from Beau's. She flinched slightly but quickly recovered. "I think you're overdue for a makeover," Bella said.

Emma's eyebrows shot up. "Right now?"

"Why not?" Isabella threw her hands up in the air. "There's never a bad time to indulge in a little beautification."

Along with his gratitude for the distraction, Beau was glad that Bella would be giving Emma an experience he could almost guarantee she'd never had before.

"Okay." Emma shrugged, letting herself be led out of the room.

13

"Ready?" Isabella asked, trembling with excitement.

"Mhmm," Emma mumbled, her eyes still closed as she sat in the swiveling office chair. Isabella had made her sit still for what felt like hours as she tested various shades of makeup. Then, she carefully applied everything from foundation to blush, eye shadow, eyeliner, and mascara, explaining that she was contouring Emma's face and giving her a cat eye—neither of which were techniques she was familiar with.

She typically wore a bit of makeup, mostly to cover up any blemishes and because she liked the way mascara made her eyes pop, but she'd always had trouble doing anything fancy. Her skin was so light that it was oftentimes hard to find products that matched her skin tone. But Isabella had pored over the makeup aisle at the drug store, picking out just the right products. After so much time spent shopping, Emma had been left with no choice but to sit back and trust her new friend as she caked her face with layer after layer of makeup.

"Okay, here we go!" Isabella swiveled Emma's chair around to face the mirror.

At first glance, she thought she must have been looking at

a face on a poster instead of her own reflection in a mirror. But no, it was really her. Looking closer, she recognized her own eyes, nose, and mouth, but all of the fading bruises had vanished, and her cheekbones were more pronounced than ever. Her golden eyes popped beneath thick, jet-black eyelashes, and her cheeks held that very light blush that she so often wore unintentionally—only, this time, it was artificial.

"Wow," she breathed.

"You like?" Isabella sounded pleased.

"Yes! Bella, this is amazing. How did you learn to do this?"

Isabella began placing makeup brushes back into a zippered pouch. "I used to be a bartender at a strip club," she admitted. "And guys gave the biggest tips to pretty girls who flirted with them. So, I learned how to dress and do my hair and makeup."

Emma lifted her chin to see how her features looked from that angle. "Well, I think you could have a career as a makeup artist. Seriously, I've never looked this good."

"Emma," Isabella chided. "You're beautiful. Makeup just enhances your natural beauty."

She turned her head side to side, continuing to inspect her face. "It *is* nice not to see the bruises for once."

"Give it time," Isabella said softly. "They'll fade—the visible ones *and* the invisible ones."

Tears springing into her eyes, Emma bit her lip to contain them. The visible bruises were one thing, but the invisible ones were a whole lot harder to get rid of. A tear threatened to fall, and she fanned her face lightly with her hands.

"No crying!" Isabella ordered playfully. "You'll make your mascara run."

Emma giggled as she wrapped her arms around her new friend. "Thanks for today."

"Of course," Isabella said. "We need to do it again sometime."

"For sure! You can do my makeup anytime."

"I'll hold you to that." Isabella winked. "But we can always hang out and do other things, too. I'm always down for a girls' night."

Emma's chest tightened at the open invitation, tears once again stinging her eyes. "I'd like that."

Just as she turned toward the mirror for another peek, Beau's face appeared in it. She almost laughed out loud at his astonished expression. Perhaps she would have if the heat in his gaze hadn't absolutely scorched her.

"Wow," he whispered, his laser-sharp stare unrelenting.

"I'll leave you two alone," Isabella said as she scooted out of the room.

"You look…incredible," Beau murmured.

Emma turned away from the mirror to face him. "Thank you."

"I mean, you're always beautiful, but…wow."

His gaze felt hot on her skin, and she couldn't help but smile. Without all the visible bruises, she actually felt beautiful, and she liked that Beau thought she was, too.

Her smile faded as she took in his attire. He was wearing the same clothes he'd been wearing the night he'd rescued her—black cargo pants, t-shirt, and work boots, and he had a bulge beneath his shirt shaped suspiciously like a Kevlar vest.

A breath whooshed out of her, all the air leaving her lungs and her prior joy escaping with it. "Why are you dressed like that?"

Beau pursed his lips before answering. "Diego and I have decided to go scout out some of the buildings we think Mason and his men could be hiding in."

Emma's heart rate picked up. "Tonight?" She knew they had to work quickly, but she hadn't expected them to take any real action so soon.

"Yes," Beau said. "Now that we know Williams is involved, we can't lose any leads. We've narrowed our search down to a few buildings that match the traffickers' M.O., and we think they're likely in one of them. Nighttime is the best time to check them out without being seen."

"But won't it be dangerous?" Emma asked, her heart pounding as her ears began to ring. There were so many things that could go wrong, so many ways Beau could wind up hurt.

"We'll be fine." Beau placed his hands on her shoulders. "We're not going to do anything reckless—just a little surveillance, and we'll set up some covert cameras."

"But what if you see Mason?" Emma asked, panic welling up in her throat. "You're going to want to go after him. What if you go after him, and you get inside the building, and he has tons of men waiting for you?"

Beau's big hands stroked up and down her arms. The gesture did little to soothe her racing mind. "Angel, we aren't planning to pursue anyone tonight. And no one will be waiting for us because no one knows we're going to be there." His calm tone wasn't helping much either.

"But what if you're just doing surveillance and somebody sees you? And what if they have a gun and they shoot you?" Emma cried.

"I have a gun, too. I'll shoot them first."

Beau's arrogance, which was usually entertaining, scared her half to death in this moment. "But what if you don't see them? What if you get hurt, Beau?"

"I'm going to be fine," he insisted.

"What if you die? What am I going to do? I couldn't handle that, Beau. What—"

He cut her off by pressing his lips against hers.

The kiss started out the same as their first—gentle, his firm lips guiding hers softly. But Emma's emotions were running high, and her intense worry had her seeking more. She needed more than a quick distraction or a ploy to pacify her. She needed reassurance that he would come back to her.

Wrapping her arms around Beau's neck, she opened her

mouth wider, inviting him in. When she felt his tongue against her bottom lip, she rejoiced. One of his hands slid into her hair, the other snaking around her waist to pull her in closer. Their once sweet meeting of mouths morphed into a passionate kiss.

Emma licked into Beau's mouth, and he groaned into hers. His hand at her waist kneaded her flesh as if he couldn't stop touching her, but she suspected he was carefully controlling himself. As she pulled back for air, Beau dropped his forehead against hers.

"Angel," he panted, taking her face between his calloused palms.

Placing her hands on his chest, she stared at that spot where their bodies met. "You'd better come back safe and sound," she whispered.

He tilted her chin up until his gaze bore into hers. "We're going to be fine. We won't do anything foolish. We'll be home by morning."

"Morning?"

"Yes," Beau said. "You'll sleep here. Isabella will show you the guest room and make sure you're comfortable. Everything will be alright."

Emma bit her bottom lip, knowing she had to let him go despite her profound worry.

"Trust me," Beau begged.

And because she couldn't lie, she responded, "I do."

"Good girl," he replied with a soft smile. "Isabella will take good care of you. And I'll be back when you wake up."

"You'd better be." Emma looked up at him through her lashes and found nothing but certainty and confidence in his expression.

"I'll see you tomorrow." He pressed one last kiss to her forehead, and then he was gone.

Standing in the middle of the room, Emma tried to process

the sudden change in events. Of course she'd known Beau planned to catch Mason—he had been collecting and inspecting potential evidence all week—but she'd never actually considered what it would take to bring him down. She hadn't considered the danger Beau would have to put himself in.

In such a short amount of time, he had come to mean so much to her. He made her feel things she'd never felt before—strong, beautiful, trusting. No man had ever made her feel so good, and now that she had him, losing him would be unbearable.

Isabella walked quietly into the room and guided Emma to the bed to sit down. "They're gone," she said. "But they'll be fine. Beau and Diego are tough, smart men."

"I know." Emma's voice was barely above a whisper. "But I never thought about the possibility of losing Beau until now. What if he gets hurt? Or killed?"

"I know how you feel." Isabella pulled her into a side hug. "Every time Diego walks out that door, I worry. Every single time. It took me a while to accept that he works a dangerous job, but I just have to trust him. I have to trust that he'll do everything he can to stay safe. And you have to trust Beau, too."

"I do trust him, but I certainly don't trust Mason not to kill him."

"Neither do I," Isabella said. "But I think our trust in our men outweighs our mistrust in Mason, don't you?"

Emma's head jerked up at the mention of Beau being "her man." He wasn't, but then…what was he? Her protector? Guardian? Bodyguard? But bodyguards didn't kiss their protectees. At least, she didn't think they did.

"How do you live with always wondering if he'll come home?" she asked.

"I'll be honest, it's hard," Isabella replied. "I fear for Diego every time he goes on the job. But you can't let fear rule you.

You can allow the fear to be present, but you can't allow it to overcome you. Otherwise, the fear wins."

Emma grimaced, thinking of how long she'd lived in fear, allowing her father to mistreat her. "I think I've let fear win for most of my life."

Isabella placed a hand on her shoulder. "I understand. I let fear rule me for quite some time, too. I think that's a natural reaction to horrible events. But the important thing is that you eventually recognize that you're letting the fear rule you and stand up to it."

"How did you stand up to it?"

Isabella smiled warmly. "By giving Diego a chance. I met him at a very scary time in my life. I was undocumented and working for a really shady guy because he would pay me under the table. I was actually assaulted while I worked there, and between that and seeing how men treated the dancers like objects, I was afraid of all men."

"I'm so sorry," Emma said, understanding all too well how awful men like that could be.

"I know how difficult it can be to see the good in people when you're so used to seeing the worst. And what I went through was nothing compared to you." Isabella's eyes filled with tears.

"You can't compare the two," Emma said, quick to comfort her new friend. "What you went through was probably the worst thing that happened in your life, and what I went through was the worst thing that happened in mine. It doesn't matter how bad events compare to each other, only how significant they are in our own lives."

Isabella smiled sadly at her. "You're stronger than you think," she said. Then, she took Emma's hands in hers and looked her square in the eyes. "We're survivors, Emma. Not victims. We've been to hell and back and lived to tell the tale. We'll probably always have some degree of fear from that, but we can't let it stop us from living our lives. We've both been given something that so many aren't—a second chance."

Emma nodded, giving Bella's hands a squeeze. She'd never quite thought of this as a second chance, but in a way, it was. She had been too afraid to fight back against her father's abuse the first time around, but she wouldn't let him get away with it again. Beau and Diego already knew the truth and were working on catching the traffickers, even as they spoke.

"My second chance happened when I met Diego. Everything changed that night," Isabella said. "He saw something in me that had been dormant for a long time. He realized that I didn't belong in that repulsive strip joint, and he convinced me that I was worthy of better."

"You two are great together. I can only imagine what it's like to love and trust someone so much."

"It's the best feeling in the world." Isabella's grin grew. "And now that you have your second chance, you can find it, too."

Emma's eyebrows inched up. Could she? She *was* free now. Her father no longer held her back from living her life the way she wanted to. And she was determined not to waste this second chance by being cowardly, as she had been before.

Maybe her fortune cookie's prediction had been right, and there *was* love in her future.

Then, she thought of all the other women the traffickers had no doubt ruined the lives of, and her wave of hope came crashing down. "Sofia didn't get a second chance," Emma muttered.

"No," Isabella sighed, her eyes once again filling with tears. "She didn't."

"Will you tell me about her?"

Isabella smiled through her moment of grief. "Sofia was a spitfire—beautiful, strong, but so loving. She adored her family. She and Diego were like two peas in a pod. The rest of their family still lives in Mexico, and she visited as often as she could, but she and Diego only had each other here in the States. And she had me, of course."

"And Beau," Emma said. "They were friends, right?"

Isabella's teeth tugged at her lip, and she remained uncharacteristically silent as she shifted on the bed beside her.

"What, they weren't friends?" Emma asked.

"Well…" Bella began, dragging the word out dramatically. "Actually, they were more than friends."

Emma's heart dropped into her stomach. "They were…together?"

"Sofia and Beau dated for a little while a few months before she died," Isabella explained. "When they broke up, Sofia was so sad that she fled to Mexico to be with her family, and that was when she was taken."

Emma covered her mouth to try and contain a gasp. "Oh my gosh. I had no idea. Beau must have been crushed."

Isabella nodded and picked at a loose thread on the bedspread. "They weren't right for each other. Their relationship was all fire and no depth. Then, Sofia wanted more, and Beau…didn't. He cut things off, and she was heartbroken. He blames himself for her abduction. The way he sees it, she would never have been in Mexico if he hadn't broken up with her."

"It's not his fault," Emma argued. "It's not like he delivered her into the arms of the human traffickers. She was just in the wrong place at the wrong time."

"Exactly," Isabella agreed. "No one blames Beau except himself. Same with Diego. But I think it still haunts him. It's why he's so dedicated to catching Sofia's killers. He may not have loved her, but he did care about her."

"Then, why did he break up with her?"

Isabella sighed out a long, pent-up breath, as if she'd been mulling over the exact same question. "Beau…he doesn't often let himself get close to women." She paused, perhaps afraid she was sharing too much, but Emma's curiosity only grew.

"Why?"

"I'm not sure," Isabella confessed. "But he tends to go for women who are…how can I describe it? Brazen? Brash? I guess he likes that they're forward and outspoken, but they always come along with lots of drama and high emotions, and Beau can't stand that side of things. I think he purposely chooses women that he knows will eventually drive him away."

"Like self-sabotage."

"Exactly like self-sabotage."

"And that's what happened with Sofia?"

"Yes, I think so. Sofia had a big personality. When she and Beau first got together, it was all sparks and fire, but you can't build a relationship on just that. Eventually, the fire will burn out, and all you've got left is a pile of ash. Ultimately, he got fed up with the drama and ended things."

"Wow." Emma pursed her lips as she thought that over. "How did he and Diego manage to stay friends after he broke his sister's heart?"

Isabella smiled shrewdly. "Diego was well aware that their relationship was doomed from the start. He knew his sister's track record with men. Of course, he was pissed at Beau when the breakup happened, but after everything went down, I think he needed a friend to lean on more than he needed someone to be angry with."

Emma nodded, relieved the ordeal hadn't negatively impacted their friendship. She was still taken aback by the fact that Beau had been in a relationship with Sofia, simply because he hadn't mentioned that detail when he'd told her his version of the story, but it made perfect sense. Beau was a vibrant, virile man, and she could see him going for a fiery woman like Sofia. His was a personality that needed to be matched. But it also didn't surprise her that he didn't put up with drama. As patient as he'd been with Emma and her various problems, she couldn't see Beau caring about more frivolous issues.

Isabella sighed. "Despite his problems with women, Beau's a really great guy. I wish he could find someone that's actually good for him."

"He *is* a great guy," Emma murmured, thinking of all he had done for her.

"He needs someone…sweeter," Isabella decided. "Less… audacious. Someone to soften out his hard edges, not sharpen them."

That made sense to Emma, too. Perhaps instead of needing someone whose personality matched his, he needed someone whose personality balanced his out. "It seems like what Beau wants and what he needs are total opposites."

Isabella smirked and tossed her long brown curls carelessly over her shoulder. "He just needs to get his head out of his ass and realize what's good for him."

Emma let out a nervous giggle, then sighed as she thought of Beau and what he was doing that night. "I hope he's okay."

Isabella reached over and squeezed her hand. "I'm sure he is. They both are." She hopped off the bed, pulling Emma with her. "We need to get our minds off our men. What do you say we end this pity party and open up a bottle of wine? Just to take the edge off."

"Yeah, that sounds good."

14

Emma had never had a glass of wine with a girlfriend before, but it seemed like a darn good time for one. In fact, she'd never had a glass of wine at all. Though her father was a voracious consumer of substances of all kinds, he'd strictly forbidden her from drinking.

Isabella procured a bottle of white and some cheese and crackers, which she arranged artfully on a plate.

"Ooh, very fancy," Emma said, grabbing a slice of cheese and nibbling the corner.

"Only the best for you, my darling," Isabella replied as she carried their snack into the living room.

Emma took a seat on the couch and tested her wine with a small sip. It was light, crisp, and delicious. She took a second, healthier sip and decided that it was dangerous how easily the wine went down.

Isabella flopped into an armchair, her wine sloshing precariously in her glass, and began flipping through the channels for something mindless to watch. "Ever seen *Bridesmaids*?"

Emma shook her head. "No, is it good?"

"Oh, it's hysterical. We've got to watch it." Isabella hit the button to rent the movie, and a loud moan sprang from the television. Emma's eyes widened at the rambunctious sex scene that opened the movie. Isabella cracked up at her bewildered expression and assured her the whole movie wasn't like that. Thankfully, that was true, and Emma found herself giggling at the absurd antics of a crew of mismatched bridesmaids.

The cheese and crackers were long gone by the time the movie finished, the bottle of wine polished off. The combination of wine and laughter had relaxed Emma into a state of fuzzy bliss.

"Well," Isabella said, stretching her arms overhead and letting out a big yawn. "I'm exhausted. Wine makes me sleepy." She rubbed her belly in a slow circle as if coaxing the wine to behave.

"Same," Emma said reluctantly. The wine had made her sleepy, too, but she hated to see the night end. She feared that sleeping in a new location might spur on her nightmares. The last thing she needed was to wake Isabella up with one of her unconscious screaming and crying fits.

Isabella showed Emma to the guest room and made sure she had everything she needed before turning in for the night. Emma took a quick trip to the bathroom to remove her makeup, wash her face, and brush her teeth, then climbed under the covers and switched off the light on the bedside table.

Closing her eyes, she settled into the unfamiliar bed as best she could. At first, she rested her head on a single pillow, but that didn't offer quite enough cushion, so she added another. As she lay on her back, she tried resting her arms by her side, then up above her head. She tried crossing her legs, then uncrossing them. With a long, drawn-out sigh, she rolled over onto her belly, resting her right cheek on the pillow. That didn't feel right either, so she flipped over onto her left. Then, the pillow began to feel too warm, so she flipped it over. The flip side was cooler, but then her body felt like it was overheating.

"Ughhh," she finally groaned out loud. Glancing over at the clock, she found that only half an hour had passed, and she'd spent the entire time tossing and turning. Flipping the covers off, she swung her legs over the edge of the bed and stood, resting her hands on her hips.

Since sleep evaded her, she returned to the living room to try and get out of her head. Tiptoeing out of the bedroom, she snuck down the stairs. The large evidence board was still the focal point of the kitchen, so she avoided that area and headed straight for the living room. Sagging onto the couch with a sigh, she flipped on a lamp and grabbed the local newspaper from the end table.

Two Dead in Dorchester Shooting, read the top headline.

Good grief. Emma quickly shut the newspaper. She couldn't seem to get away from thoughts of death. Images flashed through her mind of Beau lying on the ground, bullet holes riddling his body like Swiss cheese.

A shiver shot down her spine, and she hopped off the couch, rubbing her eyes hard before pacing around the room in circles. "God!" she whispered loudly, unwilling to risk waking up Isabella by shouting as she wanted to.

Unable to stand herself any longer, Emma forced a deep breath into her lungs and marched past the evidence board to the wine rack, grabbing a new bottle. She rejoiced upon realizing it had a screw-off cap. She didn't trust her shaking hands with a corkscrew. Pouring herself a glass, she prayed it would take the edge off as it had earlier.

Upon her first sip, she saw an image of Beau diving behind a concrete wall, a hailstorm of bullets firing toward him. Her second sip conjured a picture of Beau throwing himself in front of Diego, taking a bullet for his best friend.

She shuddered, knowing all too well that Beau was the type to do something like that. He would absolutely take a bullet for a friend, but selfishly, she hoped that if it came down to that, he wouldn't do it. Then, she felt guilty because she really liked Diego and Isabella. She wouldn't wish harm on either of them.

Gulping down the rest of the glass, she grabbed a refill, then turned the TV on low. It wasn't hard to find a late-night talk show full of celebrity news and interviews. She didn't know much about pop culture, so she tried to dedicate her full attention to learning about it. Before she knew it, she'd been fully educated on all the latest Hollywood break-ups and make-ups, and her glass was empty again. A glance at the clock revealed that another two hours had passed.

Jumping off the couch, she wobbled and found herself a bit off balance. A giggle escaped her mouth, and then a hiccup, which only made her laugh more. She'd never felt quite that ludicrously giddy before. Thoughts of guns, bullets, and death had long since dissipated. Clips of Beau getting hurt no longer reeled through her mind.

No, instead of thoughts of Beau getting hurt, thoughts of him touching her now filled her consciousness. She remembered the kisses they'd shared, his soft lips contradicting his rough edges. His strong hands on her shoulders, holding her steady as he rocked her world.

Emma hugged her arms around herself, pretending they were Beau's. Though he looked the part of a dangerous bad boy, he'd been nothing but kind and gentle with her. The perfect juxtaposition of tough and tender.

Happy thoughts of Beau had her skipping to the kitchen to pour herself another glass of wine. There wasn't much left in the bottle, so she just emptied it, giggling as she tried to walk back to the couch without spilling her too-full glass. When she finally made it, she set the glass down on the coffee table and rewarded herself with a pat on the back. Then, she chuckled because she was all alone and patting herself on the back.

The minutes ticked by. By the grace of God, they seemed to be moving faster and faster. By the time she finished off the last of the wine, Emma had gotten a full recap of the last season of *The Bachelor*, learned how to choose the right swimsuit for her body type, and gotten a frighteningly complete education on the history of Angelina Jolie and Brad Pitt's relationship.

She was just nodding off to sleep on the couch when the sound of the front door opening jolted her to attention. She sat up as the hall light clicked on and illuminated the otherwise pitch-black entryway. It was very late—or rather, extremely early.

Her gaze flicked from the clock to the door, waiting for Beau to appear. Until she saw him healthy, whole, and in one piece, she would worry. She heard Diego say a quiet goodnight in the darkness, and then Beau stepped through the entryway and into the living room. His shoulders drooped with exhaustion, and there was dirt streaked across his cheeks like camouflage.

Emma sprang up off the couch. "Beau!" she exclaimed, grabbing hold of the chair beside her for support.

His gaze shot to hers. "Emma?" He studied her for a moment. "You're awake? What are you doing down here?"

"I'm s'glad you're okay!" she slurred, completely ignoring his questions as she staggered across the room and flung herself into his arms.

Beau caught her as she hurled her body at him. "I'm okay. Are *you* okay?" he asked.

"I'm fine. More 'n okay," Emma babbled as she pulled away to look up at his face. "I'm so relieved. I was so worried. But I'm much better now."

She swayed slightly on her feet, and Beau held tight to one of her arms. His concerned gaze traveled from her, to the television, to the empty bottle of wine on the table. A slow smile spread across his face as amusement replaced concern. "Are you drunk?"

Emma couldn't help but giggle. "I think I am."

Beau shook his head, his grin widening. "Wow."

"Yeah. I've never been drunk before. I had no idea it would feel like this. I don't have a care in the world. I mean, really, you were out there scoping out maniacs, and I wasn't even worried." She frowned. "Wait, no, that came out wrong. I was really worried. But then, you know, the wine, and then I wasn't so worried. And now I'm just so relieved! You're here! You're okay!" She put her hands on Beau's chest, partly to steady herself and partly to remind herself that he really was there.

"I'm here," he repeated. "I'm okay. Why don't we get you up to bed?"

"Oh, yeah, bed. That was the problem." Emma babbled. "I couldn't sleep because I was so worried. I was afraid I'd have another nightmare. Because when you're not sleeping with me, I have nightmares. And so, I was waiting for you to come back so I could sleep with you." She slapped a hand over her mouth. "I shouldn't have said that. You don't have to sleep with me. You're probably so tired. I'm sorry."

"Hey." Beau ran a gentle hand down her arm. "Slow down. Stop worrying. You've had a lot to drink. Why don't we get you a big glass of water, and then we'll go up to bed, and I'll sleep with you."

"Okay," Emma said easily, swinging her body toward the refrigerator. "Whoa. I'm a little dizzy."

"Yeah." Beau laughed. "That happens." He took her arm and led her to a stool. "Sit."

Emma did as she was told and watched intently as Beau got her a glass of ice water.

He slid it over the counter to her with another command. "Drink."

"Yes, sir." She chugged most of the glass before letting out a big belch. "Holy crap!" she exclaimed, and Beau burst out laughing. "Whoa," Emma added, putting a hand on her chest.

"Drink the rest," Beau said, watching her with soft eyes and an amused smile. "Good girl," he said as she finished. "Now, up to bed."

"Yes, sir," Emma said again, sliding off the stool. Beau scooped her up in his arms before she could crumple to the floor. She squealed as her center of gravity shifted, throwing her arms around Beau's neck and hanging on tight.

"Shh," he reminded her, pointing toward Isabella and Diego's closed bedroom door. She let go of one arm to mimic zipping her lips. Beau chuckled, and she felt the reverberations of his laughter on her cheek.

"What am I going to do with you, Emma Anderson?" Beau murmured as he easily climbed the stairs with her in his arms.

Emma wrapped her hand around his thick bicep and felt the muscles working beneath her fingers. "I've got an idea," she whispered as she buried her face in his neck and pressed kisses to his exposed skin. She took a deep inhale, soaking in his scent. He was back, and he was unharmed, and whole, and *hot*.

Beau groaned but quieted as they passed by Isabella and Diego's bedroom. When they reached the guest room, he deposited Emma gently on the bed. "Angel, it's time to sleep."

At eye level with his stomach, she allowed her gaze to travel up his body, taking in his incredible physique. He was so sexy, and so considerate, and so *right there*. Thinking back to her conversation with Isabella, Emma remembered what she'd said about the type of women Beau usually went for. *What would a brazen woman do right now?* she asked herself.

When her eyes reached Beau's, she found them dark and intense. It would have scared her just days ago, but now she knew the intensity was not a malicious one, but a carnal one.

Liquid courage coursed through her, and she reached for Beau's waist to pull him in.

"What if I don't want to sleep?"

"Emma," he warned, even as he allowed himself to be led onto the bed beside her. She ignored his scolding tone and brought her face up to meet his, licking her lips before pressing them against his.

Beau stayed stiff at first, not pulling away but not kissing her back. She brought one hand to the back of his head and licked at his lips in an effort to get them open. Frustrated when he didn't, she nipped at his lower lip ever so gently.

Beau groaned and returned her kiss, his resolve cracked. His lips parted, and Emma slid her tongue through them. All the relief that had flooded her body at his safe return flowed into the kiss. Her lips spoke of her bliss, her tongue of her passion. Long and slow, she kissed him, and when he pulled back, her lips found his neck once again. She kissed and licked and sucked at Beau's skin because he had come back, and being close to him made her feel safe.

Emma kissed her way up his jaw to just below his ear. "I need you," she murmured, angling her face toward his to kiss him again. Beau shocked her by turning his cheek and tearing his head away. Staring at the floor beside the bed, he heaved a big breath. Mortified, Emma realized he'd turned her down.

Beau's rejection stung like a slap in the face. Sure, she was a little drunk, but she didn't think her comprehension was *that* off. She'd thought they were on the same page with their attraction, but now it was obvious Beau didn't see her the way she saw him. Perhaps he'd kissed her back out of pity, but that was where he drew the line.

Tears stung Emma's eyes as she backed away from Beau in an attempt to scramble off the bed, needing to get as far away from him as possible. Of course, she had nowhere to go, but her intoxicated mind hadn't thought that far ahead.

"Emma," he sighed, wrapping his hand around her arm in

a gentle but firm grasp that effectively immobilized her. "Come here, sweetheart."

She fought against him as he pulled her into his arms. Beau's hold on her was strong, but the kisses he pressed to the top of her head were tender. To her dismay, Emma felt one tear escape, and then two. She continued her attempt to wiggle away from Beau, but he held on tight.

Tears of humiliation turned to anger as she failed to escape his embrace. "Lemme go," she slurred, pushing at his chest. Small tear stains had begun to form on his shirt.

"Stop fighting me," Beau insisted, tucking the top of her head under his chin, his embrace unrelenting.

Emma groaned in frustration but used the opportunity to wipe her tear-stained cheeks on his shirt. Finally, she was still, and he slowly released her. She sat up beside him, resigned to wallow in her embarrassment.

Beau took her face in his hands and lifted her reluctant gaze to his. "Listen to me," he said vehemently. "I will never not give you what you need. But trust me, this isn't what you need right now. It's incredibly late, I'm dirty as hell, you're drunk, and you were scared."

Emma swallowed and shifted her gaze downward, ashamed that she'd been silly enough to make an advance on Beau. Of course he didn't want her. She was just a weak, scared, shy little girl. Not a brazen, fiery woman like Sofia.

"Hey, look at me," Beau insisted, stroking her cheek to get her attention. Given no other choice, she warily met his eyes. "Angel, you have to know that I want you. Hell, I've wanted you since you walked out of the bathroom that first night wearing my t-shirt and sweats."

Emma's eyes widened slightly at his confession. She'd seen the way he looked at her but never dared to imagine he was actually attracted to her.

"But I would never, *ever*, take advantage of you," he told her fiercely. "No matter how much I want you, I would never do anything you weren't one hundred percent ready for and willing to do. And that means being willing to do sober."

Emma grimaced, cursing herself for going back for the bottle of wine.

Beau stroked her cheek again, his thumb rough against her delicate skin. "You've been through hell, Emma—and not just these past few weeks. I need to know that you're ready before I do anything that could scare or hurt you. I need to know that you're fully with me."

Emma considered that, satisfied that at least he wasn't flat out rejecting her. If she could prove to him that she wanted him and was ready to have him, then he would be on board. It wasn't that Beau *didn't* want her; he just didn't want her under these circumstances.

Unable to form a coherent response, she let out a pathetic hiccup.

Beau smiled fondly at her and pressed a kiss to her forehead. "Let's lie down," he suggested. "We can talk more tomorrow, when you're clear-headed. We both need to rest."

Emma obediently slipped under the covers, a yawn escaping her mouth. She managed to keep her eyes open long enough to watch Beau strip his t-shirt and pants off and turn off the light. When he settled in beside her and wrapped one arm protectively around her waist, she finally closed her eyes and settled into his side.

"Thank you for coming back to me," she whispered.

"Always," he promised.

15

Beau awoke with a crick in his neck the size of Texas, but the warm body lying against his made it much more bearable. Glancing down at Emma's sleeping figure, he found her head resting delicately against his chest, her hair lightly tickling his skin. She breathed evenly as she slept, showing no signs of waking.

Though he could have stayed there and watched her sleep all day, Beau was filthy from his surveillance mission the night before and desperately needed a shower. He and Diego had spent hours camped out in the dirt, staying out of sight while they watched various abandoned buildings for signs of life. They'd detected activity in one, which was a promising sign that they may have found Mason's new headquarters.

Carefully lifting Emma's head from his chest, Beau rested it on a nearby pillow, then slowly slid out of the bed. She shifted slightly with the loss of his body but quickly settled into a new position. When she let out a sweet sigh, Beau couldn't help but run his hand over her silky-smooth hair and brush his lips against her forehead.

A long shower was exactly what he needed to soothe his sore neck, remove the layer of grime from his body, and take care of his hard-on. It had taken all of his willpower to turn Emma down the night before. He wanted her so badly already, and hearing her say that she wanted him, too, practically undid him. But it was neither the time nor the place for him to try to take things further with her.

Taking care of himself in the shower it was.

Afterward, Beau climbed back into bed with Emma. She stirred as the mattress dipped beneath his weight, her body shifting toward him. Yawning, she stretched her legs out long before opening her eyes, immediately squinting against the morning light. It took a few moments for her to gain her bearings before looking up at Beau.

He was immediately relieved that he'd thought to put two Tylenol and a glass of water on her nightstand when her hazy, hungover eyes met his.

Grinning down at her, he moved a strand of hair off her forehead. "Hi, you."

"Hi," Emma murmured, her voice raspy. She sat up slowly, her hair falling messily over her shoulders.

"How are you feeling?"

She slowly massaged her temples. "My head hurts."

"I thought that might be the case." He nodded toward the nightstand. "Take those Tylenol and drink the water. All of it."

She dutifully swallowed the pills and a couple gulps of water. Turning to Beau, she took in his clean, clothed state and shot him an accusing glare. "How long have you been up?"

"Half an hour. I wanted you to sleep as long as you needed to. You were in rough shape last night."

She blinked a few times before groaning and falling back against the pillows. "Oh, God. I'm remembering now," she cried, throwing her hands over her eyes. "I made a complete fool of myself."

"Emma, no." Beau reached for her hands. "You weren't thinking clearly, and you got a little ahead of yourself. It's nothing to worry about. I've done my fair share of silly things while drunk."

She peeked out from under one hand to assess his answer.

"Look at me," he ordered, working to disentangle her arms. "Like I told you last night, I need to know that you're ready if we're going to be...intimate. I won't risk scaring you away."

Emma's lips bent into an adorable pout. "You would never do anything to scare me away."

His chest puffed with pride at her trust in him. "Not on purpose," he amended. "But you've been hurt by men before, and I'm afraid of accidentally triggering bad memories, no matter how much you may trust me."

Emma opened her mouth to argue some more, but Beau silenced her with a quick kiss.

"Not to mention that we're in my best friend's house," he said. "No way would I allow our first time to be in somebody else's house, in the middle of the night, while I'm coming off a job and you're drunk. I'll do this right, Emma. I won't half-ass things with you. You deserve way more than that. Honestly, you deserve more than me. But I'm selfish enough that if you want me, I'll accept it graciously."

Emma gazed up at him through her eyelashes. "I do want you."

Beau closed his eyes for a moment, soaking in those words before leaning in to kiss her nose. "And that makes me a very happy man. We'll get there, sweetheart, when you're ready."

She seemed to accept that and began pulling back the covers. "If you get to shower here, then I do, too."

Beau grinned at her obvious comfort with stating her needs. "I left you an extra towel on the side of the tub. But make it quick—I smell Isabella's famous French toast cooking."

Emma wiggled her eyebrows, making him chuckle, and scurried to the shower.

Damn, she was cute. And she wanted him. How fucking lucky was he?

Beau lay back in the bed with his hands under his head, content just to relax while Emma got ready for the day. He hoped she wasn't too hungover, because he had some plans that would require her to be alert and lively. When she returned from the bathroom after a few minutes—apparently, the promise of French toast was enough to hurry her up—her hair was wrapped up in a towel that looked like a beehive on top of her head.

Beau grinned at the sight. "Feeling any better?"

She nodded. "I think the Tylenol and water really helped."

"Good." He cracked his knuckles. "Because you have your first self-defense class today."

Her brow creased. "What?"

"When we get home, we're exercising and practicing some self-defense moves."

Emma groaned, and he chuckled at her irritation. "You're the one who asked me for help," he reminded her.

"I didn't think you'd choose to give it to me on the day of my first hangover."

He tried and failed to hold back his laughter. Grumpy Emma was adorable. He hoped he got to see her through many more hangovers. "At least you're having new experiences. This is a great learning opportunity for you."

"Trust me." She grimaced. "I'll never drink that much again."

He watched intently as she unwound her hair from the towel, then sat on the edge of the bed where he was sprawled.

Emma fidgeted with the corner of the bedspread. "Maybe I wouldn't be driven to drink if you didn't do such dangerous things," she said softly.

Beau sat up and met her gaze. "Angel, I hate that you were so scared, but if Diego and I don't go after Mason, then no one will. The P.D. isn't doing shit because of goddamn Williams. I promise that I'll always do my best to stay safe and come back to you."

She seemed to consider that before shrugging her shoulders. "I just…I don't want to lose you."

Beau tugged at her arm. "Come here." He pulled her into his embrace and whispered in her ear, "You're never going to lose me."

Emma sighed and melted into his arms. His stomach dropped when he heard a sniffle, thinking she was crying, but when she pulled away, she wore a lively grin.

"I smell the French toast."

Beau grinned back at her. "Well, let's get our asses down there before they eat it all." He stood and swept Emma up with him as he did. She let out a shriek of delight before he placed her on her feet and led her downstairs. With Emma's hand in his and the promise of his favorite French toast, he couldn't be happier.

꧁꧂

Isabella presented her French toast with her signature flourish—topped with assorted berries and slathered in maple syrup and powdered sugar. Emma's eyes lit up as Bella placed a heaping plate in front of her.

Beau shoved a big forkful into his mouth, groaning as the sickening sweetness hit his taste buds. He watched Emma cut hers meticulously into tiny little squares before placing one daintily on her tongue.

She chewed thoughtfully, then swallowed and turned to Isabella. "This is so good, Bella."

Isabella grinned. "Thanks, *chica*. It's a little strange—a Mexican being known for her French toast—but it's always been my favorite dish to make."

Emma took another bite, this time loading her fork with a few of the small pieces. "Well, you're a pro."

Isabella plunked down beside her husband, running a hand affectionately over his arm. "So, how did it go last night? Did you figure out where Mason's new headquarters is?"

Beau swallowed hard, disappointed the friendly talk had turned to Mason so quickly. He preferred Emma to be smiling and giggling, not having to think about the awful man who still haunted her dreams.

"It went well," Diego answered. "We checked out a few buildings and found some activity in one. We hid security cameras across the street to hopefully catch a sighting of Mason. If we can ensure that he's there, we can make a plan to move in."

Isabella took a long sip of her tea. "And if you can't prove he's there?"

Beau fielded that question. "Then we keep surveilling. If we move in too soon and only catch some of Mason's cronies and not the man himself, we could spook him and blow the whole operation. Mason could flee to another part of the country, and then we'll never get him."

Isabella waved her fork around in front of her, flinging syrup across her plate. "So you just sit back on your asses and watch the security tapes like some kind of home movie and wait to catch a glimpse of that *pendejo* before doing anything?"

Diego placed a soothing hand on his wife's shoulder, steadying her fork to stop the trail of syrup from ruining the tablecloth. "Bella, *mi amor*, you know how this goes. We can't rush this. Beau's right. If we tip our hand too soon, we could lose Mason forever. They're probably already on high alert after losing Emma, so we need to be extra careful."

"I know it sucks balls," Beau added. "But this is how investigations work. First, we gather information, then we can move to action."

Emma shifted beside him. "How do we know they aren't

abducting other women as we speak? What if they have a new shipment coming in?"

Beau ran a reassuring hand down her arm. "We're doing our best to monitor that. We have all the intel the police have, and there's no evidence of any new shipments coming in. Plus, I have some other tricks up my sleeve." He winked.

Emma quirked a brow. "What kind of tricks?"

He smirked and patted her shoulder. "Nothing you need to worry about. The first step is keeping an eye on those cameras to see if Mason makes an appearance. If he does, then we prep to move in and capture. If he doesn't, then tomorrow I play forgetful former cop again and go back to the police station to 'grab something I left in my locker,'" he said, bending his fingers in dramatic air quotes.

Emma rolled her eyes. "I have this funny feeling that you get away with everything," she muttered.

Diego howled with laughter, the sudden outburst causing him to practically choke on his French toast. Beau slapped his friend on the back as he continued laughing. Finally, wiping his eyes, Diego said, "You have no idea."

Isabella smiled to herself and speared her last square of French toast, popping it into her mouth. "Beau never gets in trouble," she said. "It's one of the advantages of being the youngest child."

Beau snorted. "It has nothing to do with birth order," he argued. "I'm just sneaky as shit, and no one can be suspicious of this face." He smiled innocently, placing his hands under his chin.

Emma rolled her eyes again. "Sure."

Beau chuckled, loving that she was giving him shit.

Diego stood to clear the table, piling the sticky plates atop each other. "What are you two up to today?" he asked, nodding toward Beau and Emma.

Emma pressed her lips together.

Beau leaned back and interlaced his hands behind his

head in a casual pose. "I'm giving Emma a crash course in self-defense today."

Isabella's eyes widened, and she clapped her hands together. "Oh, that's great! Diego has taught me lots of self-defense moves. God willing, I'll never have to use them, but they definitely make me feel safer."

Emma nodded quietly, looking down at the empty space where her plate had been. "That's what I'm hoping for. I just don't want to feel that helpless ever again."

Beau placed his hand on her upper thigh, squeezing it lightly. "I'll never let you feel that way again," he said in a low voice.

Emma met his gaze as her mouth curved into a shy smile. He couldn't help but lean in to kiss her forehead.

Diego and Isabella shared a look that Beau didn't miss. He knew his friend would give him shit for being so soft, since he was always dishing it out to him, but Beau didn't care. Or maybe Diego thought he was a fool for getting involved with Emma. Either way, he would happily deal with any comments from his friends if it meant Emma felt safe and loved.

Pulling away before he lost all semblance of self-control and started making out with her in front of his friends, Beau stood. "We'd better get going. We have a busy day of self-defense to get to, after all."

Emma groaned and looked to Isabella for support. Bella patted her sympathetically on the arm. "It's gonna suck while you're learning, but you'll be happy you did it when you feel like you can protect yourself."

"I know." Emma sighed, placing her hand in Beau's.

16

Emma gave excuses all day about why she couldn't do the self-defense class yet. She was full of French toast. Her headache had come back. She was still hungover. By four o'clock, she was out of ideas for holding Beau off.

The truth was, as much as she wanted to learn to protect herself, Emma worried that the process of learning self-defense moves would put her in too vulnerable a situation. She was still tender from her injuries, and having a man come at her in an aggressive way, touch her, pin her down... She wasn't sure she was ready for that, even if he was just pretending and she trusted him implicitly.

Finally dressed and ready, she joined Beau in the living room. Her heart began to race as she took in his strong figure wearing nothing but gray sweatpants. Her gaze roamed over his muscular torso, from the hair that dusted his chest and drew a line down his sternum to the V-shaped muscles pointing like an arrow to his...yeah. If she was going to torture herself this way, at least she got to admire Beau's abs of steel while doing it.

"Okay." Beau clapped his hands together like a high

school physical education teacher trying to rally a group of rowdy kids. "We're going to start with a few bodyweight exercises to increase your strength. Then, we'll go over some basic self-defense moves. All this stuff takes practice, so don't get discouraged if it feels hard today. It takes time to build up strength."

Emma nodded toward his six-pack. "How long did it take you to look like that?"

Beau smirked. "I've been lifting weights since I was fifteen."

"So, I shouldn't expect a six-pack after today's workout."

Beau wagged his head. "All you should expect from today's workout is to feel pretty sore in the morning."

Emma groaned theatrically.

"Hey, it's no worse than waking up with a hangover."

She rolled her eyes. "What's the first torture mechanism?"

"First, we stretch." Beau reached an arm above his head into a tricep stretch. Emma stared at the way the movement defined his chest, her thighs rubbing together of their own volition. If she poked one of his pecs, it would probably be hard as a rock.

"Emma," Beau interrupted her imaginings.

"Right," she said, quickly raising her own arm to mirror the stretch. Still distracted by Beau's chest, she couldn't help but ask, "Can you do the thing?" She moved one side of her chest up, then the other. "You know, this thing?"

Beau burst out laughing. "You mean, can I pop my pecs?" He dropped his arm to his side.

"Yeah."

Looking her dead in the eyes, he popped one pec and then the other.

Emma squealed and clapped her hands together. "You *can* do it!"

Beau shook his head, but his lips tipped into a smile. "I

think you're trying to distract me from my mission." He raised his other arm to stretch it, and she did the same.

"Is it working?" she asked.

"No way. Now let's stretch the quads."

Beau bent one leg at the knee and held his ankle in his hand. His balance was impeccable. He barely wavered, even while standing on one leg. Emma grabbed the back of the couch to hold herself steady while she imitated the stretch, feeling like a clumsy flamingo. They repeated it on the other side, then bent forward to stretch their hamstrings.

"Let's do some lunges," Beau said. He showed her how to step forward into a lunge, making sure to keep her knee over her ankle and not go too far forward. Emma mimicked the movement once on each side while Beau watched her form.

"Perfect!" he said. "Now we'll do ten on each side, then three sets of each exercise I showed you."

Emma gaped at him, eyes wide and mouth hanging open. "Ten on each side? Three sets? I have to do thirty of these?" Her muscles already felt strained from a single one.

Beau smiled knowingly. "No pain, no gain."

She rolled her eyes but continued to lunge alongside him.

After the first set, they moved on to squats. Then jumping jacks. Then Beau broke out some little weights and had her do bicep curls. And overhead presses. And tricep extensions. Then, they got on the floor and held planks for a minute—Emma only lasted thirty seconds, which Beau said was fine for her first time—and then they did the whole thing all over again two more times.

Emma was panting and dripping with sweat by the end of the workout. She sat on the floor and chugged a bottle of water beside Beau. He was barely winded, with only a light sheen of sweat covering his bare skin.

Emma shot him an accusing glare. "I think you're trying to kill me."

He chuckled. "Actually, quite the opposite. I'm trying to help you *not* get killed. Hence the term self-defense."

She pursed her lips. As much as she wanted to learn to defend herself, she wasn't looking forward to the process.

Beau eyed her as he took a small sip of water. "I need you to take your shirt off so I can see where your bruises are. I don't want to hurt you by pressing on one of them."

Emma frowned and looked down at her shirt.

"You have a sports bra on, don't you?" he asked.

She did. She'd borrowed one from Isabella. "Yes," she said, taking the hem of her shirt in her hands, then hesitating.

Beau's eyes softened. "Angel, I don't mean to make you uncomfortable. But I couldn't bear to hurt you, and if I catch one of those bruises, I'm going to."

His logic made sense, and she certainly didn't want to exacerbate any of her bruises right when they were finally starting to heal. She skimmed the shirt off and laid it over the side of the couch. Beau sucked in a breath, and for a split second, Emma worried that he didn't like what he saw, but she quickly realized he was eyeing the dark spots on her ribs. If you looked closely enough, you could even see defined fingertips in the bruising.

Emma chewed on her lip while he assessed the fading injuries. Then, he looked up and swallowed, his Adam's apple bobbing under the weight of his anger. "Okay, let's do this."

He stood, and Emma took his outstretched hand to pull herself up, too.

"What should I do?" she asked.

"You're going to pretend I'm a bad guy that's coming to hurt you. Show me how you would handle the situation."

She nodded, and Beau began walking toward her at a clipped pace. Instinctively, she reached out an arm to whack him. He grabbed her outstretched arm and quickly apprehended the other as well. She yelped—not hurt but surprised by his agility. With both hands cuffed around her wrists, Beau held her immobile.

"Darn it," Emma grumbled.

"It's okay," Beau assured her. "I wanted you to see what not to do. You don't want to give an attacker any advantages over you. Flailing out a body part without a plan is a surefire way to get yourself in trouble." He let go of her hands and stepped back. "Now, what body parts do you think are most vulnerable on me?"

Her cheeks heated, and she knew she'd turned bright pink. It was the curse of being so pale. "Well, I'd assume your… groin would be pretty vulnerable."

Beau smirked. "That's right. The balls are always a good place to start. Eyes, nose, and neck are also vulnerable spots, but a foot or knee to the nuts will do it almost every time. Just remember, as soon as you get the poor sucker on the ground, run. A kick in the groin only incapacitates a man for so long. Use that time wisely."

Emma nodded as her face cooled. "Got it."

"Okay, now we're going to practice that scenario again, except you're going to go for the groin this time. Just please don't actually kick me. I'd like to have kids someday."

Emma blinked, then realized he was making a joke and smiled. "Okay."

Beau walked back across the room, then stalked toward her once again. This time, she kept her arms pinned to her sides and raised one foot toward the apex of his legs as he approached. Beau reached down and cupped himself, falling theatrically to the floor. She giggled at his dramatics.

"That was much better," he said. "And what would you do once I was on the floor?"

"Run," Emma answered.

"That's right." Beau stood up and high-fived her. "Now, if for whatever reason he doesn't go down, if he's wearing a cup or something and the blow to the balls doesn't immobilize him, your next line of defense is a hand to his nose. Hit it hard enough and you'll break it."

He showed Emma how to use the heel of her hand to create enough force to do just that. "A staggered leg stance is going to give you the most stability," he explained. "So, keep one foot planted in front of the other, and push against the base of the nose with all your might."

Emma got into position and held the heel of her hand just beneath Beau's nose. Each huff of his breath flowed over her skin like spring air.

"Just like that," he said, kissing her open palm before stepping back. "You can also strike the neck with your elbow. If you're lucky, you'll knock the wind out of the guy."

She lifted her elbow toward Beau's thick neck, stopping just before it came into contact, and looked up at him for approval.

"Good." Beau kissed her forearm. "What else did we say was vulnerable on the face?"

"Eyes?"

"That's right. A poke in the eyes can be totally disorienting."

Emma lifted two fingers to Beau's cheeks, just below his eyes.

"Nice." He winked and kissed each fingertip. "And remember, you can always bite or headbutt, too. Whatever you have to do to disorient and incapacitate."

Emma nodded her understanding. "I just hope I can actually get myself to poke somebody's eyes or bite them."

"Trust me, in a situation where you're in danger, the adrenaline kicks in, and you kind of go on autopilot."

"But what if I don't remember what to do?"

"That's why we're practicing," Beau said. "Eventually, it just becomes muscle memory. You won't even have to think about it—your body will just do it."

"Okay," Emma replied skeptically.

Beau gave her a quick peck on the lips. "Trust me, angel. You're so much stronger and braver than you think. You can do this."

She was glad at least one of them thought so.

"Now, those moves are for if you're standing. Ideally, you can take someone down before they take *you* down. But if they manage to get you on the ground, you need to know how to get out from under them."

Emma swallowed hard. "How do you do that?"

"I'll show you," Beau said. "Why don't you lie down on the carpet here?"

She tentatively stepped over to the area he gestured at. Her eyes found Beau's, and he nodded encouragingly. After a deep breath, she sank to the ground and lay flat on her back.

Beau approached her cautiously, as if he sensed how difficult it was for her to put herself in such a vulnerable position. He arranged himself on his hands and knees above her. Emma was not immobilized—she could easily scoot out from under him if she wanted to—but the position still felt eerily familiar.

Realizing she was holding her breath, she let it out in a gasp of air.

Beau ran his thumb over her jaw. "You doing okay down there?"

"Yes," she choked out.

His eyes softened. "If you feel scared at any point, just let me know, and we can stop."

She took a breath, bracing herself. "I want to learn."

"Good girl," Beau breathed. "Now, in this position, you can still go for the groin, eyes, nose, and neck. But if you're pinned, you won't be able to use your hands, elbows, or knees. If you buck hard enough with your hips and then roll quickly, you can actually flip someone over. Then, when you're in the dominant position, you can go for those vulnerable areas, then run."

"That makes sense," Emma said, though she had no idea how she would ever be able to buck someone as large as Beau off of her. He easily had a hundred pounds on her.

Beau gently guided her arms up by her head and placed his hands over hers, effectively pinning her down. She focused on breathing.

"Now try and buck me off," Beau said.

Emma lifted her hips but was met with much resistance in the form of Beau's hard body. She dropped her hips back down to the floor with a grunt.

"Not bad, but you need to put some more force into it."

She tried again, harder this time. Beau's body shifted slightly above her.

"Better," he said. "It may take a few strikes until you're able to roll me. This time, buck up three times in a row, then push your hands into mine and roll your whole body over."

Emma did as he said, lifting her hips three times with force, then tried to roll, but Beau's body felt like a boulder on top of her.

"You're getting the hang of it," he said. "Now, pretend you're actually fighting for your life."

Closing her eyes, she took a couple of deep breaths. She pictured Mason's face in her mind. Then, Detective Williams' face. Then, the faces of all of the men she could remember from her time in captivity. Each new image that popped into her mind enraged her more than the last.

She thought of the way they had spoken to her, degraded her, and touched her in ways she longed to forget. She thought of the bruises that dotted her skin and how they had gotten there. She thought of the way she had let her father walk all over her all those years. Anger bubbled and bubbled until it finally boiled over.

Emma's eyes flew open, and she dug deep, bucking her hips at Beau's big body three times, then one extra for good luck, before pushing against him with all the power of the rage she held inside her. She vaguely registered him grunting, and suddenly, she was on top of him, straddling his hips, her hands over his fists.

She gasped. "I did it!"

He smiled beneath her. "You sure did."

Emma grinned triumphantly. "I can't believe I actually did it."

"I knew you could," Beau said, and judging by his tone, he actually meant it. He looked up at her as if she was a gold-medal winner at the Olympics.

Emma let go of his hands, and they fell down to her hips. He held her to him, though she was now in the dominant position and could once again easily remove herself.

Instead, she leaned down and kissed him.

Their lips met, and Emma opened her mouth, allowing Beau's tongue to slide in and explore. As it did, his hands made their way from her hips up to her ribs. His grip loosened to accommodate her bruises, but the feel of his hands against her bare skin still sent a jolt of heat down her spine.

Emma brought her hands to his chest and pressed against those delicious pecs. To her delight, he popped each one beneath her fingers. Laughing against his lips, she rubbed her fingers over the flat, hard disks of his nipples.

Breaking away after a moment, she pressed her forehead to his.

"Thank you," she whispered.

"For what?" Beau asked. "Popping my pecs? I know how much you love it."

Emma grinned. "No. For teaching me all those moves. It really does make me feel more confident."

Beau brushed her hair behind her ear and kissed the tip of her nose. "I'm glad."

Frowning, she glanced down at her sweaty skin. "Sorry," she muttered. "I'm gross, and I'm all over you." She started to get up, but Beau held on tight.

"Angel, I'll take you however I can get you."

Her eyes flicked to his, only to find them utterly sincere. He craned his neck up to find her lips once more. This time, though, it was just a quick smooch.

"Why don't you shower while I make us some dinner?" he suggested.

Emma hopped up and headed to the bathroom while Beau made his way to the kitchen. The elation of her victory put a skip in her step, as did Beau's now obvious interest. The previous night at Diego's had been a fluke. Beau was a gentleman and had refused her because she'd been drunk. But tonight, she wouldn't be drunk, he wouldn't be returning from a mission, and she hoped they would once again be sharing a bed—and not just because it was the only thing that kept her nightmares at bay.

17

Beau was no chef, but he knew how to make a mean burger. He flipped the patties in the pan when they sizzled, then headed to the counter to chop tomatoes and onions for garnish. After a beat, he realized he was humming as he cooked. He was actually fucking humming. And what song? "My Girl" by The Temptations. No fucking clue why. It had popped into his head when Emma left for her shower.

He watched the knife slice through the vegetables, trying his best not to get distracted by the thoughts of Emma running through his mind. He was apt to accidentally cut his finger off if he thought too closely about how sexy she'd looked in her sports bra and shorts—minus the bruises, of course. Not that he cared that her skin wasn't perfect, but they made him think about Mason, and then he got downright pissed.

He was so proud of Emma for putting in so much hard work. Not all women were willing to get sweaty like that, and her joy when she'd been able to flip him was contagious. He couldn't stop smiling like a fool as he traipsed around the kitchen.

His smile only got bigger when Emma emerged, drowning in his Boston P.D. t-shirt. It fell below the hem of her shorts, making it look like a dress or a skimpy nightgown. Her hair was already out of its towel beehive and cascaded down past her shoulders in soft blonde tendrils.

"Hey," she greeted him as she peeked around his arm into the pan on the stove. "Whatcha makin'?"

"Burgers," Beau replied as he flipped them again, careful not to let them burn.

Emma rubbed her stomach. "Mmmm. Sounds perfect. I worked up an appetite."

"Exercise will do that to you. Remember, you'll probably be sore tomorrow. We won't practice again for a few days to give your body a break."

"Okay." Emma filled up two cups with water and placed them on the island.

"Can you grab the ketchup and mustard?" Beau asked.

"Done." Emma got the condiments and set them out while he plated the burgers. He dressed his burger with onions, tomatoes, lettuce, ketchup, and mustard. When he put the top bun on, Emma giggled at the finished product.

"What?" he asked, an amused grin stretching across his face.

"How will that even fit into your mouth?"

He pursed his lips, holding back the lewd comment he really wanted to make, and shrugged. "Like this." He shoved one end of the burger into his mouth and took a large bite. Emma's giggles turned into full-on laughter as he attempted to chew it without looking like a cow.

"That was probably a bad idea," he said when he'd finally managed to swallow.

She shook her head and squirted a small amount of ketchup on her own burger, along with single slices of lettuce and tomato.

"Do you want to watch another movie tonight? Or would you rather read?" he asked.

"Oh, actually, I'd love to read." Emma smiled at him as if delighted by the fact that he'd suggested it.

"Sure," he said with a shrug. "I may just tool around on my phone for a while. I haven't watched ridiculous YouTube videos yet this week."

Emma grinned, shaking her head, and finished her burger.

After dinner, they decided to relax in bed instead of on the couch. Beau figured Emma was probably worn out from all the exercise, so he queued up the top ten viral videos from the past week while she read quietly beside him. He felt like a jerk for sitting there watching silly videos of cats and pranks and people falling down while Emma read what looked like a very serious and academic book from Fletcher's collection.

He had to admit that he loved watching the way she squinted her eyes and furrowed her brow as she read, though. Sometimes her nose scrunched up like a little bunny, and he almost wanted to ask her about what she was reading but feared he wouldn't be able to carry on a conversation about literature. Instead, he continued watching foolish people doing foolish things because that was just about the level of intelligence he could handle.

After the second video, in which a dog had been chasing its tail and had gotten it stuck in its mouth so it turned in perpetual circles, he looked over at Emma. "Are you sure the background noise doesn't bother you?"

She looked up from her book and shook her head, her blonde curls bouncing. "Not at all. When I read, I kind of zone out and don't notice anything else that's going on."

Beau shook his head. "I don't know how you do that." He'd never been a big reader, partially because he couldn't sit still for long, but also because he was easily distracted.

Emma shrugged. "I've always been able to stay very

focused on it, even when I was a little kid. Reading was always my escape. Even if I couldn't go anywhere or do anything I wanted to do, I could experience all those things through books. I guess maybe I didn't want to miss anything, so I learned to pay really close attention."

Beau's chest grew tight at the thought of a little golden-eyed girl who only ever experienced life through books. Not wanting to dwell on that thought, he replied, "I guess I never read enough to learn to do that."

Emma studied him for a moment, then shut her book and placed it on the nightstand. "Fletcher told me your dad taught him to love reading."

Beau's eyebrows drew together, unsure why that was relevant. "I guess that's probably true."

"You never got that chance because he died when you were so young," Emma added.

"Also true."

She let out a soft sigh. "I'm so sorry, Beau. It must have been really hard to grow up without him."

Her sincerity and wide, innocent eyes made her the cutest thing Beau had ever seen.

"This might sound awful," he said, "but it wasn't as hard for me as it was for Fletcher or even Jack. I was only two when my dad died. Jack was four, and Fletcher was fourteen. I don't even remember my father. The only life I've ever known is a life without him. Of course that makes me sad sometimes, but it's not like I'm missing anything specific about him, because I can't remember anything. I just missed out on having a dad altogether."

Emma nodded, her eyes downcast. "That doesn't sound awful. It makes perfect sense." She picked at a nail, and Beau realized her thoughts must have drifted to her own father.

Trying to think of a way to distract her, he tipped her chin up with his fingers until she met his gaze. "You looked so sexy sitting there reading," he murmured.

A light blush painted her cheeks.

"Seriously," he said. "I never knew I was into smart girls, but damn." He looked her sitting form up and down once. "I definitely am."

Emma smiled shyly, and he brushed a finger over her cheek. Her blush deepened, then her smile faded.

"Isabella told me that you tend to go for…louder, more confident girls," she said, tilting her head to the side.

Beau ran a hand over his face. *Fuck*. He didn't want to talk about his relationship problems right now. Not when Emma was beside him in bed, all warm, and soft, and wearing his t-shirt, looking like a woman who was ready to make love. "Uh, yeah, I guess that's true," he said, scratching the back of his neck.

Emma pouted, and he wanted to kiss the frown right off her face, but she was clearly disturbed about something, and he had to get to the bottom of it first.

"I'm not your type," she said matter-of-factly.

Beau couldn't help but snort at that. "That's for damn sure."

Emma's frown deepened, and she began to roll away, but he caught her and pulled her into his chest before she could follow through.

Wanting to reassure her again that what had happened at Diego's really was just bad timing, he planted a kiss on the crown of her head. "Angel, you're so much sweeter, kinder, stronger, and braver than any woman I've ever been with. It's so incredibly sexy. I have never been so turned on by someone."

She blinked. "Oh."

"Yeah, oh," he said with a smirk, running his hand down the length of her arm to her hip. "You're so fucking sexy I don't even know what to do with myself."

Emma's eyes widened for a moment, as if she couldn't quite believe the words she was hearing, then her lips curved into a coy smile. "I know one thing you could do," she said before leaning in to kiss him, her lips soft and pliant against his.

Beau took the lead, directing her lips with his before coaxing them open with his tongue. She sighed into his mouth as she melted against his body, her hands skimming over his arms, shoulders, and chest.

Though he was focused on the kiss, Beau couldn't help but notice as her hand made its way under his shirt. One petite palm pressed against the bottom of his abdomen like a hot brand, and Emma charted his abs with her fingers as he traced her lips with his tongue. Beau shivered beneath her touch, and she nudged his shirt higher up to access more skin.

Pulling back, he checked her face for any signs of discomfort, but all he found was a look of drugged pleasure. Biting her lip, Emma pulled his t-shirt off over his head. Beau sat still as she stared at his abs, then his chest. He popped his pecs a few times and triumphed when Emma giggled—his favorite sound in the world.

"Come here," he said, placing a hand on the back of her neck and pulling her in for another kiss, her lips like satin against his. Emma's hands wandered over every inch of his exposed skin as they kissed. He fought to keep one hand on the back of her neck and the other on the small of her back, though he longed to explore further.

Hard as a rock, Beau positioned himself carefully so he didn't press into her. One wrong move and he feared he would scare her away. Emma's hands wandered up to his shoulder blades, and she pulled him in even closer, testing his resolve. When her knee came close to bumping into his hard-on, he pulled back.

"Hold on," he panted. "I need to take a beat."

Emma leaned back with a frown. One of her hands slid to the back of his neck and stroked over the short hair there. "Why? What's wrong?"

"Nothing's wrong," he said quickly, not wanting her to think he was rejecting her again. "I just need to stop for a second."

Her lips tugged into a sensual smile, and she pulled at him to come closer. "You don't need to stop."

"Angel," Beau groaned, throwing his head back. "I only have so much self-control." Returning his gaze to hers, he was stunned by the heat he found in her eyes. Her golden irises licked like flames at her dilated pupils.

"You don't need to control yourself, Beau," she said. "I want you. Right now. I *need* you." Leaning in, she closed the distance between them and licked at his lips until they opened, kissing him greedily. Her hands ran up and down the length of his back as her tongue did the same to his.

After a moment, Beau pulled back and cradled her face in his hands. "Are you sure you want this? There's no rush. I want you to be sure."

"I'm sure," Emma insisted. His eyes roamed her face and found nothing but certainty in her expression. "I've never trusted someone like I trust you, or wanted someone like I want you, Beau. I want you to show me what it's supposed to be like. Show me what it's like to be with a good man. Please, Beau."

On a long exhale, he dropped his forehead to hers. He wanted nothing more than to lay Emma down and make her his. Every instinct in his body was screaming at him to claim her, possess her, take her. But the rational part of his brain worried that she wasn't ready. She was still fragile and so inexperienced.

Emma seemed to sense his uncertainty, because she went on to remind him, "You told me to tell you what I need, and you said you would always give it to me. I'm clear-headed, and I'm telling you that this is what I need."

With a sigh, Beau ran his hand over her soft curls and

down to her upper arm, goosebumps blooming on her skin beneath his touch. "Are you positive?" he asked.

In response, Emma reached down and grabbed the bottom of her oversized t-shirt— looking him dead in the eye —and stripped it off. Beau sucked in a breath when he realized she wore no bra. Her bare breasts captured his gaze— perfect little mounds peaked with rosy-pink nipples.

His eyes flicked up to hers, which were watching him with piqued interest. Slowly, Beau raised one hand toward her chest, allowing her plenty of time to stop him. Instead, Emma pressed forward and into his touch. He could easily fit one of her breasts in each palm, and he did so, gently testing their weight in his hands.

"So beautiful," he breathed as he ran his thumb over a blush-colored nipple. It grew hard, and she looked down at where their skin met, equally as fascinated as he was by the contact. His gaze roamed over the rest of her skin, and he frowned at the map of bruises on her ribcage—the same ones that had caught him off guard when she'd taken off her shirt to exercise. He could make out some fucker's fingerprints on her skin, and it killed him. Gently, he ran his own fingertips over the dark spots, and Emma shivered beneath his hands.

"Lie back," he instructed softly.

She swallowed hard, losing her bravado for a moment, but did as he'd said and stretched out on her back. Beau observed her for a moment, with her hair spread out over his pillow, her breasts bared to his gaze, and her hands fisted in his sheets. He never wanted to forget this moment, when this beautiful angel gave herself over to him.

Hoping to distract Emma from any demons trying to fight their way into her mind, he lay beside her, propping his hand on his fist. "You know," he said, his voice gravelly, "I think my 'type' has changed."

Emma peeked up at him. "Oh yeah?"

"Yeah," Beau said, a wolfish grin breaking out across his face. "See, I've realized that I'm really into sweet, blonde angels." He stroked his hand over her hair. "With perfect pink nipples." He tweaked each one between his thumb and forefinger, making her squeak. "And I've also discovered that I really dig pale, creamy skin," he continued, running his fingertips along her side from her chest to her hip, then across her waist.

Her amber eyes blazed up at him, and a slow smile worked its way over her perfect lips. "You know, I think I've found my type, too."

Beau's heart lit up like a fucking Christmas tree, but he did his best to stay calm, cool, and collected as he asked, "Yeah? And what's that?"

She traced his six-pack lazily with her fingertip. "Well, I think muscles are incredibly sexy." Her finger drew a path up to his chest. "And I really like a guy who can pop his pecs."

Beau indulgently popped his pecs beneath her finger, eliciting his favorite giggle.

She placed her palm on the cluster of tattoos on his chest, though her fingers were too short to span their entirety. "And I never really knew I liked tattoos before, but I've discovered that they're a major turn-on."

"I'm very happy to hear that," Beau murmured, relieved to see Emma's playful side emerging—a sign that she was growing more comfortable. Cautiously, he leaned over and pressed his lips tenderly to a bruise on her shoulder, then lower to her ribs, and lower still to a dark spot on her waist.

Emma shuddered and sighed.

He slowly shifted over her, hovering a moment before settling himself between her legs and catching her gaze. "Is this okay?"

"Mhmm," she mumbled dreamily.

Grinning, he whispered, "Good," then prepared to do

exactly what she'd asked for. "A real man"—he pressed a kiss to the side of one breast—"puts his partner's pleasure"—he kissed the other side—"before his own." His mouth descended to the valley between her breasts, leisurely licking the column of skin there before moving to hover above her other breast. "A real man"—he placed a kiss on the inside of her breast—"finds pleasure"—his tongue dragged a rainbow over the top of her breast to the outer edge—"in giving his partner pleasure."

Beau swiftly glanced up and found Emma watching him beneath half-hooded eyelids. He took that as a sign that she was enjoying his kisses as much as he was and returned his attention to her breasts. Reaching up, he rolled a nipple between his thumb and forefinger to harden it before placing a kiss on it.

Emma gasped, and Beau grinned at her responsiveness. "Does that feel good?"

"*Yes*," she sighed.

Satisfied with that answer, he kissed her nipple again, then sucked it tenderly between his lips. Emma arched up involuntarily, giving him the go-ahead to suck harder. As he did, she brought a hand to the back of his head and tugged at his hair. He usually kept it much shorter, but with the events of the past few weeks, Beau hadn't had a chance to get to the barber. Now, he was quite glad for that fact because Emma tugging on his hair was a huge turn-on.

Moving across to her other breast, he gave that nipple the same treatment. When he was done, Emma was breathless and ready for more.

He leaned back and fingered the bottom of her shorts. "Is it okay if I take these off?"

She nodded silently.

"Tell me out loud."

"Yes," she said softly.

"You know we can stop at any time, right? You just say the word and we stop."

She nodded. "I know."

Tucking his thumbs into her shorts, Beau tugged them off, watching her facial expressions for any sign of panic as he did so. His eyes widened when he looked down and realized she wasn't wearing any underwear either.

"No panties? You're naughty," he said.

Emma's face turned bright red, and her knees knocked together.

Beau chuckled and ran his hands over the tops of her thighs. "Don't worry. I like it." He ran soothing circles over her upper thighs, gently encouraging her to open her legs for him. Tentatively, she drew her knees apart and bared herself to his gaze, which dropped to the apex of her inner thighs, already glistening with need. The downy hair above was the color of honey, and Beau was willing to bet she tasted just as sweet. Her light coloring made her look like some sort of ethereal creature—a goddess, a siren, luring him out to sea, or, as he liked to think of her, an angel come to Earth.

"Beautiful," he said again, unable to come up with a word that aptly described how incredibly stunning he found her.

Emma's face remained flushed under his appraisal. He felt her tense beneath his hands, and he continued stroking circles on her inner thighs while he checked in with her. "How are you feeling?"

"Good," she said quickly. "Just…I'm not used to this."

"I know," he said softly. "I'm going to take good care of you."

Her muscles relaxed as he kneaded a bit deeper with his thumbs. Dragging one a bit higher, he hovered over her seam as he waited for some sort of permission to touch her there.

Emma lifted her hips into his touch, and Beau heard her sharp intake of breath when skin met skin. He stilled for a moment to let her acclimate to the feeling of his finger on her, then ran it through her slickness. Just that light touch had her squirming beneath him, but he took his time touching her, leisurely getting to know this most intimate part of her.

Emma moaned when he reached the bundle of nerves above her damp lips. Using his thumb to drag moisture over it, he massaged it in a slow circle. "Do you like this?" he asked as he circled her again.

She nodded.

"Tell me out loud."

"*Yes.*"

Beau grinned. "Then I think you'll *really* like this," he said as he slid onto his stomach, positioning himself just above her. With one hand on each of her inner thighs, he didn't hesitate before bringing his lips to cover the area he'd been stroking just moments before.

Emma gasped in surprise. Licking up her seam, he reached her clit, and her hips jumped.

"Fuck," he muttered. "You're sweet."

His lips returned to lap up her wetness, which tasted even sweeter than honey. Emma's gasps and moans let him know he was doing a good job, as did the hand she brought to the back of his head to hold him there. He ate her hungrily until she was wriggling and bucking desperately against his mouth.

Pulling back slightly, he ran his hand over the smooth skin of her inner thigh. Her eyes, which had been sealed shut, opened to peer down at him.

"Angel," Beau murmured. "I'm going to put a finger inside of you now."

Emma's eyes widened, but her muscles remained relaxed, which he took as a win.

"Are you ready?" he asked.

"Ready," she whispered.

Maintaining eye contact, he trailed a finger up her inner thigh and over her lips. Her eyes were on fire and alight with curiosity, not an ounce of fear to be found. Ever so slowly, he pushed the tip of his pointer finger inside of her. She gasped but showed no signs of discomfort.

"My beautiful, brave angel," Beau crooned as he slid his finger all the way in. Emma's eyes snapped shut, and she groaned at the same time he did.

"Fuck," he hissed as she clenched around his finger. "How is that?" he asked, withdrawing his finger and pushing it back in. It glided easily through her slickness.

"It's... It's good," Emma mumbled. "Really good."

Beau grinned like a man who'd just won the lottery. "Good." He slid a second finger in, and Emma moaned as she ground down on them both.

"There you go. Good girl," he murmured, bringing his mouth back down over her while he continued to stroke his fingers in and out. Emma arched into him, squeezing around his fingers, and he knew she was getting close. He continued his teasing touches while he alternated sucking on her clit and licking circles around it.

Emma's thighs tensed and began to shake, so he doubled down with an extra-long suck, and then she was coming with a long moan, head thrown back, eyes screwed shut, looking every bit the goddess that she was.

Beau kissed her lightly on her inner thighs, bikini line, and that honey-colored hair, working her down from her orgasm before gingerly withdrawing his fingers. Her knees remained wide and eyes shut as she lay there, limp and boneless.

He grinned at her satisfied sigh and lay down beside her, face to face. As he stroked his thumb over her jaw, Emma opened her eyes, blurry with pleasure, and smiled at him. Beau didn't think he'd ever seen a more satisfied woman.

"Wow," she whispered. "That was...wow."

He leaned in to kiss the tip of her nose. Her cheeks had turned the loveliest shade of pink. Pride surged through his blood at the pleasure he'd given her. "That's what it feels like to be with a good man," he said. "Every single time."

"Every single time?" she asked in astonishment.

"Yep." Beau couldn't help but lean in again to kiss her cheek. "Sometimes there are extenuating circumstances, like you've got a lot on your mind or something, and you may not always climax, but for the most part, yeah, it should feel that good."

She raised her eyebrows. "Oh."

He grinned at her revelation, his heart soaring.

"I didn't know it could feel like *that*," she admitted quietly, eyes downcast.

Though he didn't know quite how inexperienced Emma really was, she clearly hadn't had many, if any, pleasurable sexual interactions with a man.

"Come here." Beau pulled her in closer to his chest, and her knee brushed against his raging erection—a natural but unfortunate byproduct of having the most beautiful woman he'd ever seen take her shirt off and ask him to show her what sex was supposed to be like.

Emma's gaze flew down to the bulge in his shorts, her eyes growing wide as saucers. "Oh, right. You're...you're still...you didn't..."

Beau ran his hand over her soft hair. "It's okay, angel. That was all for you. Though, trust me, I enjoyed it every bit as much as you did, if not more."

"But...don't you want to..." She was staring at his lap but couldn't bring herself to finish the sentence, both of which made Beau's lips lift into a smile.

"No. I'm fine, really," he said.

Finally, she looked back up at him, her nose scrunched in consternation. "Does it hurt?"

Her inexperience was charming, and her concern evident. It was the sweetest damn thing.

"No, sweetheart, it doesn't hurt. It's a bit uncomfortable, yes, but I've been through far worse."

She stroked a hand over his chest. "Are you sure you don't want me to..." she trailed off.

"No." Beau pecked her on the lips. "That was for you."

"Well...next time it will be for both of us, okay?" There was a hopeful tinge to her voice, and Beau wanted to pump his fist in the air and scream, *She wants me!* Instead, he settled her against his chest and tucked her head under his chin.

"Okay."

18

Emma hadn't realized how incredibly entertaining it would be to watch a macho man do a domestic task. As she sat on the closed toilet lid, wearing only Beau's t-shirt, he poured a scoop of Epsom salt and a capful of lavender-scented bubble bath into the tub full of warm water. The muscles of his arms undulated as he lifted and poured the jug of bubble bath.

She'd woken up sore from exercising, as Beau had warned her she would, and he'd insisted she take a bath to relax her muscles. He claimed he took them all the time when he was sore from a workout or a strenuous day on the job. Emma couldn't quite imagine the large man soaking in a bath, but she wasn't averse to seeing it for herself.

"The bubble bath is Christa's," Beau explained as soapy bubbles began to fizz under the running faucet.

"Christa?"

"Fletcher's girlfriend. All the girly stuff you see in this bathroom is hers." Beau stuck a hand into the bath to test the water. "It feels good—warm but not scalding." He turned the faucet off and twisted toward Emma. "Do you need anything else?"

Looking around at the clean towel he'd slung over the towel rack and the line of shower products on the tub, she shook her head.

"Good," Beau said. "I'll make us some breakfast while you soak. Take as long as you need." He pressed a kiss to her forehead and turned to leave.

Emma grabbed for his hand, and he spun around.

"Will you…join me?" she asked, gesturing to the inviting, bubble-filled bath.

His eyebrows drew up. "Are you sure you want me to?"

"Yes." After the night before, she wanted nothing more than to be pressed against Beau's body, skin to skin. His eyes searched her face as he took it in his hands, the calluses on his palms rubbing against her cheeks. There was something so hot in the scrape of his rough skin against hers.

"I would love to." Beau leaned down for a quick kiss, then pulled back to remove his shirt, revealing the toned body that Emma couldn't get enough of. She didn't think she'd ever get tired of that view.

Turning slightly, she averted her gaze as he pulled down his shorts. She wasn't sure why she bothered with modesty when they were about to be naked in a bathtub together, but luckily, Beau didn't acknowledge it as he stepped into the bath. She tugged her own shirt off, and by the time she turned around, his lower half was already hidden by a mountain of bubbles.

Emma sighed in relief. Gingerly stepping into the water, she sat with her back to Beau's front, groaning as the hot water hit her tired muscles. The heat from his body and the bath enveloped her, and he let her get settled a bit before taking her palms and placing them against his knees. The position allowed her to relax back into him, her head resting on his chest.

"This is a lot more comfortable than sleeping in here," Emma said after a beat.

Beau chuckled, and she could feel the movement in his chest beneath her head. "I'll bet."

One of his hands came to cover hers, and she turned her palm up so their fingers could intertwine. "You know that first night when you rescued me, and you were driving me home in your car?" she asked.

"Yeah," Beau said quietly, squeezing her hand.

"Well, I noticed your hands that night, on the steering wheel. They looked so huge, and I couldn't stop thinking about how you could probably kill someone with your bare hands."

His grip on her loosened. "I could."

The way he said it sent a shiver down Emma's spine. She unwound their fingers so their palms were pressed together. His fingers dwarfed hers.

Beau spoke softly into her ear. "The thing is, hands that can hurt can also protect. People always have a choice of how they'll use their power. It takes just as much effort to hurt someone as it does to help them."

Despite the delightfully warm water, Emma shivered again as his breath teased over her neck. She intertwined her fingers with his once more. "I'm really glad you found me."

Beau placed a chaste kiss on the top of her head. "So am I."

They continued to soak for long minutes, their hands occasionally wandering over each other's skin. Emma could feel Beau's hard length pressed against her back, but instead of bothering or scaring her, it aroused her. He was hard for *her*. He thought she was beautiful and strong, and he *wanted her*.

Beau shifted behind her, and she realized he'd grabbed a bottle of rose-scented body wash off the ledge of the tub. Squirting some into his big palm, he began rubbing it over her back and shoulders. She moaned as he hit a particularly sore spot, and he rewarded her with some extra-deep pressure.

Pressing a kiss to each of her shoulder blades, he massaged the knots in her back.

Emma sighed as his hands made their way to her belly, then began inching upward, soaping every inch of her skin with the luscious, fragrant scent. Calloused palms ran over her breasts, and the rough skin of his thumbs perked her nipples right up. A light pinch made her jump and tighten her hold on Beau's legs.

He chuckled low in her ear. "This is why I shouldn't have joined you. I'm supposed to be letting you soak your sore muscles, but I can't keep my hands off you."

Emma stroked his thighs, feeling the coarse hair there, and turned her cheek to his chest. "Luckily, I like having your hands on me."

Beau groaned and kissed her hair as he dragged his hands lower, down her legs and then back up again, stopping at the junction of her thighs, waiting for permission.

Emma allowed her legs to fall open and her head to loll back against Beau's chest. The hot water, the heady scents of lavender and rose, and his tantalizing touch had lulled her into a state of utter bliss that was only heightened when his hand brushed over her slick opening.

"Yes," she whispered, knowing he'd require her verbal consent.

Without skipping a beat, Beau's fingers skimmed over her, grazing her clit but not stopping to lavish it. His hands remained in motion, one below her belly and the other wandering over her breasts, rubbing and pinching. Before she knew it, she was grinding against his hand, eager for more.

Beau's excitement was evident in the press of his erection against her back, but he touched her patiently, caressing the parts of her he'd discovered the previous night and working her into a frenzy. Emma let out an impatient noise, and Beau kissed her temple as he carefully slipped a finger inside of her, working it in and out slowly and steadily.

Mewling, she clutched onto his legs as she rode his finger, and then fingers when he added a second one. She knew her nails were probably digging into his skin, but she couldn't stop herself from squeezing even harder as his thumb found her sweet spot. She cried out loudly with pleasure.

"Shhh," Beau whispered in her ear as he held her close and continued working her over with skillful hands. "I've got you." One kneaded a breast while the other both penetrated her and rubbed her clit at the same time. Though Emma didn't quite comprehend the logistics of that, it felt incredible.

She climbed higher and higher, completely at the mercy of the pleasure Beau gave her until, surrounded by flowing water and hot, hard man, she came.

Beau grunted when she clenched and spasmed around him. She made a guttural sound, and his hand stilled, letting her ride out her orgasm without overstimulating her. It felt like falling, but not hard and fast like a heavy object falling from a great height. More like a feather floating down lazily as the wind carried it ever so gently to the ground.

Vaguely aware of Beau stroking her inner thighs, Emma opened her eyes and watched his hands move over her skin. She relaxed her own, resting them atop his thighs, and frowned when she caught sight of the little red half-moons indented in his skin where her nails had been.

"I'm sorry," she whispered as she ran a finger over the imprints of her desperation.

Beau caught her hand and kissed it. "It's okay, angel. Did you enjoy that?"

Though her cheeks were already flushed from the bath and the orgasm, she felt the color deepen. "I think you know I did."

He chuckled and nipped at the shell of her ear. "Just making sure," he whispered, his breath hot over her skin. He remained rigid against her back, and Emma squirmed against the thick column.

"The next time was supposed to be for both of us," she reminded him.

Beau kissed her hair and hit the lever to drain the tub with his big toe. "This one didn't count because we were in the bathtub. Next time we're in bed, it can be for both of us."

Though she didn't really follow that logic, Emma didn't have a chance to object before Beau was lifting her by the hips to stand. Grabbing a fluffy towel, she wrapped herself up in it and waited for him to do the same.

"Why don't you go get ready, and I'll rinse off in a cold shower?" he suggested.

Emma frowned, her eyebrows drawing together. "But we just took a bath."

Beau shot her a wry smile. "The cold shower isn't to get clean."

Her cheeks heated, and she hoped the color could be blamed on the humidity in the bathroom. A quick glance at the mirror confirmed that they had, indeed, turned tomato-red. "Okay," she murmured, scurrying to the bedroom to get dressed and apply a bit of the makeup Isabella had bought for her.

Once again, she felt bad about leaving Beau hanging, even though it was at his insistence. She would just have to make sure that the next time they were in bed together, she blew his mind.

A few minutes later, Beau entered the room with a towel wrapped around his waist and his hair damp. A few water droplets spilled down his chest, and Emma watched them trail down his abdomen.

"Feeling better?" she asked.

"I was until I came in and saw you looking so beautiful," he muttered, prowling over to where she sat on the bed and pulling her in for a healthy kiss.

Emma grinned mischievously. "Sorry about that." Just

because she felt bad didn't mean she didn't enjoy driving him wild. It made her feel powerful and desirable.

Averting her eyes while Beau pulled on his boxers, Emma watched him as he dressed the rest of the way. It was a shame to hide away all that toned goodness, but she knew she would get her chance to explore it all soon enough.

Beau cooked them a big breakfast of bacon, eggs, toast, and fruit. He even squeezed a few oranges to make them fresh orange juice. It was an impressive spread that Emma was thrilled by until she learned that it was an advanced apology for the fact that Beau would be gone for a good part of the day.

"I'm sorry, angel. I wish I could stay here with you, but there are a few things I have to do that Diego can't," he said between sips of his juice.

"Like what?"

"Well, I have to go into the station again, like I said."

"Do you think you'll find any information you don't already have?"

Beau shrugged, his massive shoulders brushing the bottoms of his ears. "Maybe. You never know. But I also plan to put a bug in Detective Williams' office while I'm there."

Emma's nose scrunched in confusion. "A bug?"

"A recording device," Beau said, his lips twisting into a smile. "Not a cockroach."

"Ah, I see." She nodded once before muttering, "I wish he'd walk in to find his office full of cockroaches."

Beau chuckled at the thought. "So do I. If Diego went down to the station, it would be too noticeable. I still have the excuse of forgetting something, so I have to do that"—he rubbed the back of his neck—"and then I have to go talk to your father."

"What?" Emma shrieked, too shocked to worry about how horrifyingly shrill her voice sounded.

"Relax, sweetheart," he said in a calm, soothing tone, as if he was talking to a scared animal he'd backed into a corner. "I'm not going to tell him I have you, or know you, or anything like that. I'm just going to question him and see what I can get him to admit to."

"What will you question him about without bringing me into it?" she asked.

"I'm going to ask him about his association with Williams. Diego staked out one of the illegal card games your father loves last night. He got video footage of him playing, so we have some leverage. I'll tell him I'm investigating a detective from my department that we suspect has some illegal dealings. Maybe I can get him to turn on Williams and admit he's in the human-trafficking game. Down the road, he could be a really helpful witness."

Emma's stomach twisted. "You're not just going to let him be a witness and then get away, are you?"

"Angel." Beau scooted closer to Emma. "If you think I will, for one second, even entertain the thought of your father spending any more of his life outside of a jail cell, you're dead wrong, because I'm going to put him there myself. He'll never see the light of day again if I have anything to say about it. But it's not just him I want. I want Williams, and Mason, and the whole damn operation to go down in flames. If I can get your father to spill the beans, he might be able to get himself some kind of deal, like more outdoor time or some money in his commissary, but he will be gone for good. I'll make sure of it."

"What if he runs away before then?" she asked, the knot in her stomach growing tighter. "What if he gets spooked because the police are questioning him, even if it's about someone else, and he gets away?"

"I hate to break it to you, sweetheart," Beau said, "but your father is an addict. His whole network is here. If he ran away, he'd have to find new games and all new connections."

Emma chewed on her lip. "I guess that makes sense. I just don't want him to get away."

"He won't," Beau promised. "If I can manage it, I'll set up a bug in his house, too. If he packs up to leave anywhere, I'll know, and he won't be able to get far. But I really don't think he'll try."

"And you promise you'll get him eventually?"

Beau leaned down to kiss her forehead. "I promise. We'll use him for all he's worth, then lock him up for good."

Emma stiffened. "Just like he tried to do to me."

Beau bowed his head until their foreheads connected. "I will never let him hurt you again."

Emma wrapped her arms around him and pressed her face into his warm neck, soaking in his strength. Engulfed in Beau's embrace, she felt like she could breathe deeply. The rest of the world seemed to fall away, her troubles included. Not only could she trust him to protect her, but now she knew he desired her, and somehow, that had become equally as important.

Beau waited until her arms loosened to pull away. "Fletcher will come stay with you."

"Doesn't he have school?"

"It's Saturday," Beau said gently.

"Oh," she mumbled. With so much else to keep her mind occupied, she really hadn't been keeping track of the days.

Beau smiled softly and brushed her hair behind her ear. "It's okay, angel. No one expects you to be in tune with the real world given all you've gone through."

Emma sighed and returned to her breakfast. As much as she would love to return to normal life, she knew she wouldn't be returning to the life she had known. She would never live in her father's home again. She would never rely on his money, but instead would have to find a job to support herself. It felt like she'd reached a turning point. There was no looking back now.

As scary as it was to look into the unknown, she had hope that the future could be far better than the past. Free from her father's influence, she could pursue whatever her heart desired. Perhaps she would finally get a job at the local library, or maybe even try out some college courses. She'd always done well in school and enjoyed learning. She could have friends, and they wouldn't be scared off by her father or her unorthodox lifestyle. She could even find love, like Isabella had said.

The endless possibilities excited Emma almost as much as the prospect of Beau's return, when she would finally get him in bed and give him the same pleasure he'd given her.

19

Beau resented the disapproving glare he got from Fletcher when he kissed Emma goodbye. It wasn't like it had been over the top—just a peck on her lips. Okay, and maybe he'd slipped a little tongue in there, but he needed to give Emma something to remember him by while he was gone all day and she was hanging out with his older, wiser, more intelligent brother.

Beau had grown used to Fletcher's judgment. Having practically raised him, Fletcher had seen him do a million foolish things and called him out on every single one. Getting involved with a woman he definitely shouldn't have been involved with was pretty much par for the course. Fletcher thinking he was a fool—and probably an ass, too—wasn't all that surprising.

What he didn't realize was that Beau was attracted to Emma in a way he'd never been attracted to anyone before. Emma wasn't outspoken, or overly flirtatious, or blatantly sexual. But her quiet strength, utter sweetness, and subtle sensuality called to him like a siren. He wanted to teach her everything. *Show* her everything. Give her every experience she'd ever missed out on.

And unlike any other woman he'd been with, Beau would rather die than hurt Emma.

The memory of her spread out before him, open to his touch and kiss, with that lusty look in her eyes, almost had him driving off the road. Goddamn, she had looked gorgeous in his bed. And then getting to hold her in the bath, her wet *everywhere*, so soft beneath his hands, left him aching. She'd bared herself to him so bravely, bold in an entirely new way. When Emma did things that Beau would normally take for granted, they meant all that much more because he knew what she'd been through.

For all intents and purposes, she should have sworn off men forever. But she'd refused to let the men who'd made her life miserable continue to have a hold on her. She had asked him to show her what it was like to be with a good man, and he hoped to hell he had. He longed for more. The thought of filling her, claiming her, nagged at him like a dog with a bone.

It was going to be a long day until he could return to her.

※

Emma glanced at the clock to find that only a couple of hours had passed. Fletcher had arrived after breakfast, and they'd been lounging on the couch ever since, first catching up on the morning news, then reading. Fletcher had kindly brought her a box of Christa's books, including a series of historical-fiction romance novels that Emma had been dying to get her hands on prior to her ordeal with Mason. She dove into one of those while Fletcher flipped through a book about education for elementary students.

He'd been acting off since his arrival. He wasn't all that talkative, and he kept giving her odd looks when he thought she wasn't watching. She tried to ignore his behavior, but when she caught him staring at her as they read their respective books, her curiosity got the best of her.

"What's up?"

"What?" Fletcher blinked fast a few times. "Oh, nothing. Everything's fine."

"You sure?" Emma pressed.

Fletcher ran a hand through his overlong blond hair. "I guess I'm just trying to figure out how you're really doing."

Emma closed her book and placed it on the table beside her. "I'm good," she assured him.

Fletcher put down his own book and leaned his forearms on his thighs. "You seem good. You seem…happy, which should be impossible, given your circumstances. And I'm glad to see your bruises are healing." His gaze roamed over the faded bruises on her arms.

"They were pretty nasty. But I really am doing better every day."

"I'm really glad to hear that." Fletcher's sincere smile confirmed his words. "I just worry about you. It was… shocking to see you all bruised up that first time we met, and then to learn about what you've been through…it's a lot. I want to make sure you're doing as well as you seem to be."

Emma smiled softly at Fletcher. "I am. I mean, I obviously still live with a lot of fear, but Beau's been really helpful with that. He's gone out of his way to make me feel safe. Yesterday, we even practiced some self-defense moves."

Fletcher's eyes narrowed, and she tried to read his expression. "What's really bothering you?" she asked.

"You and Beau are…together," he said slowly.

Emma pursed her lips. "Um…I guess we are. It's…new."

"I was taken off guard when he kissed you this morning," Fletcher admitted. "I just didn't realize you'd gone beyond… whatever you were before."

"I know it's complicated because of how we met," Emma said carefully. "But he's been really amazing, and I guess we just kind of clicked."

"He's not pressuring you?"

Horrified at the thought, Emma waved her hands back and forth in front of her. "No! Not at all. In fact, if anyone's doing the pressuring, it's me."

As soon as she uttered the words, her cheeks grew hot.

Fletcher tilted his head to the side, his lips tipping up at the corners. "I can't imagine you having to pressure him very much."

Looking down at her hands, Emma chose a nail to chew on nervously. "Beau has been…cautious with me."

"I'm very glad to hear that," Fletcher said gently. "I got concerned when he kissed you, because you've been through a lot, and Beau doesn't always make the best decisions, especially when it comes to women."

A lump formed in Emma's throat. "I know Beau has made some mistakes with women. Isabella told me what happened with Sofia. But he's never been anything but kind and careful with me."

Fletcher's eyes widened fractionally. "You know about Sofia?"

Emma nodded. "Beau told me about her before he introduced me to Diego. Then, Isabella told me that Beau and Sofia dated. I think her death really affected him—made him want to be better. He's been nothing but caring and thoughtful with me."

"That's good to hear," Fletcher replied. "Sofia's death hit him hard, and I wasn't sure how it would affect him. With Beau, it could have gone either way—either his grief could have made him lean on bad habits, or it could have made him grow up. He's been acting much more mature than usual. It's nice to see."

Emma couldn't help the shy smile that formed on her face. "I really like him."

"And you're happy with him?" Fletcher asked, his eyebrows raised.

Thinking about how good Beau made her feel, both physically and emotionally, had Emma's smile widening. "Very happy."

Fletcher curled one hand into a fist, mock-punching the air. "You know, if he hurts you, I'll kick his ass, right?"

Emma giggled at the easygoing threat. Fletcher may not have been as muscular or as tough as Beau, but he was his older brother, and that had to count for something. "I like the sound of that."

Planting the bug in Williams' office was a piece of cake. Beau had once again gotten an old buddy to escort him into the station under the guise of visiting with old coworkers. He chatted up a few of the officers, asking about their families or discussing the results of the latest football game—Pats won by a landslide—then slid right into Williams' office, stuck a dime-sized listening device on the underside of his desk, and slid right back out.

The conversation with Emma's father was sure to be a less pleasant task. Beau parked his truck a couple of doors down from the address he'd found for Earl Anderson. The ramshackle, ranch-style house was an eyesore for sure, with a couple of boarded-up windows and green paint that had faded to a color reminiscent of barf. The disarray wasn't all that surprising—there couldn't have been much money left for home improvements when one owed an absurd amount to various bookies.

Cracking his knuckles over the steering wheel, Beau mentally reviewed the questions he would ask Earl, then patted his pocket, feeling for the second small listening device he hoped to plant somewhere in the house. When he had all his ducks in a row, Beau hopped out of the truck and ambled down the street to the ranch.

It took two rings of the doorbell before the door swung

open to reveal a tall, wiry man with white hair, bright as snow. The mid-day sun glinted off of it, practically blinding Beau. He raised a hand over his eyes to block the sun and finally got a good look at Earl's face. The man was only fifty-eight—Beau had done a background check on him—but he looked well over his age, with dark bags under his eyes and wrinkles marring his forehead.

When Earl opened his mouth to speak, Beau noticed he was missing more than one tooth. "Can I help ya?" he rumbled.

"Earl Anderson?" Beau asked in his well-practiced authoritative voice.

Earl scratched at his ear. "Who's askin'?"

Beau flashed the fake badge he'd obtained.

Earl squinted at the badge but didn't question it. *Doofus.* He narrowed his eyes in suspicion. "I ain't done nothin' wrong, officer."

"I think we both know you have," Beau said with a conspiratorial smile. "But I'm not here to talk about you, Earl. I'm here to ask you a few questions about one of my fellow officers."

Earl let out an undignified cackle, clutching his hand to his chest as if he might keel over. "You're here to ask *me* questions about a *police officer?*" he howled.

"Yes, sir," Beau confirmed with a sharp nod. "We're running an investigation on Detective Isaac Williams, and we have reason to believe you might have information that could assist us."

Earl looked Beau up and down with a sneer. "Why would I tell you anything?"

"I thought you might ask that." Beau pulled out his cell phone and located the snippet of video footage Diego had given him of Earl, holding the screen so the man could see it. "This is footage of you participating in an illegal card game. There are no less than six drug dealers in attendance with you, and I'm willing to bet that you utilized their services that night. In fact, if we kept this video playing for another twenty-seven or so minutes, we would see footage of just that." Beau narrowed his eyes, giving Earl his best stare-down. "I think my fellow police officers would be very interested in this video, don't you?"

"I, uh, well…" Earl stammered, scratching at his ear again. Beau noticed he pulled out a small lump of yellow goo and tried to pretend like he hadn't seen it. Earl flinched and shrank back when Beau stepped toward him.

"Now, may I come in so we can talk about this like civilized adults?"

Earl nodded, wide-eyed, and stepped into the house. Beau entered behind him, sweeping his gaze around the interior. It was just as dilapidated as the outside, with wallpaper that looked as if it would flake off at the lightest touch and filthy wall-to-wall carpeting. The air was stale, smelling of moth balls marinated in humidity. There was a distinct lack of furniture, giving the home an eerie feeling. Perhaps Earl had sold it all off for drug or gambling money.

The thought of Emma growing up there horrified Beau. That hazy image of a blonde-haired girl formed in his mind again, and this time, he pictured her in the corner of one of these rooms, cowering as Emma had been when he'd first found her. The image made him want to put his fist through a wall.

Beau turned to Earl, who was leaning against the front door with his arms crossed over his chest. "Do you think you could grab me a glass of water?" he asked. Oldest trick in the book: get a suspect to leave the room for a glass of water so you have a moment to look around.

"Uh, yeah. Yeah, sure," Earl mumbled, tripping over himself to get to the kitchen.

As soon as he was out of sight, Beau began looking for a good place to hide the bug. The lack of furniture made placement tricky, as it had to remain hidden so Earl wouldn't notice it. There was only one chair in the room, which Early presumably used frequently, so he might notice a bug on it. There were a few pictures on the wall that might be a good spot.

Beau ran his finger over the top of a frame. It came back covered in dust, but he'd found the perfect flat spot to stick a little bug. No one would ever find it unless they took down the photo, and judging by the layer of dust, it hadn't been touched in years.

The water turned on in the other room. Knowing he only had a few more moments, Beau pulled the bug from his pocket and secured it to the top of the frame. Stepping back, he was pleased to find that it wasn't visible at all. With that mission accomplished, he took a moment to look at the photos on the wall.

The frame he'd bugged housed an ancient wedding photo. The bride and groom both wore straight faces, and their attire placed them somewhere in the '40s or '50s. Earl's parents, perhaps? Next to that was a photo of a handsome Great Dane with its tongue hanging out of its mouth. There were a few other photos, but Beau quickly realized Emma wasn't in any of them.

A frown tugged at his lips. Emma had grown up in this house, and Earl had continued supporting her until very recently. Why didn't he have any photos of his beloved daughter displayed?

Obviously, the bastard didn't care about Emma at all—that much was clear by the way he was willing to sell her for gambling money—but it still stung that there was no trace of her in this house. Seriously, there was a photo of a fucking dog, but no photos of Emma?

Earl returned with a cup of tap water. The glass shook in his hand as he passed it to Beau.

"Thanks," Beau said, flashing Earl what he hoped was an evil smile. "Shall we get started?"

"Right, right," Earl said, wringing his hands as he sat on the lone chair in the room. Beau leaned against the wall nearby, holding his cup in his hand. Earl didn't even notice that he hadn't taken a sip.

"So, Earl," Beau began. "Obviously, we know that you're into some unseemly stuff."

Earl chewed on a dirty fingernail. How long had it been since this dude took a damn shower? "Well, I mean…you know…I just have some vices, but I'm…I'm working on them."

Beau held up his hand to stop Earl's nervous babbling. "Like I said before, I'm really not here to talk about you. Tell me about Isaac Williams."

"I don't know no Isaac Williams," Earl said, using air quotes when he said the detective's name as if Beau had made it up. Then, his hand returned to his mouth, his teeth gnawing at that nail again.

"Come on, Earl," Beau said with an easy smile. "We both know that's not true. That game we got footage of you at? I think Detective Williams goes there, too. I think you've played together. I think that maybe you're even friends."

Earl bit off a piece of his fingernail, and Beau watched him flounder with what to do with the small piece of dead skin cells now floating around his mouth. When Earl swallowed hard, Beau's stomach turned sour. Maybe he would need a sip of that water after all.

"Okay, you're right," Earl said, putting his hands up in surrender. "I know Williams. But we are *not* friends."

Beau nodded and placed his water glass on the ground, pulling out a small notebook and pretending to write in it. He wasn't asking anything he wouldn't remember the answer to, but if it looked more official, Earl might be more intimidated. "Okay, so you're not friends, but you do know him?"

"Sure," Earl said, back to chewing on another fingernail.

This one was dirtier than the first, and Beau prayed he wouldn't wind up biting off more.

Picking up the glass of water, Beau took a long slug, attempting to wash away the lingering taste of puke. "Great," he muttered. "I need you to tell me everything you know about Williams."

"Well," Earl scratched his head, and some dandruff flew out and floated onto the chair. Beau bit his lip to keep from gagging. The dude was seriously grungy. "He's a bit younger than me, and I'm pretty sure he's married. He's great at poker—wins even more than I do—and craps, too. And his lucky number is four." Earl nodded, grinning as if he was proud of himself for remembering that mundane information.

"Okay," Beau said, drawing out the word and hoping that Earl wasn't going to turn out to be a wholly unhelpful prick. "Have you ever seen him purchasing illegal substances?"

Earl paled, his leathery skin turning a ghostly white. "Uh, maybe."

"Can you recall a specific time that you witnessed him purchasing drugs?" Beau pushed, his pen hovering above the paper as he eagerly awaited the answer.

Earl covered his face with his hands. "Man, he's going to kill me if he finds out I talked about him."

"It's okay," Beau assured him. "By the time he finds out you helped us, he'll be behind bars." *And so will you*, he thought.

"Alright." Earl scratched nervously behind his neck. Beau looked away so he wouldn't have to see what sort of substances that might produce. "I have seen him buy drugs a few times. Just pot, though, I think."

"Good, that's helpful," Beau said, drawing scribbles in his notebook. He'd begun to doodle the outline of the Great Dane in that photo on the wall. "Is he into anything else illegal that you can think of?"

Earl stopped scratching, his hand frozen behind his head. "Like what?"

Beau shrugged nonchalantly. "Like, anything. Crooked cops rarely stop at one illegal thing. Now I know he was both playing in illegal card games and purchasing illicit substances. Do you know of anything else he may have been into?"

Earl's hand dropped into his lap with a light thud. "I don't know...I'm not sure, but I think maybe he hired prostitutes. Yeah, I think he was into that. That would put him in jail for longer, right?" he asked hopefully.

"Maybe," Beau answered, realizing he had Earl by the balls now. The man had already given him enough information to get Williams in trouble, but probably not enough to put him in jail for life. Earl knew Williams would kill him for tattling if he got out of jail, so he needed to provide Beau with more ammo. "But not for as long as, say, being involved in human trafficking would. That would get him a hefty sentence," Beau added.

"Yeah"—Earl nodded eagerly—"he was into that. Human trafficking."

"How do you know?" Beau asked, fake scribbling furiously in his notebook now. He was adding details to the Great Dane's face, complete with pointy ears and a droopy mouth.

Earl paled again, taking a moment to find his voice. "I heard him talking about it sometimes at the card games. He would ask us if we wanted to buy a girl to take home—that's why I mentioned that he used prostitutes. But I also know that he stole those girls from poor countries and brought them here, so that's human trafficking, right?"

"Yep." Beau nodded and let out a whistle. "Sure is. Sounds like Williams was into all sorts of shit."

"Oh yeah," Earl agreed with a nod. "He should go away for a long time."

Beau looked up from his notebook. The Great Dane was

complete. "He will, if you're willing to testify to everything you told me today."

Earl's gaze shot to his. His eyes were slightly glazed, and Beau vaguely wondered if he was high. It would help explain his squirrelly behavior, but then again, it wouldn't surprise Beau if this was Earl's typical demeanor. "What? You never told me I'd have to testify to any of this. I thought we were just talking?"

Beau tucked the notebook into his back pocket. "We are. But when I apprehend Williams, I might need witnesses to testify to all the things we're talking about, and right now you're the main one."

"No, man, I can't do that." Earl waved his hands around in a frenzy. "One of his men will kill me."

Beau shrugged. "It's either that or go to jail." He held up his phone. "Remember, we've got that video footage. If you don't help us, we'll send you to the slammer, and there's no access to those vices you talked about in there."

"Gahh," Earl screeched, scratching his head so dandruff flew everywhere. Beau stood abruptly, ready to run outside if he needed to vomit, but Earl quickly stopped and looked up at him. "Fine. I'll testify if it comes to that. But I need you to promise me protection."

"Sure," Beau lied. Actually, it wasn't a total lie. Earl would be fairly protected in prison. Perhaps he could suggest solitary confinement and make the bastard live out the rest of his days all alone. "Thanks for your time today, Earl. It's been real." He walked toward the door as Emma's father curled into the fetal position on the chair. "I'll be in touch."

Earl let out a guttural groan as Beau slammed the front door shut behind him. He shook out his clothes as he walked to his truck, as if that would remove the musty scent of the Anderson house. He would need a major shower when he got home. God knew what germs and filth he'd picked up in there. And he wouldn't touch Emma while smelling like her father.

Hopping into his truck, Beau shot off a text to Diego that the bug had been planted. Diego was monitoring the video camera at the headquarters, as well as the bugs that now sat in Williams' office and Earl's house. He would report anything fishy, which gave Beau the freedom to care for Emma the way she deserved to be cared for.

Emma. His beautiful angel who'd grown up in this absolute hell. How had she turned out so sweet? How was it possible that this house hadn't hardened her? She should have been jaded, cold, aloof. Instead, she was curious, warm, and lovely. How could one grow up in darkness and turn out like sunshine bottled up?

20

Emma and Fletcher were still in their respective seats in the living room when Beau returned. They had eaten lunch together—grilled cheese sandwiches because, as it turned out, Fletcher was as good at making them as Beau was—then gotten back to their reading like the couple of introverted bookworms they were. Emma was flying through one of the historical romance novels Fletcher had brought her while he read more for work. His thin, wire-framed glasses were balanced low on his nose as he studied the thick, academic book.

Beau flew in the door, making them both jerk their heads up. Emma blinked once, readjusting from the regency world she'd been immersed in for the past hour. Beau was already halfway through the living room when she managed to greet him.

"Hi," she called as he veered toward the bathroom.

"Have to shower," Beau huffed. "Will explain in a minute." He disappeared into the bathroom, slamming the door shut behind him.

Emma shot Fletcher a confused glance. "What's up with that?"

Fletcher shrugged and pushed his glasses up his nose. "He's weird sometimes. Who knows?"

Emma bit her bottom lip. "I hope everything went alright. He was planting bugs at the police station and my father's house," she said with a grimace.

"I'm sure it was fine," Fletcher assured her. "Beau has a knack for getting away with pretty much anything."

Emma rolled her eyes. "That's what people keep telling me."

Fletcher smirked at that. "That's because it's true. When he was little, he used to get away with everything. Mostly he blamed stuff on Jack, who was just two years older, so it was pretty believable. Like when Beau unraveled every toilet paper roll in the house or flushed an action figure down the toilet, we totally believed that Jack could have done it. Even when Beau once shoved a penny up his nose, he convinced our mom that Jack had stuck it up there. Otherwise, Beau would flash me or Mom his little puppy-dog eyes, and we'd just crumble."

Emma shook her head, a chuckle escaping her lips. "I can totally see that. He's so charming."

Beau burst out of the bathroom then, his hair still dripping wet, and made a beeline for Emma, grabbing beneath her armpits to pull her up off the chair. She gasped as he swung her into his arms and squeezed.

"You're…squishing…me," she complained breathlessly, not to mention that her shirt was soaking through with the water from his hair.

"Sorry," Beau mumbled as he set her on her feet. Taking her face in his hands, he held her gaze. "I am so sorry you had to grow up there, in that disgusting house, with that…fucking jerk wad," he barked. "I'm sorry, Emma, but your father is a major loser."

Shame heated Emma's cheeks, and she tried to drop her gaze down to her feet, but Beau wouldn't let her. He coaxed her eyes up with a light brush of his thumbs against her cheeks.

"No, look at me," he insisted. "You. Are. A. Miracle. Your father is a total fuck-up, but somehow, you turned out the exact opposite of him. I don't know how you did it, but you turned into the loveliest woman alive." His eyes softened. "I am in awe of you, Emma Anderson, and I will never let you forget it."

Her eyes widened, stunned at Beau's emphatic words, but she didn't get a chance to respond before his lips were on hers, consuming her with his expert kissing. She melted into his arms, allowing his lips to guide hers until Fletcher cleared his throat, reminding them both of his presence.

Beau turned to his brother. "In case it wasn't obvious, we're together now," he said. "And I won't hear one word about it other than, 'I'm happy for you, Beau.' I like Emma, and I'm going to protect her and make her happy, and nothing you can say will stop me from doing that."

An amused grin stretched across Fletcher's mouth. "I'm happy for you, Beau. There's no need to get defensive. Emma already told me that you're together and that she's happy about it. Lord knows *what* she sees you," he added, eliciting a friendly slap on the shoulder from Beau, "but I am happy for you, bro."

Beau grinned smugly at his brother's approval, then took Emma's hand in his as if they were a unit—joined and unbreakable. "Feel like staying for dinner?" he asked Fletcher. "I promised Emma Mexican the other day."

Fletcher's eyes lit up. "From Maria's?" he asked, rubbing his flat stomach. "I could really go for a burrito bowl right about now."

"Maria's it is," Beau said, leading Emma toward the kitchen. She relished the feel of his big hand around hers, remembering all the wicked things he'd done to her with that hand, and the wicked things he *would* do once they were alone.

Beau pulled a menu for Maria's Taqueria out of the drawer and pointed out his favorite dishes to Emma. She decided to go for some chicken tacos with pico de gallo and hot sauce on the side. Unaccustomed to spicy food, she worried about getting anything that might be too much. Beau got his usual carnitas fajitas and a burrito bowl for Fletcher. They made sure to order extra chips and salsa, which Beau explained are the best part of every Mexican meal.

Everyone's stomachs were grumbling by the time the food arrived, and they sat in a line at the kitchen island. Emma loaded her tacos up with a lot of pico and a little hot sauce. "Mmm," she moaned as she took the first bite, the flavors of spiced chicken and fresh, juicy tomato bursting on her tongue.

Beau shifted on his stool beside her. "Good?" he asked, one eyebrow raised.

"So good," Emma replied, taking another bite. "You know, Fletcher made us grilled cheeses for lunch, and they might have been better than yours," she taunted.

Beau puffed out his chest. "No way. I'm the reigning grilled cheese master."

Emma shrugged and took another bite of her taco, the thrill of provoking Beau making her bold. "If you say so. But Fletcher added a secret ingredient, and it really pushed the sandwiches over the edge."

Beau shot an accusing glare at his brother. "What did you add?"

A small, furtive smile crossed Fletcher's lips. "If I told you, then it wouldn't be a secret."

"Well, I refuse to believe that your grilled cheeses are better than mine," Beau huffed.

Fletcher turned to Emma, the mischievous tilt of his brows making her giggle. "I take back what I said about him acting more mature around you," he said. "He still has the maturity level of a seven-year-old."

"I'd argue he's more like a five-year-old," Emma teased.

Beau turned to her with a look of mock indignation. "I'm used to taking this shit from him, but you, Emma? You're supposed to be defending me!"

She shrugged and took a bite of her taco. "Nothing to defend against if it's true."

Beau's mouth dropped open playfully.

Fletcher roared with laughter. "You know," he said, "I was worried that my brother was taking advantage of you, but now I see there's no need for concern. You can obviously take care of yourself."

"Damn right she can," Beau snarled, draping an arm over Emma's shoulders. "But she'll never have to."

Fletcher departed after dinner, and Emma and Beau got themselves tucked into bed the same way they had the night before, with her nose buried in a book while he did God knew what on his phone. She knew he wanted her to relax and forget about the fact that he'd paid a visit to Earl that day, but Emma couldn't simply ignore the fact that her lover had met her father under less-than-stellar circumstances and she hadn't even been there to see how it went.

Chewing on her lip, she finally worked up the courage to ask about the encounter.

"Don't worry about it," Beau said, turning to her and running his thumb over her cheek.

"No, tell me," she insisted, rolling to her side so she could face him. "Please."

"Emma." Beau sighed. "I'll tell you anything you want to know, but I'm so afraid of dredging up old memories or saying something that might trigger you. Please be honest with me if you want me to drop it, okay?"

"Okay," she agreed, leaning over to give him a light peck on the lips.

"Good," Beau said, his eyes tightening as he recounted his day.

Shame burned like acid in Emma's mouth as he expressed his disgust at her childhood home and her father's hygiene, but his earlier words soothed her like a balm. He didn't think she was appalling for growing up there; he thought she was a miracle for making it out alive. So, she didn't stop him as he rehashed every time he thought he was going to vomit due to her father's repugnance.

Clenching his fists, Beau finished with, "And he has all these pictures up on the wall, including one of a damn dog, but there's no trace of you. What the fuck is up with that?"

Emma sighed. "That's Dolly, my dad's childhood dog. I swear, Earl cares more about her than he ever did about me."

"He's such an asshole," Beau growled.

"Can't argue with you there. But hopefully you'll catch something on that bug that will put him away for a long time."

Beau ran a hand over his face. "That's the plan. I swear to God, Emma, I will never let him hurt you again."

She softened back against the pillows behind her. "I know."

He caught her gaze, his deep-brown eyes boring into hers. "I'm serious. I will kill him before I let him hurt you, physically or emotionally."

A wry smile curled Emma's lips, because she didn't doubt his words one bit. "I know."

"Good," Beau huffed, relaxing back into his own cradle of pillows. There was something so gratifying about being the person who this hard, potentially dangerous man wanted to unwind with. "Now, try to relax and enjoy your book. What are you reading, anyway?" he asked, peering over at the book she'd laid on the other side of the bed.

Emma prayed her blush wasn't as deep as it felt as she snatched the book and answered, "Oh, just a book Fletcher brought me from Christa's collection." In truth, it was a much raunchier romance than she normally read, but she had to admit she was really enjoying it. The regency romance chronicled a whole lot of secret sex between a rake and a wallflower in great detail.

Enough detail, in fact, that she was able to picture Beau doing to her every wicked thing the hero did to the heroine of the novel. Her insides grew warm and tingly as the author described every move he made, and she imagined Beau doing the same.

While he seemed oblivious to her rising excitement, Beau clearly had needs of his own, because before long, he began running one big hand over her thigh before stopping to rest at the top of it. Emma read the same line three times as she tried to concentrate on her book instead of the weight of Beau's hand on her bare skin. Gently kneading, his fingers explored as she attempted to finish her chapter. Before a full page had gone by, Beau's lips had found her temple, cheek, and worked their way down her jaw to her neck, where he paused to suckle on a sensitive patch.

"Beau," Emma said, her eyes scanning the page to find where she'd stopped. The exercise was futile—she hadn't made sense of a word she'd read in the past few minutes.

"Hmm," he hummed against her neck.

"I'm trying to read. Just let me finish this chapter."

She felt his smile against her skin before his mouth drifted to her ear.

"I thought you didn't get easily distracted."

Faux annoyance marked her words as she replied, "I don't get distracted easily by background noise, but you kissing me is a different story."

His lips pressed against the patch of skin behind her ear, and a shiver moved through her. "I like distracting you," he whispered.

Emma groaned because—dammit—she liked it, too. She especially liked that Beau was showing his interest instead of trying to be all gentlemanly and gallant. He showed far too much discipline around her, and she wanted to make him as wild as he made her.

"Just give me one more—ah!" she cried as Beau's sharp teeth nipped her earlobe. The book snapped shut, and Emma hastily placed it on the bedside table. Beau's victorious grin made her roll her eyes, but any complaints were swallowed up by his swift kiss.

Emma wrapped her arms around his neck as he ravaged her mouth, his tongue darting into every corner and crevice, thoroughly exploring her depths as his hands roamed her body. Her own moan rang through her ears as Beau's lips found her neck once again. Sucking, licking, kissing—she was already lost to the pleasure.

She attempted to pull off his shirt, but she couldn't budge his big body as it pressed against hers. She tugged at the bottom of his shirt, but Beau remained unmoved as he continued raining kisses over her neck and jaw.

"Beau!" Emma nudged him with her knee, and he pulled back immediately. Concern flashed over his face but quickly turned into a lascivious grin when he realized her only issue was being unable to remove his clothing. Beau helped her tug off his t-shirt and then her own, his gaze heating as he took in her state of undress.

"Fuck, you're so beautiful," he rumbled, his eyes pinned to her chest.

"So are you." Emma ran her fingers lightly over his abdomen, transfixed by the way the muscles clenched and contracted beneath her touch. Beau's fingers found her nipples, and he made quick work of hardening them into firm little diamonds.

A growl escaped his throat. "You drive me wild," he admitted as he slowly lowered her back onto the bed. "All day I thought of you, in my bed, in my bathtub, spread wide open for me. Even the thought of you sitting beside me in bed reading, all serious and studious, turns me on. You are so fucking sexy, Emma, and I don't think you have any idea how much it affects me."

Her eyes widened at his honest words.

"That's why I couldn't leave you alone, even though I know you wanted to finish that chapter or some shit," Beau continued. "You test my self-control, angel."

She wasn't sure if that was a good thing or a bad thing. "I…I don't mean to."

Beau barked a laugh and kissed away her frown. "I know. And that's what makes it so goddamn sweet. You have no idea what you do to me. How you tear me apart."

Emma could scarcely believe what she was hearing. *Her* tear *him* apart? More like the other way around. She'd missed him every single second he was gone. Drowned in the fear that he wouldn't return to her. Ached with the need to be in his arms again.

She leaned up to capture his lips and show him the depth of her affection with her kiss. He groaned and kissed her back, rougher and needier than before. Emma sensed his thinly veiled desperation and willed him to give her what they both needed.

She widened her knees, and Beau settled between them, his hardness pressing against her belly. He kissed his way down to her breasts, tonguing each nipple he'd already sensitized. Emma arched into him on a moan, seeking more. More contact. More pressure. More assurance. More. More. More.

"Beau," she breathed. "Please."

His head popped up, and his gaze settled on hers. "Please what?"

She grunted in frustration. "I don't know! *Please.*"

He chuckled at her neediness but mercifully reached down and drew her shorts down her legs. When he moved down the bed to align his mouth with her belly, she stopped him.

"Wait!"

Like a well-trained puppy, Beau rocked back and waited for further instruction.

Emma scrambled to sit up and put her hands on his chest. "This time is for both of us," she reminded him. "No more giving without taking."

A mischievous glint entered Beau's eyes. "But I enjoy giving so much."

She whacked his bare chest lightly. "Beau, please. I want this. Want you. *All* of you."

Cradling her head in his hands, Beau stroked a thumb down her jawline. "Are you sure you're ready?"

She didn't know how to tell if she was truly ready, but she had surely never wanted someone in the way she wanted Beau, or trusted someone in the way she did him. "As sure as I'll ever be," she said. "I'm sure I want you."

He accepted her answer with a gentle smile and a soft kiss on her lips. Knowing she had his agreement, Emma's arms circled his waist, and she peppered kisses on his chest and abdomen, eager to reciprocate the ways in which he'd pleasured her. He sighed as her lips brushed over his nipple. A curious finger trailed its way across his waistband and stopped to caress the soft hair above his groin. Beau caught her hand and encircled her wrist with his fingers.

Emma looked up and found fierce brown eyes staring down at her. Beau's breath came out in short spurts, and she realized that he was working steadfastly to control himself. Wanting him to give it up already, she wriggled her hand free and reached for the waistband of his boxers. To her delight, he didn't protest as she tugged them over the bulge between his thighs.

She paused when his erection sprang free. Somewhat aware that she was staring, Emma worked to contain a gasp. Beau was beautiful, and he was *big*. She should have guessed. There was nothing small about the man. His rigid erection strained upward toward his stomach, and her eyes traced the prominent vein running all the way along it. Thick and pulsing, she vaguely wondered if it was painful for him, even though he'd previously assured her it wasn't.

Prodded by her momentary lapse in confidence, Beau helped Emma by pulling his underwear the rest of the way off.

"You're…big," she murmured, unable to break her gaze from his groin.

Beau caught her chin and tipped her face up. "Yes." He held her gaze. "But don't worry, angel, I'm going to make you feel so good." He brushed his lips over her forehead. "We'll make sure you're nice and ready." He reached over for something in the bedside table drawer, and Emma watched the muscles on his back and shoulders work as he procured two small objects.

"What are those?"

He held up a foil packet. "This is a condom." Then, he showed her a small tube. "This is lube. It'll ensure that I don't hurt you. And we'll go slow. If anything doesn't feel good, you just tell me, and I'll stop."

"O-okay," she stammered, watching intently as he tore open the condom and rolled it over himself. Seeing his big hands touching that part of his body sent a jolt of excitement through her veins, and unexpected heat pooled in her belly.

Beau squeezed a dollop of lubricant onto his palm. A smile tugged at his lips as he asked, "Want to help me?"

"W—with what?" Emma sputtered.

He took her hand and transferred the jelly-like substance into her palm. She stared obtusely at the small glob.

"With rubbing this on me," he explained, his fingers circling her wrist and guiding her hand to his length. She instinctively wrapped her fist around him. Beau let out a, "Hmph," then covered her hand with his and showed her how to rub it up and down until he was slick. Thinking the job was done, Emma tried to remove her hand, but Beau kept it pinned there.

"A little more," he instructed. "You can squeeze harder," he added and grunted when she did. When Beau took his hand away, Emma continued running her fist up and down a few times with a firm grip, fascinated by the way he seemed to harden even further in her grasp.

"That's enough," Beau said in a tight voice. Emma looked up to find his jaw clenched and eyes half hooded with pleasure. She let go of him, and he crowded over her until she finally lay back on the bed again. With Beau above her on all fours, the position reminded her of their self-defense class. Only, this time, she didn't want to buck him *off* of her; she wanted to buck up so he was *in* her.

Beau began by running a finger through her damp folds, and her legs automatically opened wider to accommodate him. Gently, he tucked one finger inside of her.

"Fuck, you're so wet. Maybe we didn't need lube." He inserted a second finger and seemed to be thinking for a moment. "Nah, I take that back. I liked the process, even if you were already wet enough."

Pleased that Beau seemed to enjoy having her hands on him as much as she enjoyed his touch, Emma asked, "Now do you believe I'm ready?"

A devilish smile formed on Beau's lips. "Feisty tonight, are we?"

"I want you." Maybe if she said it enough times, he'd finally get it through his thick skull.

"And have me you will, angel." He removed his fingers and slid up until their bodies were pressed together. The fuzzy hair on his chest tickled her breasts, and she could feel him hard and ready against her inner thigh.

Suddenly, a wave of trepidation washed over her. This was really happening. Everything had felt good so far, but the fact that Beau was *so* big and *so* hard and *so* close suddenly became *so* real.

He noticed her hesitation and playfully kissed her nose. "Relax, angel."

Emma took a breath, and his kisses on her lips, breasts, and belly helped loosen her up. Finally, Beau returned to his earlier position and grazed his tip over her opening.

"You ready?" he asked, his tone rough and gravelly.

Emma gazed up into his eyes, finding a compelling mixture of concern, adoration, and lust in his expression.

"Yes," she confirmed.

And then, ever so slowly, he sank into her. Emma gasped, less surprised by the full feeling and more so by the fact that she actually enjoyed it. Beau retreated a few inches, then delicately drove forward again as Emma got accustomed to his size. He watched her face closely, his eyes carefully assessing, and his teeth gritted together as he pressed into her over and over.

She accepted him easily, slick from the lube and her own excitement. Beau caught her lips in a kiss and penetrated them with his tongue, mimicking the action going on below. She found herself wrapping her legs around his waist, urging him closer, deeper. The feeling that came over her was primal and wild. All she could focus on was the feeling of Beau moving inside of her and her desire to keep him there.

Emma's eyes snapped shut as pleasure overtook her senses. A shudder moved through her when his mouth found her neck, and he sucked at her skin. His body was a pleasant weight atop her, but in the instant she allowed her guard to fall down, memories began flooding her mind. Memories of other bodies above her, hard and heavy, trapping her. Hurting her.

Her body tensed, and her eyes flew open on a gasp. Beau was off her in a millisecond, noticing her shift in demeanor immediately. He rolled to the side as if he'd caught fire and put his hands up in surrender. Wide eyes watched Emma as she came to her senses.

"What the hell just happened?" he asked quietly.

21

Emma reached for Beau, not wanting to lose that contact, and circled her fingers around his bicep.

"I—I'm sorry," she breathed. "I don't know what happened. I was fine...I was more than fine. But then I closed my eyes and...I saw someone else."

Beau's eyes softened as understanding dawned. "Ah, angel." He pulled her into his chest and kissed her forehead. "I'm sorry. Maybe it was too soon."

"No!" Emma pulled back so they were face to face. She would not let him decide that she wasn't ready. She would not let him try to do the gallant thing *again*, when all she wanted was to have this experience with him. Her momentary outburst was just a hiccup. "I don't want to stop."

Beau's mouth hardened into a thin line. "Emma, I don't want to scare you."

Bringing a hand to his cheek, she stroked over the beginnings of the stubble there. This sweet man seemed to think of nothing but her. Even with a raging hard-on (Emma knew—she had checked), he was willing to stop because she may not have been in the right frame of mind.

"You didn't scare me," she insisted. "I just had a bad

memory pop into my head. *That's* what scared me. And how am I ever supposed to get over the bad memories if I don't have good memories to replace them? I need to make new ones. With you. Right now."

Desperate to get back to the delicious sensations that had enveloped her before the mishap, Emma pushed her breasts into Beau's chest.

He huffed out a sigh and closed his eyes. He seemed to be thinking, which couldn't be a good thing. Hoping to distract him, she leaned down and kissed across his chest. When she glanced back up at him, he was watching her.

"Do you want to try being on top?" Beau asked, surprising her.

She frowned. "What?"

"Do. You. Want. To. Try. Being. On. Top?" he asked slowly, as if the pace of his words was what had led to her confusion.

She shrugged helplessly. "I wouldn't know what to do."

A slow grin spread across Beau's face. "I'll teach you." He lay flat on his back and propped a pillow beneath his head. "Come over here and kneel with one knee on either side of my hips."

Emma did as he said and paused when she was atop him, his hard body extended in front of her. She idly ran a finger over his chiseled abdomen, outlining his six-pack.

"You have bad memories of men controlling you," Beau said gently. "Now, you're on top. You're in control. We'll try this again, but if you get scared, we're stopping."

Emma nodded her agreement. Beau's hands found her thighs and urged her to rise up on her knees. She adjusted her position so his hardness was in line with her heat and, without even thinking, reached down and used her hand to guide him into her. Once he'd entered, she sat down hard and gasped. He was even deeper this way, and she briefly wondered if it was merely the position or if Beau had been holding back on her.

Rocking her hips back and forth, Emma explored the feeling of him from this angle. Beau's big hands came around to palm her ass before lifting her slightly. Catching on to the movement, she began raising her hips up and down, sheathing his hard length.

"Yes, that's it, up and down," Beau ground out, his hands traveling to her waist as she took over the movement, reveling in the fullness of the angle. The power she held in the position was intoxicating. She set the pace, the depth—everything. Though she had no doubt Beau could gain control in a millisecond, he allowed her to be in charge. And finally, *finally*, she had a chance to give him a taste of the immense pleasure he'd given her.

Reaching down, Emma caressed his chest, tugging gently on the light smattering of hair there. Beau let out a strangled moan, which pleased her to no end, and she placed her palms square on his chest for stability as she began riding him faster.

"Yesss," he hissed as she picked up the pace. "Good girl." His big hands found her breasts, and he rolled her nipples between his fingers. The sensation shot straight down to her lower belly, where heat was beginning to build. "Does that feel good, angel?"

"Yes, it's—" A gasp interrupted Emma's answer when he tugged at her nipple. "It's really good."

Beau responded by pulling her in closer and capturing that same nipple between his lips. Emma groaned as he sucked, closing her eyes as pure, unadulterated pleasure coursed through her veins. Beau was hard inside of her, his lips soft around her breasts, his hands planted firmly on her ass. The onslaught of sensations was a potent mixture of eager, needy passion and soft, sweet heat.

Emma didn't realize her movements had faltered until Beau brought his hands to her ass to help her.

"Stay with me, sweetheart."

"I'm...with...you," she panted.

"Good," he whispered into her mouth as he caught her lips in a kiss. Emma returned it feverishly, no longer worried about controlling the undulations of her hips. She simply let Beau lift her up and down at his will and poured her passion into the kiss.

The heat in her lower belly churned with the need to erupt. Beau's lips found her neck, and his tongue traced patterns on her skin. At some point, his hips had taken over much of the work, driving into her from below. Emma moaned, want and need colliding in a rush of sensation.

"What do you need, angel?" Beau's voice came out low and rough.

"Wh-what?" she sputtered.

"What do you need to come?"

Emma was quiet for a moment, unable to form a cohesive thought. "I need...gah! Beau, I don't know, but I'm so close."

"How about this," he suggested, bringing a hand between them and pressing lightly on her clit. It proved to be precisely what she needed. She rocked into Beau's hand a few times, each movement harder than the last, and then she was coming apart in his arms, pleasure rushing over her in waves.

Emma collapsed on top of Beau, limp with pleasure, his face still buried in her neck and his cock buried deep inside her. On a low groan, he wrapped one strong arm around her waist and began driving up into her, seeking his own release. His hips pumped furiously for just a few moments before he stilled, his whole body tensed beneath her. The growl Beau let out as he came was so feral it sent goosebumps coasting over Emma's skin.

With his arms tight around her waist, she melted into him like a popsicle on a hot summer day. His long fingers ran up and down her spine, and she brought her head to his chest, resting there as they both caught their breath. After long moments, she propped her chin on her hands.

Beau gazed adoringly down his chest at her, one big thumb stroking down her cheek. "How are you feeling?" he asked.

Emma beamed up at him. "I feel great."

A look of pure male satisfaction crossed Beau's face as he cradled her cheek in his palm. "You're incredible." His serene smile faltered for a moment. "I didn't hurt you, did I?"

She shook her head as she leaned in to drop a kiss on his chest. "Not at all."

Beau's previously easygoing demeanor reappeared, and he pulled Emma in tight to his chest. "Good."

She nuzzled into his warm skin, basking in the afterglow. "You could never hurt me, Beau," she whispered. "You're healing me."

22

When Beau awoke the next morning, Emma was curled up into his chest like a content kitten. The night before had been, well, monumental. Being inside of Emma was like experiencing a little slice of heaven. Wet and snug and soft—she was perfect. And her revelation about him healing her...Beau had a hard time believing that he had anything to do with her newfound strength, but he did know, without a doubt, that he didn't deserve her.

Emma had been through so much, and after meeting Earl and seeing where she'd grown up, the fact that she had turned out even semi-normal was even more astounding. Beau was more determined than ever to make up for all the things she'd missed because of her shitty upbringing. So far, he'd introduced her to new movies and television shows, they had tried Chinese food and Mexican food, she'd gotten a makeover, learned self-defense, gotten drunk, and had what Beau hoped was the best sex of her life. That was a pretty good list for just a few weeks of working on it, right?

He would give Emma anything, do anything for her. Beau knew he was wrapped around her little finger, and he didn't even care because she was worth it. Worth every second of anguish he'd endured in his life, every injury he'd sustained on the job, every single hardship he'd ever been through, because it had all led him to her. In a wacky, roundabout way, his entire life had been leading up to this. To *her*.

Every woman he'd been with in the past paled in comparison to Emma. He'd never quite known why none of those other women did it for him—why none of them made him desire to settle down or engage in anything more than a fling. But now he had his answer. He'd been waiting for someone like Emma. An angel that called to him like a siren and who he could worship like a goddess.

Stroking a hand over her light-blonde hair, Beau leaned in to press a kiss to the top of Emma's head. Her cheek laid on his chest, and she had an arm flung over him, her hand resting right atop his beating heart. One leg was hitched up and tangled between his.

Beau was usually hard when he awoke, but having Emma pressed up against him had him sporting some major morning wood. Noticing the way the sheet tented down below, he shifted and tucked himself to the side so Emma wouldn't wake up to such a blatant display of his masculinity.

She stirred, nuzzling her face into his chest, and Beau chuckled at the ticklish sensation. A large yawn escaped her mouth before she blinked her eyes open and looked up at him, her gaze hazy with sleep.

"Hi, you," Beau rumbled, his morning voice still rough.

Emma treated him to a sweet smile as she stretched out her legs. "Hi."

"Sleep well?"

She nodded sleepily. "Very well."

"Good," Beau said, placing a kiss on her forehead. Emma ran her hand over his chest, stopping to outline the tattoo above his left pec. It was a pair of angel wings with two dates written below them.

"Those are my father's birth and death dates," Beau

explained softly as Emma traced the outline of the wings with her finger.

"Oh," she whispered, leaning in to kiss each wing tenderly. He shuddered as her lips met the tattoo, and she ran her hand over the spot to soothe it. "I'm sorry, Beau."

"Thanks," he replied, glad she didn't dwell on the topic. Instead, Emma's fingers skated over his chest to his bicep, where there was a larger piece of ink. The tattoo of a snake wrapped around Beau's upper arm six times, its head appearing right at the edge of his shoulder, where its tongue stuck out as if it were mid-hiss.

"Does this one mean anything?" she asked.

Beau flexed his arm so the snake moved, loving how Emma's eyes widened as he did. "It means I was sixteen, and foolish, and a snake was the coolest thing I could think of getting tattooed on myself."

Her eyebrows drew together as an adorable frown formed on her lips. "You got a tattoo when you were sixteen? How?"

Beau smirked to himself. "I blackmailed Fletcher into pretending he was my parent and signing off on it. He was almost thirty at the time, so it was believable enough."

Emma's jaw dropped open. "How did you possibly have bad enough dirt on Fletcher that he was willing to do that? He seems so…straight-laced."

"He is," Beau said, a shrewd smile curving his lips. "Most of the time. But when Fletch is heartbroken, he makes bad decisions and does things he doesn't want my mother to find out about. It's only happened a couple of times in his life, but it's never good. He happened to have a nasty breakup right around my sixteenth birthday and decided to blow off some steam by finding an empty highway and driving recklessly. He wound up wrapping his car around a pole and totaling it. He walked away just fine, lucky bastard, but he didn't want to worry my mom. I happened to discover the crushed-up car in his garage and demanded an explanation. Then, I used the information to my advantage."

Emma shook her head but seemed to be biting back a smile. "You're terrible."

"That's not what you were saying last night." Beau wiggled his eyebrows in an attempt to make her laugh. It worked. When Emma's laughter died down, her fingers made their way to his final tattoo—a series of dots and lines running across his clavicle.

"What does this one mean?" she asked, running her finger along the line of symbols.

"It's Morse code."

She arched a brow. "Really?"

"Yep."

"Well, what does it say?" she asked, scrunching her nose and squinting as if that would help her decipher it.

"It says *protect and serve*," Beau explained. "It's kind of the unofficial police slogan. I wasn't really supposed to have any identifying information tattooed on myself in case I ever went undercover, but no one ever suspected what that one might mean."

Emma pinched the skin on his collarbone. "Yet another thing you got away with, huh?"

Beau grinned smugly. "Yep."

"Do you regret it now that you're not an officer anymore?" she asked, rubbing her finger soothingly over the skin she'd pinched.

"Nah," he answered easily. "I may not do the same job, but I still live to protect and serve others."

Emma smiled up at him, her golden eyes glowing. "Like me."

Leaning down, he kissed the tip of her nose. "Exactly like you."

She drew back and pursed her lips together. "Why did you leave the force?"

Beau hesitated, unsure just how much to tell her. She knew about what happened to Sofia, and that he'd lost faith in the police force because of their failure to protect her, but she didn't know the full extent of his upset.

Heaving a sigh, he decided it was probably best to tell Emma the truth. "After Sofia died, I couldn't trust anyone else on the force anymore. They fucking let her and all those other women down by not finding them fast enough. Now that I've familiarized myself with the case even more, I see that balls were dropped all over the place. There was no reason they shouldn't have been able to find those women in time. I blame the force for that, but"—Beau paused to take a deep breath—"I blame myself for Sofia getting abducted in the first place."

Placing her hand on his chest, Emma rubbed her thumb over his *protect and serve* tattoo. "It's not your fault," she said softly.

Beau snorted. "That's sweet of you to say, but you don't know the whole story."

Emma's gaze dropped to her hand as she drummed her fingers over his collarbone. "Actually, I do. Isabella told me that you and Sofia used to date and that she ran away to Mexico after you broke up. She said you feel like you drove her into the arms of the traffickers."

Dropping his head back against the headboard, Beau let out a groan. "That woman can never keep her damn mouth shut."

Emma pinched his nipple, making him jerk. Her cute little frown would have made him grin if he hadn't been so pissed at Bella for spilling the beans.

"She was just trying to make me understand the situation better," Emma said.

"It wasn't her place to tell you about that," Beau grumbled.

"You're right, it wasn't," Emma conceded, patting his

chest. "But I'm glad she did. It helped me understand why you're so set on catching Mason and his men."

"I would've wanted to round them up and kill them anyway, but yeah, the fact that I feel responsible for Sofia's death kicked my motivation into gear," Beau said. "And then finding you just pushed me even more."

Emma grinned sweetly at him before pressing a kiss to his shoulder. When she pulled away, she was fondling her lip between her teeth as if she was still deep in thought about something.

"Something else on your mind?" he asked.

"There was something else Isabella said that bothered me."

Beau raised his eyebrows in question. "What's that?"

"She said that you specifically choose women who you know will drive you away."

"I'm gonna kill her." Beau's fists clenched involuntarily by his sides. "You two sure talked a lot about me, huh?"

Emma grabbed one of his fists and drew it up to her mouth for a kiss. "I think she really was just trying to help me understand you better. But it got me wondering…why?"

"Why?"

"Why do you choose partners you know won't last?"

Beau was silent for a few moments, deliberating the question. Why *did* he always go for brassy broads when he knew their drama would eventually turn him off? Why had he never considered a quieter, more modest woman like Emma, when it was obvious that she complemented him so well?

"I guess I've always been a little nervous about serious relationships," he admitted. "Especially with my job, it seemed like a bad idea to let someone get attached to me. Selfish, even. Every time I stepped out the door, I was putting myself in danger, and there were no guarantees I would make it home. I grew up watching my mom live without her husband because of an incident on the job. I didn't want to be responsible for putting someone else through the same."

Emma listened intently, her golden eyes never leaving his. When Beau finished, she covered his cheek with her palm, stroking him like something precious. "You're really thoughtful, you know."

His eyebrows flew up. "Me? Thoughtful?"

"Yes," she said. "You had to see your mom upset over losing her partner, and you don't want to do the same to someone else. You don't want to hurt anyone. It makes sense. But what about what you *do* want?"

Beau crinkled his brow as she went on.

"Don't you want to find someone to spend your life with, even if it scares you?"

He smiled softly, taking her hand in his and kissing the middle of her palm. "Angel," he whispered. "I think I already found her."

Without pause, he leaned in to press his lips to hers. Emma gasped at his unexpected words, and he took the opportunity to sweep his tongue into her mouth. She recovered quickly, darting her tongue against his as she scooted closer to him.

"You've bewitched me," Beau breathed between kisses.

Emma pulled back, her wide, bright smile bringing on one of his own. "Who are you? Mr. Darcy?"

Beau scratched his head. "Who?"

"Never mind." She scooted up to press a kiss to his jaw. The movement brought her silky thigh in contact with his crotch, and he bit back a moan. The erection that had gone into hibernation during their more serious conversation raged back to life.

Emma gulped, no doubt feeling him harden against her leg, and Beau craned his neck to lick up the column of her throat. She shivered beneath his attention.

"You are so sexy," he whispered by her ear.

She caught his lips in a kiss, sliding her tongue expertly along his, and he almost forgot how inexperienced she really was. Gently cradling her head in his hand, Beau slowed down the kiss. Emma had other ideas, and she slung one leg over his, pressing his erection against her belly.

He felt her gasp beneath his mouth as his length pushed against her bare skin. "Is this okay?" he asked.

She bit her lip between her teeth and gave him a slow nod. "Yes." Leaning over, she traced his angel wing tattoo with her tongue. Fuck, why was that so hot? Kissing along his collarbone to his shoulder, she flicked her tongue over the snake tattoo, then peered up at him mischievously.

Beau took on a serious tone as he asked, "Did you just kiss my snake?"

Emma's eyes grew wide at his question. "Um, yes?"

He shook his head slowly and deliberately. "You naughty girl," he murmured. "Those lips are for me only."

A playful grin returned to Emma's face. "Oh, sorry. Let me make it up to you," she said, leaning in to capture his lips again. Beau sighed as her tongue found his, and she crawled the rest of the way atop his body, melting into him like a puddle. He wrapped his arms around her waist, covering her ass with his palms.

"I want to try something," she murmured, inches from his lips.

"Hm?" he mumbled, his attention caught on the way her skin felt so silky beneath his hands.

"You know when you kiss me…down there?"

Beau jolted back, a slow grin spreading over his lips. "You mean when I eat you out?"

Emma's cheeks blushed a furious red. "Yes."

Enjoying her bashfulness, he squeezed the round globes filling his palms. "And you love every second of it."

She sighed dreamily. "Yes, well…I'd like to try doing that to you."

Horror streaked through Beau momentarily, and he was sure the emotion flashed across his face because Emma's eyes widened comically.

"You want to eat me out?" he asked.

"No!" she cried, pressing her forehead to his chest. "I mean…I want to…" she trailed off, no doubt too shy to say what she meant.

"Oh," Beau drawled as understanding dawned along with a rush of blood to his crotch. "You want to blow me."

Emma lifted her head, but her gaze remained fixed on his chest as she replied, "I'd like to try."

Reaching for her chin, Beau lifted her gaze to his. "You don't have to, angel." As much as his body was showing them both he wanted it, he knew it was a big deal for her to go there.

"I know," she said. "I want to. I mean, only if you want me to."

"Of course I fucking want you to." Actually, Beau couldn't think of anything else he wanted more. Any material object he'd ever desired paled in comparison to the idea of Emma's mouth on him.

With a coy smile, she slid down to kneel on the bed between his legs. "You have to tell me if I do something wrong," she said, swiping her tongue across her top lip. "I want it to be good for you."

"Emma," Beau said, a hint of censure in his tone, "there is no possible way that your mouth on my dick won't be good for me."

Her cheeks grew even redder, if such a thing was possible, but she continued to lower herself onto the mattress. She shifted for a moment, seeking a comfortable position before sliding her palms over his thighs. Beau grew painfully hard but stayed silent as she coasted her hands over his skin.

Emma stared down at him, scrutinizing his cock as if coming up with a game plan. After a moment, she leaned forward, closer to giving them what they both wanted, then paused. Beau bit back a grunt, his desire for her so great that he could hardly contain it. His pulse ratcheted up as she hovered over him, the anticipation almost too much to bear.

Lifting her gaze to his, Emma batted her eyelashes once before continuing her descent. Her hands locked onto his thighs like an anchor, and Beau let out a silent breath of relief when she pressed the lightest kiss to the tip of his erection. The relief was short-lived, though, and quickly replaced by need. Need for more. Need for release. Need for *her*.

Keeping her lips on him, Emma licked out her tongue, swiping it over the underside of his tip. With her inexperience, she probably didn't realize that was the most sensitive spot, but she'd certainly discovered it quickly enough.

Beau hissed out a breath, and her gaze shot to his, holding eye contact as she licked the spot again. His eyes snapped shut as he fought for control. His instincts were pushing him to move, to rock his hips, to thrust into her mouth. Instead, he fisted his fingers in the sheets and tried to breathe deeply.

Gaining confidence, Emma wrapped her lips around the head of his cock, getting accustomed to his girth. She sucked on his tip like a lollipop, drawing him in and out in shallow pulls. Lust chased satisfaction as she went infinitesimally deeper each time.

Risking a look down at her, Beau watched inches of himself disappear into her mouth. On a groan, he reflexively lifted his hips before regaining control, willing himself to remain still and not drive into that warm, wet little mouth like he wanted to.

"Am I doing alright?" Emma murmured.

"Fuck yes," he ground out. "You're doing more than alright."

"Is there anything you want me to…do differently?" she asked, glancing up at him as she wrapped her lips around him for another suck.

Beau barely contained a moan. Her mouth was the sweetest form of torture, and he would happily lie there and take it for hours. But need clawed at him like a hungry tiger, and he knew exactly what would quell that craving.

"Remember how I showed you to use your hand on me? To squeeze it nice and tight?"

Emma nodded wordlessly, though her breaths seemed to speed up, her chest rising and falling rapidly.

Beau reached down with his own hand to show her what he wanted. "Hold the base just like that while you use your mouth on the head."

Nodding, she pressed her lips together and replaced his hand with her own. Stroking up and down with her fist, she finally settled it around the base, giving a firm squeeze. Her lips came to cover his head once again, and she worked him all the way in until her mouth hit her hand.

A low, content moan rumbled from Emma's throat, and Beau practically lost it. Need surged through him, and he reached for her head, resting his palm atop it and resisting the urge to apply pressure.

"Keep stroking while you suck," he instructed, and Emma immediately complied, pumping her hand up and down, then following the movement with her mouth. She found a steady rhythm that had him arching off the bed as pressure throbbed within him.

"Fuck, I'm close," he groaned as everything within him tightened. When he felt his balls draw up, he knew it was time to stop. "Stop, Emma. I'm about to come."

She was either so overcome with pleasuring him that she didn't hear him, or she purposefully ignored his warning. Her petite hand and mouth continued working him over until he knew he wouldn't last.

Fisting her hair in his hand, Beau drew her off of him as gently as possible. Her mouth released him with a *pop*. But his forethought hadn't taken into account where he would come if not her mouth, and before he had a chance to aim away from her, he exploded on her face.

"Shit," he breathed as moisture coated her cheeks, chin, and lips. Beau was as appalled at himself for his lack of control as he was intrigued by the sight of Emma's face covered in him. Primal satisfaction washed over him, and his chest ached with pride that this brave, radiant woman wore the proof of his pleasure.

Emma sat there, stunned, for a moment, as if still processing what had happened, before rocking back to sit on her heels. A pout tugged at her lips. "I wanted to taste you."

Beau's eyes threatened to bug out of his head as she thrust out her tongue to catch some of the moisture dripping down her chin. Sitting abruptly, he framed her face with his hands and pulled her into his lips, uncaring that her mouth was still coated in his release. He kissed her hard—probably harder than he should have—but she met him eagerly, molding her body to his as she reciprocated that kiss.

"And how do I taste?" he asked, resting his forehead against hers.

She licked her lips. "A little salty."

Beau let out a hoarse chuckle. "And you're sweet as honey. We're salty and sweet."

She looked up at him through her eyelashes and beamed. "The perfect combination."

"Yes," Beau agreed before laying her down on the bed to return the favor.

23

In the month since Emma had been rescued, she'd never felt safer. Currently sprawled out on the couch, her feet dangled off the edge as she watched trashy television. Beau was still showering off the sweat from his morning workout, which she'd happily observed over her breakfast of a veggie omelet with home fries. It was "arm day" for Beau, which had involved a lot of grunting, bulging biceps, and of course, popping of pecs.

He and Diego had been working like dogs, analyzing evidence, scrutinizing audio and video footage from the various bugs and cameras, and constantly reorganizing their evidence board. They seemed confident that they had almost enough proof of Mason's whereabouts to capture him, and they were formulating a plan for how they would prove Williams' involvement.

Despite their feverish investigating, there had still been plenty of time for Beau and Emma to bond and continue building their relationship, no matter how atypical it was. He seemed to have a never-ending list of things he wanted her to try, or watch, or do, and he spent most of their free time educating her on everything from popular board games to different sex positions that didn't involve him being atop her.

Emma had never felt more at home than she did at Beau's apartment, but she yearned for the day that Mason, Williams, and her father were all taken care of so they could finally start living like normal people. She wanted to go out to the movies. Go shopping at the mall. Go out to dinner on a real date with Beau. Until then, she'd settle for whatever she could get within the apartment, because any time spent with Beau left her feeling like she was on cloud nine.

Emerging from the bathroom in long athletic shorts and no shirt, Beau wandered into the living room. Gently lifting Emma's head, he plopped himself on the end of the couch before placing her head in his lap.

"Watcha watchin'?" he asked, stroking a hand absentmindedly over her hair.

"It's some reality show about a cruise ship," Emma answered, her eyes glued to the television. There had been a lot of drama between the captain and one of the cooks, and she couldn't wait to see how it played out.

Beau shook his head. "I can't believe you enjoy this stuff."

She reached up to smack his bare chest. "Hey, I'm making up for years of being ridiculously sheltered. You get, like, every single channel on this TV, and I'm taking advantage of it."

"Okay, okay," Beau said, laughing as he deposited a kiss on her palm. "I'll join you for a bit, and maybe then I'll understand the hype."

They watched in companionable silence for a few minutes until a breaking news banner floated across the screen along with a little news jingle indicating that the show would be paused. A female newscaster appeared on the screen, her hair tied up in a remarkably high bun. The gray A-line skirt and white blouse she wore looked pretty, yet professional. Understated makeup made her skin look flawless, and she had that cat eye going that Isabella had tried to teach Emma.

"We're sorry for this interruption," the newscaster said, "but we bring you breaking news of a missing local woman."

A picture flashed on the screen, but Emma was so busy studying the newscaster's impeccable style that it took a moment for the photo to fully register in her brain. When it finally did, she flew into a seated position, her vision blurring from either the rapid movement or the shock of seeing her face on the television screen. More likely, a mixture of both.

The newscaster was still talking on the screen, but Emma didn't register a single word she said. Her ears were ringing as she gazed at a photo of herself beneath words like *Missing* and *Have you seen this woman?* and *Please call the police with any details.*

"B-Beau," she whispered, grabbing the edge of the couch to steady herself.

"What the ever-loving fuck?" he growled beside her.

"I'm…I need…" Emma began, then slapped a hand over her mouth. Launching herself off the couch, she barely made it to the toilet before expelling the contents of her breakfast into it. She was still on her knees when Beau arrived at her side.

"Jesus," he muttered as he yanked her hair back into a ponytail. "Em," he whispered, running a hand over her back before kneading her shoulders. She sat up slowly as the nausea subsided, grabbing a tissue to wipe off her face.

"Wh-what's going on?" she choked out.

Beau's eyes were a little wild, and he continued massaging her shoulders, his fingers digging in just a little too hard. "I don't know," he said. "Someone must have reported you missing. Do you know who would do that?"

Emma stood and headed for the sink to swish out her mouth. "No," she said between gurgles of water. "There's no one in my life that would notice I was missing."

Beau hung his head, probably as upset over that sad truth

as he was that the police were now looking for her. He ran a hand over his face before looking back up at her. "I need to call Diego and talk this out. You need to pack a bag."

"What?" she asked, panic edging into her tone. Was he seriously kicking her out right now? "Why?"

"We're going to need to get out of here," Beau said.

We. Emma audibly exhaled. *Thank God.*

"Now that the police are looking for you in this area, it's not safe for us to be here," he said. "The neighbors may have seen you, and you've been out of the house a couple of times. We can't risk someone reporting you. It would mess up our whole case, and the police would try to get you back to your father."

Emma felt the color drain from her face at the thought. "I'll go pack."

❀

"Turn on the news," Beau said without preamble when Diego answered the phone.

"Okay," Diego drawled on the other end of the line. "What's got your panties in such a—" His voice died as he presumably caught sight of Emma's photo on his television. "Shit."

"Yes," Beau said tightly. "Emma's packing a bag now. She doesn't know anyone who would have reported her missing."

"Fuck," Diego said. "Do you think it could be Mason or one of his men? They must be pissed that she's gone."

"That was my first thought, too," Beau said. "It's pretty risky for someone with as many targets on his back as Mason to purposefully get involved with the police, but with Williams on his side, I could see it happening."

"I'll fast forward through the latest recordings from Williams' office and see if I can catch any chatter," Diego said. "I'll go through the tapes from Earl's after, too. I doubt he's had contact with Mason or any of his men. It's more likely that they bought Emma and never gave Earl a second thought. But there could be something helpful there."

"Yeah, might as well. Thanks," Beau muttered, running a hand over his face. "I don't know what I'm gonna do, D. This apartment could be crawling with cops any time now if someone reports having seen Emma around. We have to get out of here, but I don't know where to go."

"Why don't you go stay with Jack?" Diego suggested.

Beau sighed. It was the most logical option, as his brother lived on Nantucket, the small island where they grew up. Though still part of Massachusetts, it was thirty miles off the coast and insulated enough that the local Boston news probably wouldn't make a big splash there. Emma's face wouldn't be making the rounds on television screens like it was all over the city.

"I might have to, but I really don't want to drag Jack into this mess. It's bad enough that Fletcher could be seen as an accessory to what the police are now viewing as an abduction. Getting both of my brothers involved seems like a bad idea."

"Then don't tell him why you're going. He can't be held accountable if he doesn't know he's harboring a fugitive."

Diego's words hit Beau like a smack in the face. "Fuck, I *am* a fugitive," he groaned. *From cop to fugitive in one week... That would make a great title for a documentary*, he thought.

"Settle down, *hermano*," Diego chided. "It's all a big misunderstanding. We both know you haven't done anything wrong, but the police don't know that yet. You just have to lay low for a few days while I figure out who reported Emma missing and force them to rescind the accusation. Then, we can get back to our original mission of catching Mason."

"You think that's all it'll take?" Beau asked. "A few days?"

"Sure," Diego replied confidently. "I can almost guarantee you that there'll be at least a hint of our culprit on the tapes in either Williams' office or Earl's house. I should be able to listen through all of the recordings from the past twenty-four hours by this afternoon. The software I use allows me to skip over any long periods of silence, so it gets really condensed. I'll report back to you with what I find, and we'll get this all taken care of."

Beau breathed out a sigh of relief. "I can't thank you enough for your help, man. I'll do whatever I can to assist you once we're settled somewhere, but right now I need to focus my energy on keeping Emma calm and safe."

"Of course. That's all you *should* focus on. Tell Jack you have some time off now that you're between jobs, and you want to visit the island for a few days. He'll think nothing of it."

"You think?" Beau asked, chewing on the idea. It wouldn't be all that out of the ordinary for him to request to crash at his brother's apartment for a couple days. He tended to do it every few months when he needed to get out of the city.

Jack and his wife, Natalie, lived above their café, Danny's Place, with their adopted son, Carter. There was a spare bedroom, or at least there would be until Natalie gave birth in a few months when it would become a nursery. But for now, there was an open room for them, as long as Jack agreed to let them use it.

Of course, bringing a woman along with him would complicate matters. Beau rarely, if ever, brought women home to meet the family, and he certainly never brought any of them on a vacation. That in itself might be a red flag, but on the other hand, Emma's bruises were finally gone, and she had mostly gotten over her skittishness, so there would be no obvious signs of her distress.

It could work. There would be questions, but it could work.

"Okay," Beau agreed. "I'll give Jack a heads up while we drive over to the ferry. I don't want to stick around here any longer than I have to."

"Agreed," Diego said. "Go take care of your girl, and leave the rest to me."

"Thanks, D," Beau murmured into the phone before darting off to find Emma. He checked the bedroom and the kitchen before finding her in the bathroom, loading up a plastic bag of toiletries with trembling hands. She was dropping in a random assortment of items—a tube of toothpaste, but no toothbrush, a comb she hadn't touched once since she'd arrived, and a loose bar of soap that was probably still damp from his shower. Her movements were shaky and uncontrolled, and she jumped half a foot when Beau touched her lightly on the shoulder.

"Sorry," he mumbled, then greeted her with a gentle, "Hey." As he took Emma's trembling hands in his, she gazed up at him through puffy, bloodshot eyes.

"Hi."

"Oh, angel," Beau breathed, pulling her in for a long hug. A few of her tears hit his skin, and his heart wrenched. She had been through too damn much already. Why did someone have to go and ruin everything by noticing that she was missing? It could have been that some Good Samaritan noticed she hadn't come home in a while—maybe even a mailman or a neighbor—but it still rankled Beau that it could all be part of some elaborate plan on Mason's part to get Emma back. No way in hell would he let that happen.

"Everything's going to be okay," he promised. "I'm going to protect you."

Emma nodded against his chest, her hair tickling his chin. "Where are we going?" she asked as she pulled away.

"We're going to stay with my brother Jack on Nantucket. No one will find you there."

Her eyebrows pulled together, and Beau slid a thumb over her brow to soothe it.

"He doesn't mind us coming on such short notice?" she

asked, and the worried frown on her face was so endearing that Beau couldn't help but let a chuckle escape his throat.

"Sweetheart, you've only been out of the clutches of human traffickers for a month, and now you have God knows who looking for you, and you're worried about inconveniencing my brother?"

Mercifully, Emma's lips tipped up in a small smile. "I don't know how to react in this sort of situation. It's my first time being a missing person."

Beau grinned at her playful remark, grateful she was still able to access her sense of humor amidst the gravity of the situation. "Angel." He sighed, dropping his forehead against hers. "You haven't been missing since the moment I found you. You're right here where you belong. With me. And I'm never letting you go."

With a sweet sigh, Emma snuggled into his chest for another minute. He relished the peace and tranquility of the moment, knowing in his gut that it may be the last moment like that for quite a while.

24

Despite booking a spot on the slower ferry, which took an extra hour to complete the journey to Nantucket compared to the fast ferry's single one, Beau and Emma opted to remain in his truck rather than get out and stretch their legs or enjoy the outdoor deck of the boat. They couldn't risk anyone seeing them and recognizing Emma's face from the news.

Even being locked up tight in the truck, they each wore sunglasses and baseball caps like celebrities hiding from the paparazzi. A few minutes into the journey, Emma had climbed into Beau's lap as he sat in the driver's seat and curled into his chest, where she stayed for the rest of the trip. He idly stroked her hair as he made a couple of calls that she half listened to. He was alerting Jack to their impending arrival, as well as instructing Fletcher to stay at Christa's apartment for the foreseeable future.

When the voice over the loudspeaker announced that it was time for passengers to return to their cars in preparation to disembark the ferry, Emma slid into the passenger seat, flipping down the sun visor to adjust her disguise in the mirror. A few light-blonde tendrils escaped from beneath the Red Sox cap Beau had lent her, and the cheap sunglasses from the convenience store covered half her face, effectively concealing her identity.

"Here we go," Beau said softly as he revved up the engine in the truck and drove them onto land. They were just beginning to bump slowly over the cobblestone streets of downtown Nantucket when his cell phone rang. Flicking his gaze momentarily down at the screen, Beau answered, put it on speakerphone, and set it in the cupholder between himself and Emma.

"Hi, D. Whatcha got for me?"

Diego's voice was grave on the other end of the line. "You're not going to like it."

"Didn't think I would. Give it to me straight."

"I started with the recordings from Williams' office, but there was nothing useful there, so I dug into the tape from Earl's house. Two nights ago, he had a couple of visitors. I'm almost positive one of them was Williams. They informed Earl that Emma had gone missing, and he was going to have to repay his debt to them in cash since they could no longer make money off her. Earl told them he didn't have the money, so they shook him down until he was screaming and crying like a baby. Eventually, he promised he would find Emma and return her to them."

"Oh, *hell* no," Beau snarled, his hands tightening on the steering wheel and reminding Emma why she'd been so frightened of him that first night when he found her.

"My thoughts exactly," Diego said.

Beau banged the wheel a few times. "What possesses a man with as many potential charges as Earl to go to the police willingly? What on Earth is he thinking?"

"Well," Diego replied, "we've already determined that he's not the sharpest tool in the box, and the guy is broke and owes his bookies a shit-ton of money. At this point, he'll do anything not to have to face their wrath if he can't repay it."

Beau ran his hand over his face. "Why the fuck did he have to get the police involved?"

"I could go over there and try to threaten him into rescinding his accusation that Emma is missing, but honestly, at this point I don't think he'd go for it. He's too desperate. We just need to ride out this whole missing-person thing, and once we catch Mason, we can explain the whole story to the police."

"This is such bullshit," Beau complained.

"I agree, *hermano*, but it is what it is. Are you guys almost at Jack's?"

"Yep. We're driving to his place now. You'll keep an eye on all our surveillance cameras and bugs?"

"Of course," Diego said. "Any minute, someone's going to say something tipping off Mason's current location. I really believe that. We just need to have patience."

"Patience, my ass," Beau grumbled, then sighed. "Thanks for the call, D. Keep me in the loop."

"You've got it," Diego said. "Bye."

Beau hung up the phone and struck a glance over at Emma. "I hate your father."

She blew out a breath before replying, "Me too."

Reaching over, Beau clasped a hand over her thigh. "We'll get through this together."

Anchored by his hand, she focused on breathing as she took in the charming downtown area full of quaint little shops, vibrant flowers, and cheerful tourists. Before long, they were driving into a crushed-up-seashell driveway beside a charming building labeled *Danny's Place*. The exterior was a muted mint green, which looked dazzling against the backdrop of the blue ocean and sky behind it.

"This is it," Beau announced as he turned off the ignition. "Like I told you earlier, the bottom of the building is the café, and the apartment is up top. There's a guest bedroom where we can stay, and we can retreat there at any time, but I'd really like you to meet Jack and Natalie."

"Of course. I want to meet them, too," Emma said. "If we're going to make this look as normal as possible, we're going to have to put on happy faces and hang out with them like we really want to be here. Not that I don't—like I said, I want to meet them—but the circumstances could be better."

Beau reached over to tuck a lock of her hair behind her ear. "I get it. Don't worry. They're going to love you."

Emma tugged her lip between her teeth. "You really think so?" She had a hard time believing that anyone would see a weak, timid woman like her and think she was a good match for Beau. Then again, hadn't Isabella said he needed someone to soften out his sharp edges? And she wasn't really weak or timid. Not with Beau. He made her feel strong and beautiful. Maybe they really were the perfect combination.

He leaned in to brush a kiss over her forehead. "I *know* so. Trust me, once they get over the shock that I brought such a nice woman home, they'll be thrilled to have you here."

Hopping out of the truck, he came around to pull open the passenger side door and help her onto the driveway. The salty scent of the ocean filled her nostrils as she stepped down from the truck. Beau grabbed their overnight bags from the back and hoisted them over his shoulder. Emma appreciated the sight of his biceps and shoulders as he hauled the bags around as if they weighed nothing.

The seashells crunched beneath her feet as they made their way to the apartment door. Beau knocked twice, then took Emma's hand in his, squeezing it reassuringly as the door swung open to reveal a man leaner than Beau and with slightly longer hair but the same dazzling brown eyes.

"Hey, man," Beau greeted his brother jovially, pulling him in for a one-armed hug while he kept Emma's hand contained firmly in his. A woman appeared as they pulled apart, bouncing into the doorway. Her long, blonde hair was collected into a braid running down her back, and a very pronounced baby bump jutted from her slim body with a colorful maxi dress tented over it.

"Hi!" the woman squealed, pulling Beau in for her own one-armed hug while Emma stood awkwardly to the side, hanging on to his hand like a life preserver.

"Jack, Natalie." Beau gestured to each of them, then swept his arm toward Emma. "This is Emma."

Keeping the fingers of her left hand laced with Beau's, Emma reached out with her right to shake Jack's and Natalie's for just the required amount of time to be polite. "It's so nice to meet you both."

"You as well," Natalie said cheerfully, pumping Emma's hand up and down.

"We had no idea Beau was seeing anyone," Jack added as he retracted his own hand and ran his fingers through his brown curls. Emma's cheeks heated, but the subject was quickly dropped when Natalie surreptitiously stomped on her husband's foot. She frowned at him until he amended, "But we're so glad he is."

"Yes," Natalie said tightly. "We are." Turning back toward Beau and Emma, her face brightened. "Why don't you two come upstairs and get settled in? I just had Derek make us a fabulous cheese board." She spun around and began waddling her way up the steps.

"Derek's the cook at Danny's Place," Jack explained as they trudged up the stairs behind Natalie. Dropping his voice to a whisper, he added, "Her pregnancy cravings are out of control. If she doesn't get a cheese board at least once a week, she turns into a monster."

"I heard that," Natalie called from the top of the stairs. "Make fun of me all you want, but you reap the rewards of my cravings, too," she said, popping a cracker loaded with multiple types of hard cheeses into her mouth.

"Drop your bags here," Jack said, pointing beside the couch, "and we can enjoy this food while we catch up."

Beau set their bags down and led Emma to the kitchen, depositing her on a stool at the island, right in front of the impressive array of crackers, cheese, nuts, and fruit that Natalie was chomping on. Gazing up at Beau from her spot on the stool, Emma smiled to reassure him that she was doing alright.

His eyes softened as he took in her expression, and he leaned down to kiss the top of her head. "Do you want some water?" he asked softly as he pulled away, finally dropping her hand.

"Yes, please." She watched his large frame as he strolled through the small kitchen to grab her a glass. Jack and Natalie exchanged glances, looking puzzled at the interaction. Emma couldn't figure out why, but before she had the chance to dwell on it, they were turning back to her.

"So!" Natalie exclaimed. "How did you two meet?"

"Oh, uh, well…" Emma trailed off. Her brain wasn't functioning fast enough to come up with a fake story. *He rescued me from the human traffickers that my dad sold me to*, just didn't seem like it would make a great first impression. *Oh, and the only reason we're here is because the police are searching for me.* Yeah, that definitely wouldn't work.

"We met at a bar," Beau chimed in as he poured water into a glass. "Some guys were hassling Emma, and I came in and saved the day." His cocky smile and confident tone made the story sound believable even to Emma, and it wasn't *entirely* untrue, if you swapped out the bar for an abandoned warehouse.

"No way!" Natalie smacked a hand against Jack's chest, and he rubbed the spot with faux hurt. "We had a similar experience. This jackass was hitting on me at a bar, and he even kissed me, and then Jack punched him in the face. That was the night of our first kiss." She glanced fondly up at her husband.

"I'll never forget it," Jack replied, leaning down to smooch her on the lips.

"That's so funny that it happened to both of us," Natalie said as she shoved a handful of nuts into her mouth.

"Yeah…so funny," Emma mumbled with as much enthusiasm as she could muster, grabbing a cracker to chew on so she wouldn't need to answer any more questions for a few moments.

"I'm pissed that it happened, but glad it brought us together," Beau said as he slid the full water glass in front of Emma. She gratefully accepted it, chugging a few mouthfuls to wash down the dry cracker.

"That's the spirit." Jack reached out his fist and bumped it with Beau's. "If that night at the bar hadn't happened, my baby wouldn't be cooking in her belly right now," he said, placing a protective hand over Natalie's stomach. She leaned back into his chest with a soft sigh.

Emma watched the interaction wistfully. The two were obviously so in love and eager to expand their family. She only hoped she would one day be safe enough to do the same.

"How many months along are you again?" Beau asked.

Natalie placed a hand over Jack's, and together they rubbed over her bump. "Seven. If all goes according to plan, this baby will be born in July."

Beau shook his head. "That's so cool. And you're not finding out the sex in advance, right?"

"No, we want to be surprised," Jack said. "Although, Carter is convinced it's a boy. He can't stop talking about playing ball with 'baby brother.' I don't have the heart to tell him the baby won't be able to play ball with him for at least a year after it's born."

Beau chuckled. "Where is the little man today?"

"He's at Mom's," Jack explained. "She still takes him for a

day every week. Did you tell her you were going to be on island?"

"No," Beau answered a little too quickly, and Emma froze, a cracker balanced between her teeth as she waited for him to expand. "I don't really want her to know we're here. I'm not ready for her to meet Emma yet."

Emma bit the cracker in half, grateful that Jack and Natalie seemed satisfied by that answer, and chewed it.

"Whatever you say, man," Jack said. "But Mom would be stoked that you have a girlfriend."

"That's exactly why I'm not ready. She's going to have a lot to say about it, and I just want these few days to be relaxing for us."

"I respect that. But you can't keep her hidden forever," Jack added with a wink.

The double meaning in that statement, that only Beau and Emma would realize, sank into the pit of her stomach. They couldn't stay hidden forever. There were only a couple of options. Either Beau and Diego would catch Mason, or the police would catch her and inform Earl of her whereabouts, who would inevitably inform Mason. The situation was a ticking time bomb, and Emma prayed that when things blew up, the explosion worked in their favor.

25

After an afternoon walk on the beach, during which Beau and Emma both stayed fully disguised and held hands like one of them might float away on an ocean breeze, and then a delicious barbecue dinner with Jack and Natalie, the four of them found themselves settling onto the cozy lounge furniture in the living room.

Natalie had maneuvered herself into an armchair, propping pillows all around to support her back and sides, then settled into them with a long sigh. Jack sat in another armchair by her side, watching her with eagle eyes for any sign of discomfort, or perhaps just getting ready to jump up a moment's notice to fetch her cheese. Emma had taken a seat next to Beau on the couch, just close enough so their thighs touched. The slight pressure of his arm around her shoulders anchored her, and she settled into his side, resting her head on his shoulder.

"I am *so* full," Beau announced, rubbing a hand over his flat, muscular abdomen.

"You only ate that much because no one else wanted your steak tips. Obviously, mine were superior," Jack said with an impish smile.

Beau snorted. "Mine were exceptional. That's why I didn't want to share them with anyone." Apparently, his competitive spirit extended beyond grilled cheese. The two brothers had split a bag of steak tips, and each prepared them in their own ways, then stood side by side at the grill, rotating their skewers at precise intervals and talking trash the entire time.

"Sure," Jack replied in a tone that implied he very much did not agree.

"Let's ask Natalie," Beau suggested. "She tried both. Whose steak tips were better?"

Natalie shifted in her chair, placing a pillow on her lap beneath her protruding stomach. "I'm not interested in being a part of this dick-measuring contest," she said breezily. "Besides, a pregnant lady would eat anything you put on her plate. You could have served me something out of the garbage and I probably would have enjoyed it."

"Thanks for the lovely compliment, babe." Jack shot her a good-natured glare.

"How about you, Emma?" Beau asked, squeezing her shoulder. "You tried both as well. Which one was better?"

Her cheeks warmed as she thought back to Beau feeding her a bite of his steak tips. He'd lifted the fork to her mouth, then watched her lips hungrily as she sucked the piece of steak off, no doubt remembering her sucking off something else entirely.

"They were both fantastic," she said. "But I tend to prefer sweet over spicy, so I think I like Beau's marinade better."

Jack shook his head in mock disdain while Natalie smirked.

"I thought you preferred salty," Beau whispered in Emma's ear, which only increased the blood flowing to her cheeks. Without preamble, he pulled her into his lap, tucking her head beneath his chin. Emma glanced over at Jack and Natalie, worried they would find the public display of affection inappropriate, but they only grinned knowingly. Content,

Emma melted into Beau's chest, feeling the steady beat of his heart beneath her cheek.

"Whatever," Jack said haughtily. "You're only saying that because you're dating him. Apparently, married people don't have to support their significant others anymore." He gave Natalie a dirty look, but she just smiled brightly at him.

"So, Emma," she said, rubbing her bump. "I want to know all about you. What do you do?"

Emma tensed at the question because, once again, the answer was something she simply couldn't say. *I'm fully supported by my overly controlling father because he never let me get a job or keep my own money.*

Beau must have felt her change in demeanor, because he smoothly intercepted. "She's in between jobs right now," he said, stroking up and down her arm soothingly. Would he ever stop saving her? She hoped not.

"Ah, the job market's so tough right now," Natalie said, shaking her head.

"You could always move back here," Jack said, his eyebrows climbing up hopefully as he glanced at Beau. "I know Mom would love to have another son living on the island." He looked toward Emma. "And there's always a job opening for you at Danny's."

"Thanks," Emma said, touched by Jack's kindness. "I've been thinking about looking for a job at a local library, though. It's always kind of been a dream of mine to work at one."

"Oh, that sounds lovely," Natalie said.

Beau kissed Emma behind her ear, eliciting a shiver that rolled down her spine. "I think that's a great idea," he said softly.

She tipped her head up to meet his gaze, and Beau indulged her with a brief kiss. Apparently not brief enough, though, because Jack cleared his throat forcefully, receiving a smack on his chest from Natalie as a reward.

"Ouch, woman!" Jack cried, rubbing at his chest. "You've become utterly violent in your pregnancy."

"Stop goading your brother," she scolded. "I will never forgive you if you drive away the only woman he's ever introduced us to."

"I was just going to offer to show them to the guest bedroom in case they wanted to continue their salacious pursuits in private," Jack said with faux innocence.

"Jack," Natalie chided.

"Ignore him," Beau whispered in Emma's ear, then turned to Jack and Natalie. "Actually, I think we're about ready to turn in for the night. We had a long day of travel, and I, for one, am exhausted." He let out an exaggerated yawn and stood, still cradling Emma in his arms. She grabbed his shoulder to steady herself as he placed her feet gently on the floor.

"Me too," she added. "Thank you both so much for letting us stay here. We really appreciate it."

Jack waved off her gratitude. "Of course. We're always happy to host. A little more notice might be helpful next time, but—"

"Don't listen to him," Natalie interrupted, unmoving from her nest of pillows. "You're welcome any time."

"Of course," Jack agreed in a sugary-sweet tone. Natalie angled a fierce frown at him that immediately softened when he winked at her.

"Jack and I will both be working down at Danny's all morning, but help yourself to whatever's in the kitchen," Natalie offered. "Or come downstairs and grab some breakfast and coffee if you'd like!"

"Thanks," Beau said, walking over to give his sister-in-law a goodnight kiss on the head. When he straightened and returned to Emma's side, Natalie had a gleam in her eyes that Emma couldn't quite read.

"See you in the morning, man," Jack said, clapping Beau

on the shoulder. He returned the gesture with just a little more force than his brother had. And the competitive streak continued.

Beau led Emma to the guest bedroom, and they took turns using the bathroom to get ready. Emma couldn't help but giggle to herself as she took in the random array of toiletries she'd packed in her haze. Luckily, the bathroom was stocked with anything she might have forgotten. Once her face was clean and her teeth were brushed, she returned to the guest bedroom to find Beau sprawled across the sheets in just his boxer briefs.

The sight of his bare, brawny body would never cease to captivate her. His powerful thighs were almost as impressive as his massive biceps, which were on display as he rested his head back against his hands. Emma's gaze caught on his face, where his lips were drawn into a concerned frown.

"What's wrong?" she asked, placing her bag of toiletries on the bedside table.

Beau's core muscles coiled like snakes preparing to strike as he sat up in the bed. "Come here," he rasped, holding his arms open for her. Emma hurried into his embrace without hesitation, melting into his arms. "Let me hold you," he requested as he stroked his fingers over her hair.

She was all too happy to oblige, sinking into Beau's body and finally releasing the mask she'd worn all day around his brother and Natalie. They were alone together for the first time since they'd arrived, and all the fear and worry she'd felt earlier in the day began rushing back. While Jack and Natalie had been great hosts, and Emma had genuinely enjoyed spending time with them, she hadn't forgotten the real reason they were on Nantucket.

Her eyes began to burn with unshed tears. She fought them but lost the battle, a small whimper escaping her throat as grief and sorrow gripped her.

"Oh, angel," Beau sighed, pulling her in closer. A sob

wracked Emma's body at the tenderness in his tone, and she buried her face in his chest as she cried herself to sleep.

※

The first rays of sunlight were just filtering through the blinds as Beau opened his eyes. A quick glance at his watch told him it was five-thirty a.m.—way too early to be awake, but it would be impossible to fall back asleep. His mind was already running a mile a minute as he thought about the events of the day before and anticipated pretending everything was fine around Jack and Natalie for another day.

Emma was nestled into his side, her chest rising and falling peacefully. His throat tickled, and he didn't want to wake her by clearing it, so he carefully withdrew from the bed to grab a glass of water. Tiptoeing through the house, he soon realized that Jack and Natalie had already left the apartment. The morning rush at Danny's began early, so they must have already gone downstairs to work.

Making his way to the kitchen, Beau poured a glass of water and stood before a window, sipping it as he watched morning begin to unfold. At the early hour, the sun was just barely peeking over the horizon, but the ocean already reflected the bright-orange orb as it began its ascent into the sky. Setting the empty glass on the counter, Beau stretched his arms overhead with an exaggerated sigh. Hopefully Emma would be able to get a few more hours of sleep than he had, and he decided to lay beside her and scroll on his phone for a while as she did.

As he padded back to the bedroom, a small noise set him on high alert. It almost sounded like a quieter version of the shrieks the seagulls liked to let out on the beach, but it was coming from inside the apartment. When he poked his head in the guest bedroom doorway, Beau realized the sounds were coming from Emma.

"Please, no!" she moaned, her eyes scrunched up tight as she thrashed from side to side. "Stop!"

It was the first nightmare she'd had in a while. The stress of running from the police must have put her on edge. Beau tiptoed toward the bed, determined not to startle her, but eager to pull her from her bad dream.

"Please don't," Emma pleaded in her sleep. "I love him!"

Beau froze in his tracks. *Love him? Who?* More curious than ever about what was going on in her dream, he slid into the bed and ran a gentle hand over Emma's cheek to rouse her. She whimpered and threw her head to the other side of the pillow.

"Angel," he said loudly, shaking her shoulder. "Wake up."

Emma's blurry eyes popped open, and she blinked a few times before focusing on his face. "Beau?"

"I'm right here," he assured her, stroking her soft hair. "It was just a bad dream."

Her gaze burned into his for a moment before she launched herself at him. Startled at the abrupt change in demeanor, Beau allowed himself to be rolled onto his back. All of a sudden, Emma was atop him, straddling his thighs and pecking at his lips, sliding her tongue across them until he opened his mouth and returned the kiss. His hands automatically found her hips as she began to grind into him, but after a moment, he came to his senses and tried to slow her down.

"Emma," he mumbled beneath her lips. When she didn't pause her pursuits, he squeezed her hips to still them. "Emma, stop."

She rolled off of him as if he'd slapped her, but Beau quickly pulled her into his side. "Sweetheart, you're still half asleep, and you were having a nightmare. Let's slow down."

Emma turned her gaze, which had admittedly cleared, up to his. "I don't want to," she argued, her lips pulling into a pretty pout. "I need you, Beau." Her hand skimmed over his briefs, and Beau's eyes snapped shut at the zing of pleasure.

"Do you need me?" she asked quietly, and the vulnerability and hopefulness in her voice both tore Beau's heart in half and sewed it back together in the span of a single moment.

"Always, angel," he answered, craning his neck to find her lips. Keeping the kiss light and sweet, he brushed his lips over hers with care, but her hand was still on his crotch, and when she squeezed slightly, he couldn't help but rock into her touch.

"Then take me," she whispered, and the slightly dirty edge to her words revved Beau's engine. Who was he to deny her what she said she needed? Emma's body was heaven, and he could use the release himself.

Bringing his lips to her ear, Beau whispered, "Okay."

26

Settling onto his back, Beau motioned for Emma to get on top of him, but she hesitated. Suddenly shy, she bit her bottom lip between her teeth.

"What's wrong?" he asked.

She took a deep breath before answering. "I want to try with you on top."

Beau's eyes shot to hers. "Are you sure?"

"Yes." While her expression appeared unwavering, he wasn't willing to risk doing something she might not be ready for. Then again, she had been ready for far more than he could have ever hoped for already.

"Why do you want me on top?"

She heaved out a sigh. "Because I want to be able to do it without freaking out. I want to have a normal sex life."

Beau tucked a curl behind her ear. "Angel, it's okay to modify things to make them more comfortable for yourself."

"I know," she replied. "But I'll never get over the bad memories unless I make new ones to replace them. I want this. I *need* this."

He let out an exasperated sigh and pinned her with his gaze. "Okay." Her face lit up at his acquiescence, and he almost forgot what he was going to add. "But," he said sharply, "you have to make me a promise."

Emma nodded sincerely. "Anything."

His heart softened at her earnest pledge. "You have to promise me you'll stop me if you're at all nervous."

Her gaze dropped to his chest. "I know. I'm sorry I didn't say anything last time, but it all happened so fast. I was fine…better than fine…and then, in a split second, I wasn't."

"I know," Beau soothed. "You don't have to apologize. I'm glad I was able to read your body language so well. I'm just afraid that, at some point, I'll be so into it that I won't realize that you're uncomfortable."

Emma reached over to run her hands over his biceps. "I know you would never hurt me, Beau."

He ran a hand over his head. "Not intentionally."

"Not at all," she argued. "But I promise I'll tell you if I need to stop."

"Good." Beau sat up and crawled toward her. "Let's get this off," he murmured, tugging her t-shirt up and over her head. Her little pink nipples were already perked up with pleasure, and he couldn't wait to get his mouth on them. "Lie down, sweetheart," he said.

Emma complied, lying back until her curls splayed over the pillow like the sun's rays. She gazed up at Beau adoringly, and he probably could have come just from staring into her eyes for too long. Unwilling to embarrass himself like that, he averted his gaze to their lower halves, sliding off both sets of underwear.

When he revealed her pink, glistening core, he felt his erection bob up toward his stomach. Damn, his self-control was totally shot. Emma's eyes widened to the size of quarters as she watched his member move like it had a mind of its own.

"Are you sure you want to do this?" he asked.

She licked slowly over her top lip, her gaze glued to his crotch. "Yep."

"Fuck, you're naughty." He grunted as he crawled over her and finally got her to meet his eyes again.

"Only with you," she whispered, and Beau dropped his forehead to hers as he soaked in those sweet words. Only with him did she feel safe enough to explore that side of herself. Only with him did she feel the desire to try new things, to push her limits.

"Good girl," he whispered as he settled himself between her legs. Propping himself up on his forearms so Emma wouldn't feel trapped, he leaned down to catch her lips in a tender kiss. Her palms found his face, then looped around the back of his neck. They kissed for a long, leisurely minute before Beau pulled away.

"Is this alright?" he asked, rolling his hips so she could feel his erection.

"More than alright," she answered.

"Good," he murmured, shifting to bring his mouth to her breasts. Her nipples were already pebbled, and he laved each one with his tongue before sucking on them. When Emma was writhing and whimpering below him, Beau rolled to the side, reaching for his bag to locate a condom. Rolling it on swiftly, he navigated himself back on top of her.

"Remember, we can always modify if you get uncomfortable," he reminded her.

"I know," she whined. "*Please* get inside me, Beau."

Her impatience made him chuckle, but his laughter cut off abruptly as soon as he pushed inside of her, returning to his very own wet, plush heaven. Keeping himself supported on his hands above her, Beau rocked into her slowly and carefully, inch by inch, as she acclimated to him. Emma's eyes fluttered shut, and the look of sheer bliss on her face had his chest swelling with pride. When she opened her eyes again, though, her mouth fell into that cute little frown of hers.

"Come here," she prodded, tugging at his arms, which were extended straight to keep as much of his bodyweight off of her as possible.

"Emma..." Beau groaned, wanting so badly to be as close to her as possible, but unwilling to risk scaring her again.

"Please," she added with another tug. "Kiss me."

Unable to reject that request, he dropped to his forearms, still keeping most of his weight off of her but allowing him to reach her lips. Beau kissed Emma tenderly, but she had other ideas. Slipping her hands behind his neck, she pressed her lips to his, licking along the seam until he couldn't help but open them. When her tongue slid along his just as he was driving into her, Beau shuddered, pleasure surging through his veins.

Lowering her hands to his shoulder blades, Emma attempted to pull him even closer. "Please, Beau," she begged. "Come closer. Stop holding back."

"Angel." He sighed, nuzzling his nose into her neck, then placing a kiss there.

Emma responded by wrapping her legs around him, her heels digging into his lower back. "I want all of you," she whispered.

His heart throbbed. "You have me," he murmured as he released the tension in his forearms, laying himself over Emma and giving her his weight, trusting her to tell him the truth about what she needed.

She moaned as Beau slid in and out of her, the angle deeper now. She was moving as much as he was, and together, they found a tempo that served them both. All thoughts of caution floated away as Beau thrust into her again and again, relishing the feel of her silky snugness and the erotic moans that assured him she was enjoying it as much as he was.

With both arms now free, he was able to bring one hand to Emma's clit, giving her just the right amount of pressure to set her off. Two flicks of his finger and she was trembling beneath him, calling out his name and bucking wildly as she rode out her orgasm. He followed immediately, shattered by Emma's cry as she clenched around him. No bad memories this time. She knew exactly who was on top of her, bringing her the most pleasure she'd ever had.

Spent, Beau lay atop her as he caught his breath, then rolled to the side to remove the condom. When he looked back at Emma, she had tears in her eyes, and her lips were quivering as if she was trying to hold them in.

"Shit," he muttered, pressing his face into her neck in shame. Had those not been moans of pleasure? Had he scared her again? *Hurt* her, even? "I'm so sorry, angel."

"Wh-what?" Emma sputtered, tugging at his hair to lift his head. "Why are you sorry?" Tears were trailing down her cheeks when he finally looked up.

"Because I was too rough with you," he said. "I shouldn't have let myself go like that."

"Beau," Emma said, shaking her head as if she was disappointed he would say such a thing. "That's exactly what I wanted you to do. I want all of you. I want to experience everything with you. I'm not a porcelain doll. I'm not going to break. You made me feel so wanted just now, so *desired*."

Beau crinkled his brow. "Then, why are you crying?"

She grinned at him, even as tears continued spilling from her eyes. "Because I had no idea it could feel that good."

"Ah, angel." He pulled her into his chest and stroked her back as her tears subsided. Even though they were apparently joyful tears, he couldn't stand to see Emma crying. Pride at being the one to make her feel that level of emotion soon overtook his worry. Emma was a strong, resilient woman, and every day he was learning to trust that more. He may never lose his sense of protectiveness over her, but he was realizing that he didn't need to treat her with kid gloves the way he sometimes did.

When Emma's breathing evened out, Beau pulled away to

look at her face. "Want to shower, then go down and grab some breakfast at Danny's?"

"Yes," she replied, licking her lips. "I think I've worked up an appetite."

❦

Emma was still finishing getting ready when Beau went down to Danny's to order them breakfast sandwiches and coffees. Catching her reflection in the mirror, she relished the fact that there were no longer any bruises on her face, just cheeks that were a healthy shade of pink. A small smile tugged at her lips as she recalled the strenuous activity that had put the color in her complexion.

She felt a keen sense of accomplishment for getting Beau to finally release some of his tightly reined control. While she always appreciated his careful treatment, sometimes a woman just needed to feel *needed*. She wanted Beau to crave her as much as she did him—to feel that wild yearning that she did whenever he was near.

With a grin on her face and a bounce in her step, Emma headed downstairs to meet him at Danny's. She was just about to cross the threshold when voices floated out from the office at the back of the café. Emma paused when she caught her name in the conversation. Quickly realizing it was Jack and Natalie talking, she shrank back into the stairwell to listen.

"It's just kind of weird, you know?" Natalie said. "He hasn't made one inappropriate joke or sexual remark since he got here. It's so unlike him."

Jack's laughter echoed into the stairwell. "I know. Where did my baby brother go? It's like a polite, civilized alien has invaded his body."

Emma froze. What did he mean by that? Jack spoke as if Beau was some uncivilized barbarian, when she knew him to be a kind, gentle giant. Sure, he was a little rough around the edges, but he wouldn't hurt a fly...unless maybe the fly was threatening her in some way.

Natalie snickered before replying, "Maybe Emma's changed him."

"Maybe," Jack agreed. "I just hope that when his façade breaks and he's back to his usual self, she doesn't dump him."

Emma frowned. Why would she ever dump Beau just for being himself? He was the most incredible man she had ever encountered. She couldn't imagine ever willingly losing him.

"Maybe he's truly changed," Natalie said. "Maybe the crude remarks are gone for good."

"Wouldn't that be something," Jack replied. "Maybe our boy's finally growing up."

Unwilling to listen to their defamatory conversation any longer, Emma tiptoed toward the door out to the beach and gently pushed it open, letting it shut delicately behind her. Beau would come looking for her soon, but he'd just have to glance out the back door and he'd see her.

Once she was out on the beach, Emma plopped herself down on the sand and placed her chin on her fists. Had she changed Beau? She'd only known him for a short time, so she had no way of knowing what he'd been like before, but it nettled her that he may not have been acting like his true self with her. She'd finally gotten him to break down a bit in the bedroom, but what if he was still holding back pieces of himself in other areas?

Beau was constantly telling her that she wasn't an imposition, that she wasn't burdening him, but what if she was forcing him to be someone he wasn't?

The back door swung open with a *whoosh*, and a moment later, Beau was lowering himself to the ground beside her. "Hey," he said, concern etched onto his features. They both wore their required hats and sunglasses, but worry was written on the parts of his face she could see. "You didn't meet me at Danny's."

"Sorry," Emma murmured, turning her gaze toward the ocean.

He handed her a brown paper bag and Styrofoam cup. "Here's your breakfast."

"Thanks," she replied, taking the offering from his hands.

"What's wrong?" Beau asked as he placed his own meal on the ground, twisting the coffee cup to create a little hole in the sand to keep it steady.

"Nothing," Emma said, and her voice sounded weak even to herself.

"Tell me," Beau pressed, scooting a bit closer until their thighs touched.

She looked up at him and let out a sigh. "I overheard Jack and Natalie talking inside, and it kind of…upset me."

Beau's gaze darkened. "What did they say?"

"It's nothing bad," she hurried to say. "Just…" She trailed off.

"Talk to me," Beau said softly, planting a hand on her thigh and squeezing gently.

"They were saying that you seem different."

"Different?" His eyebrows drew together in confusion.

"Yes, different. They seemed to say that you weren't acting like yourself."

Beau's frown deepened. Scratching the back of his neck, he asked, "What would make them say that?"

Emma shrugged. "Natalie said something about the fact that you hadn't made any inappropriate or sexual jokes since you got here."

Beau shook his head, removing his hand from her thigh and running it over his face. "Yeah, I haven't always been the most mature person in the family."

"Do you not feel like you can be yourself with me?" Emma asked, her tone laced with uncertainty and a touch of hurt.

"Of course not," Beau said. "I—" his voice cracked. "I'm more myself with you than with anyone else."

Her heart fluttered, but she didn't trust the warmth spreading in her chest. "I'm afraid that you're changing who you are because of me, and I don't want that."

Beau was so virile, so vibrant, and the last thing she wanted to do was dull his personality. He had already sacrificed so much for her. She wouldn't let him sacrifice himself, too.

"Emma," Beau said, taking her hands in his. They were heated from carrying the coffee cups, and they enveloped her hands like a warm hug. "You *are* changing me."

Unshed tears blurred her vision, and she tried to pull her hands away, but Beau held on tight.

"Listen to me," he pleaded. "You're changing me for the better. I've been a little lost for a while now, and when all the shit with Sofia happened, I realized that I haven't been living my life the way I want to. I don't want to work for an organization I don't believe in, and I don't want to date women that aren't right for me. I want to be a better man. *You* make me want to be a better man. I may not be able to talk about literature with you like Fletcher can, or resist being overly competitive with Jack, but I'm trying to find my own ways of being mature. I want to be a man you can count on. Someone you can trust. I want to be a new Beau. A better Beau."

Tears dripped down Emma's cheeks as he spoke, his words tugging her heart in a million different directions. While she didn't want him to feel like he had to be someone different with her, she believed him when he said that he wanted to be better. And it wasn't just about her. Sofia's death had changed Beau forever, and that would have been true whether he'd met Emma after or not.

"Beau," she said around a sniffle. "I…" She paused, three little words on the tip of her tongue. The three words she'd said about Beau during her nightmare that morning, during which she had dreamt that Mason held a gun to his head. *I love him.* But it was too soon. She was getting ahead of herself. All the adrenaline from the past twenty-four hours must have gone to her head. Biting back the words she truly felt, she said, "I think you're already an amazing Beau."

He released her hands to frame her face with his palms, wiping her tears away with callused thumbs. "Let's make a deal. I'll start making some inappropriate jokes again, but I'll also continue being a more decent guy."

Emma snorted a laugh. "Deal."

Wiping away the last of her tears, he pulled her close to kiss her lightly on the forehead, then dipped his mouth close to her ear. "What did the hot dog say to the bun?"

Emma scrunched up her nose as she tried to think of a punchline but couldn't come up with anything. "What?"

"I want to be inside you," Beau breathed.

Heat painted her cheeks as she pushed him away, more of a reaction to the spike of longing that surged through her than embarrassment at the joke.

Beau retreated with a chuckle. "Hey, you asked for it."

Emma shook her head, but before she had a chance to come up with a retort, Jack was sticking his head out the back door of Danny's. "Heads up," he hollered. "Mom's on her way here with Carter. You'd better get out of here if you don't want her to see you."

"Thanks, man," Beau called to his brother before turning back to Emma. "Want to get out of here? There's a place I want to show you."

She beamed up at him. "Sure."

27

Emma watched the lush landscape pass them by through the passenger side window. Once they got out of downtown, with its cobblestone streets and cute little shops, the scenery became wilder—raw and untamed. Patches of verdant forest were followed by stretches of sand hidden behind large beach rose bushes. It looked magical—like the sort of place you'd find fairies flitting about and little doors at the bases of the trees for elves to enter.

A pang of jealousy struck Emma's chest at the fact that Beau had gotten to grow up here, while she'd been stuck in a rickety shack with Earl. Beau had probably spent his childhood frolicking in fields and learning how to fish, not evading abuse and escaping into books.

"Everything okay over there?" Beau squeezed her thigh, pulling her from her memories.

"Yes, sorry," she answered. "Just excited to see where we're going."

He flashed her a full-toothed grin. "I think you're going to love it." Turning onto a tree-lined dirt road, his truck bumped over the uneven ground.

Emma gasped as they rode past field after field of low-growing shrubs dotted with twisty trees. The dirt road wound through the foliage, eventually turning to sand. There wasn't another car or person in sight. It was as if they had entered their own little world.

"What is this place?"

"It's called Madequecham," Beau said. "It's one of the most remote parts of the island."

"It's gorgeous," Emma breathed, her gaze glued to the passing scenery. Eventually, Beau maneuvered the truck down a half-hidden passageway, and they arrived in an empty, dirt parking lot.

"There are usually some cars here during the summer," he said, "but it's still the off-season right now. Looks like we're alone."

He rounded the truck and opened Emma's door, extending a hand to assist her as she stepped down onto the sandy terrain. Hand in hand, they mounted the small dune that led them onto Madequecham Beach. A slight hazy fog floated over the water, and the waves were much harsher than those at the beach near Jack and Natalie's.

Beau led Emma toward the water but stopped a few feet away from where the waves hit the shore. "It's freezing right now," he said with a grimace. "My brothers and I used to do a polar plunge here around this time every year."

"What's that?"

A mischievous smile split Beau's face. "We would strip down to our underwear and get in the water as fast as we could. The rules were no wetsuits or rash guards, and you had to go all the way under. Whoever lasted the longest won a hundred bucks from each brother. I won almost every year," he boasted.

Emma's eyes rolled heavenward. "Why am I not surprised?"

He pulled her in for a playful squeeze. "Because I'm good at everything."

As she looked out over the thrashing ocean, a wave of trepidation washed over her. "We're not doing that right now, are we?"

A chuckle escaped Beau's throat as he hugged her tighter. "No, angel, we're not. Unless you want to?"

"No," she answered quickly. "I'm good."

They stood like that for a few moments, watching the waves roll in beneath a blanket of fog, until Emma spotted something moving in the water. Squinting her eyes, she tried to make out the shape of it, but all she could see was what looked like an animal's head.

"Look!" She pointed excitedly at the dark object bobbing amidst the waves. "Is it a dolphin?"

Beau grinned down at her, his lips pulling toward his ears. "Sweetheart, it's way too cold for dolphins around here. It's a seal."

"Oh," Emma muttered with a frown. She hadn't spent much time at the beach and, embarrassingly, hadn't realized there weren't dolphins in the area. Her humiliation was soon forgotten, though, as she spotted a second creature weaving through the water behind the first. "Look, there's another!" The two seals seemed to be chasing each other, dipping below the water, then crashing through the surface again as they trailed each other.

"Let's follow them," Beau suggested, looping his arm through hers and leading her down the beach. They kept their pace relaxed, enjoying the seals' performance as they trudged through the sand. After a few minutes, Beau pointed a few yards ahead of them. "Check it out."

Emma followed his finger, noticing there was another seal heading toward the two they'd been following. As it got closer, she realized its head was significantly smaller than the heads of the other two.

"It's a baby!" she cried, watching as the smaller seal pup reunited with what she assumed to be its parents. "That's so cute."

They stopped to watch the family of seals glide through the water together for a few minutes until they disappeared under the surface.

Emma turned to Beau. "Thank you for taking me here," she said with a bright smile.

He returned one of his own before wrapping her in his embrace. "I'm glad you like it."

"It feels so safe here," she murmured against his chest. "Like no one will ever find us or hurt us."

Beau's lips pressed against the top of her head. "I will never let anyone find you or hurt you," he promised.

Emma melted into his arms, relishing the refuge they provided. His embrace felt like home. If kissing him was like taking a deep breath, being held by him was a long exhale.

As the ocean roared before them, large waves crashing to shore and spilling foam onto the sand, Emma and Beau stood entwined with one another—an unbreakable unit. Out on this remote beach, with his strong arms wrapped around her, Emma almost believed that his words were true.

❀

A few hours later, they returned to reality. Carter was back home, and Beau couldn't wait for Emma to meet him. His nephew was the cutest child in the world, if he did say so himself.

They walked up the steps to the apartment and were greeted by a cacophony of childish giggles and deep, booming laughter. Jack was tossing Carter up the air and catching him while Natalie watched nervously to the side.

"Hey," Beau called out. "Where's my favorite little guy?"

"Uncle Beau!" Carter shouted from his position in Jack's

arms. The man placed him on the floor, and he came barreling over to Beau, who swung him up in his arms for a hug and a noogie.

"What's up, little dude?" Beau asked as Carter threw his arms around his neck.

"I'm two!" Carter announced.

"I know." Beau chuckled. "I was at your birthday party." The boy had turned two back in the winter, and Jack and Natalie threw him a big birthday bash. They had only officially adopted him about six months prior, so they went all out with a gourmet cake, decorations galore, and a deluge of gifts.

"I had cake, and presents, and cake," Carter said proudly.

"I remember," Beau said. "I ate about six pieces of it." Placing Carter back on the ground, Beau turned the boy's little body toward Emma. "I want you to meet someone." He gestured toward Emma, who stood quietly off to the side. "This is Emma."

"Hi," the little boy said. "I'm Cawtew." Trotting over to Natalie and pointing to her bump he added, "That's my baby bwothew."

Emma's radiant smile lit up her face in response. "Hi, Carter. You are going to be such a great big brother!"

The little boy beamed at her, then wrapped his arms around his mother's leg, showing a hint of shyness. Emma grinned back at him, kneeling down to the floor to be on his level. Beau watched as she silently charmed the boy by sticking out her tongue and making silly faces.

"How was your day?" Jack asked.

"It was great," Beau said, tearing his gaze away from Emma. "We went over to Madequecham. Saw some seals. It was deserted."

"No polar plunge?" Jack smirked, no doubt remembering all the years they had frozen their asses off in the Atlantic Ocean.

"Nah. Didn't want to risk the cold water shriveling me up.

I've got a lady to impress." Beau wagged his eyebrows up and down.

Jack replied with a groan. "We were about to throw hot dogs and burgers on the grill," he said. "Will you join us for dinner?"

Beau looked over to Emma, but she was busy hiding and revealing her face in a game of peek-a-boo while Carter watched with a timid smile.

"Yeah," he answered. "We will."

❦

Emma loved having dinner with Beau's family. Jack and Natalie's banter was beyond entertaining, and Carter was so adorable. She was sad when the little boy had to go to bed but enjoyed the fact that it meant they were getting closer to her and Beau going to bed together.

After clearing the table, the four of them moved into the living room, each settling into the spots they'd sat in the previous day. Jack wielded the remote, clicking through channels to try and find something for them to watch. Eventually, he landed on one of those trashy dating shows.

Beau groaned as the screen showed a line of contestants—men of all shapes and sizes, all of whom were surely losers. "Do we really have to watch *this*?" he whined.

"I like this show," Natalie said.

"I know you do," Jack said, leaning over to peck his wife on the lips.

"Have you ever even seen it?" Natalie asked, her eyes trained on the television, where each man in the line was listing his top three qualities and top three areas in which he wanted to improve.

"No, but Emma's been learning all about reality TV lately," Beau said, shooting her a smirk.

"Ooh!" Natalie squealed. "What shows? That's all I've wanted to watch since I've spent more time resting during pregnancy."

"I've been catching up on the Kardashians and *Beneath the Deck*," Emma answered, and Natalie immediately launched into a conversation about the two outrageous shows.

The women's dialogue was interrupted when a loud *breaking news* jingle blared from the television. That same female reporter in her preppy outfit and ridiculously high bun appeared, jabbering on about a missing local woman.

"Shit," Beau muttered under his breath, trying to come up with a plan to get the remote out of his brother's hand before Emma's photo appeared on the screen. "Seriously, let's change the channel. This show sucks."

Natalie turned to glare at him. "No way. It's over in half an hour. That is, if this news report doesn't take too long."

Emma clutched Beau's arm tightly, and he saw that she had turned sheet-white, her eyes wide and panicky. He gave her a quick squeeze of reassurance before trying again.

"Jack, toss me the remote," he insisted, but it was too late. Emma's face popped onto the screen, her halo of blonde curls cascading above eyes the color of honey.

Jack and Natalie's jaws were on the floor as they exchanged confused glances. Beau's gaze darted from their shocked expressions to the television, vaguely wondering where the picture had come from since Earl obviously didn't prioritize having photos of his daughter around. But his irrelevant thoughts were cut off when Emma flew from his lap, her hand clasped over her mouth.

Shit. Not again.

She bolted for the bathroom, no doubt to empty her stomach as she had the last time she'd seen her face on the news.

Unprepared for Emma's abrupt exit, it took Beau a few

seconds to pry his own body up off the couch to follow her. Somehow, even in her pregnant state, Natalie was faster than him, and she hurried after Emma. Maybe it was some sort of motherly superpower—you hear someone vomiting, and your body flies into gear. Jack was closer to the bathroom, and he was up on his feet and blocking Beau's path by the time he got to the hallway.

"Move," Beau roared.

"No," Jack boomed, his arms outstretched to block the hallway. Emma's retching could be heard from where they stood, as could the low hum of Natalie's soothing words that Beau couldn't quite make out.

"I swear to God, Jack, move or I will move you," Beau snarled. Nothing would stop him from getting to Emma, but he preferred not to cause bodily harm to his brother in the process.

"What the fuck is going on?" Jack demanded.

"It has nothing to do with you," Beau snapped. "Now *move*."

"I'm not moving until you tell me what's going on," Jack said, like the annoying brother he was. "Why are the police looking for Emma? Did you do something?"

Anger simmered in Beau's chest at the accusation, and he tried to dart under his brother's outstretched arms, only to be shoved in the chest. Fuming, he grabbed Jack by the shoulders and tried to move him aside, but Jack, though less bulky than him, was fast. He grabbed Beau's waist and pushed with all his might, pressing his head against Beau's chest like a charging bull. Beau stumbled back a step as the brothers found themselves in a stalemate, each of their protective natures preventing them from backing down.

When Jack lifted his head, Beau caught a glimpse of what his brother had often looked like back in high school, his eyes wild and chest heaving as he fought against whatever demon was plaguing him. In this case, that just so happened to be some misguided belief that Beau had done something to harm Emma. The mere thought caused his stomach to churn, nausea roiling in his gut.

"*Fuck. You*," Beau barked, shoving his brother back using the shot of adrenaline his accusation had sent through him. Though Beau had grown stronger over years of grueling workouts in the precinct's state-of-the-art gym, Jack still possessed a scrappy flair for fighting, and he didn't seem to be in any mood to surrender.

Beau opened his arms wide, just about to attempt a new tactic, when Emma came shooting from the bathroom, right into his outstretched arms.

"Stop!" she screamed, burying her head in Beau's neck, her hands plastered on his chest. "Just stop, please."

Beau instinctively wrapped his arms around her as Jack looked on with narrowed eyes, a scowl etched onto his mouth. Natalie waddled out from the bathroom, placing an arm around her husband's shoulders.

Still tucked into Beau's chest, Emma turned toward Jack and Natalie. "Please don't be mad at Beau. He saved my life. If you want to be mad, be mad at me. I'm sorry we brought this trouble to your door, but we had no other choice."

"Emma," Jack said, his expression softening. "No one is mad at you. We're worried for you. And very confused."

Natalie nodded her agreement. "We want to help, but we're a little startled by all this. Please tell us what's going on."

Beau placed a kiss on Emma's head. "Why don't we sit down," he suggested, and the four of them slowly returned to their spots in the living room. Once Emma was settled as close to him as possible, with her legs draped over his lap and her head resting against his shoulder, Beau began to explain. "Last week, I went after the men who were responsible for Sofia's death."

Jack and Natalie exchanged mystified glances. They knew about Sofia and that her death was the reason for Beau leaving the force. There were no secrets between the McNally men—well, except the one Beau was about to share.

"I knew the police were slacking on the case, so I took matters into my own hands. I located their headquarters, and I went there one night to hopefully catch Mason—the mastermind behind the human-trafficking ring. Instead, I found Emma there, locked in a concrete room."

Natalie let out a small gasp as she clutched Jack's knee. His face had hardened to stone. The two of them sat up a little straighter as they processed what Beau was telling them. Emma buried her face in his t-shirt as he went on.

"She was dirty and covered in bruises. They had tortured her and planned to sell her. I knew I couldn't leave her there, so I gave up my chances of getting Mason and took her instead. I brought her home to Fletcher's and my apartment, and we've been mostly hiding out there. But then she was reported missing, and we couldn't risk someone who may have seen us turning her in, so we ran. I didn't think the news coverage would make it all the way out here."

There was silence for a few moments as the almost unbelievable story created a thick tension in the room.

"Who reported her?" Jack finally asked.

Beau nudged Emma's head with his nose, looking for a sign of affirmation that she was alright with him explaining.

Emma looked up at him, her amber eyes glassy as she nodded. "My father reported me missing." She took a deep breath. "However, he was also the one who sold me to the human traffickers in the first place."

Natalie gasped again, louder this time. For one horrifying moment, Beau worried the shock would send her into labor or something, but she just clasped Jack's knee tighter. "What?"

"I know." Emma let out a nervous chuckle, and Beau

smoothed his hand over her thigh, using his thumb to draw small circles on her skin. "What an asshole, right?"

"That's..." Jack shook his head in disbelief. "That's fucked up."

Emma smiled sadly. "My whole life's kind of been that way. My dad, Earl, is a real piece of work. I can't let the police return me to him. He'll just give me right back to Mason."

"Of course we can't let that happen," Jack said before flicking his gaze over at Beau. "That's not going to happen, right?"

"Of course not," Beau said. "We've got surveillance cameras on the building where we think Mason's currently hiding and audio bugs in Earl's house and the office of a cop on the case who we discovered is crooked. I think that bastard's the reason the case hasn't gone anywhere. Anyway, Diego is monitoring the feeds for relevant information. Once we have everything we need, we'll catch Mason, disband the human-trafficking ring, and send everyone involved, including Earl, to jail. Then, Emma will be safe."

"You say that like it'll be easy," Natalie scoffed.

Beau shrugged, Emma's head bobbing up and down on his blocky shoulder as he did. "We have no other choice."

Natalie turned sorrowful eyes toward Emma. "You two are welcome here as long as you need. And we'll do anything we can to help."

"Of course," Jack agreed. "As long as you two are careful and don't let anyone recognize you, it's no problem."

Emma sat up straighter beside Beau. "Thank you. Thank you both. That means so much to me. We would never do anything to put your family in danger. The second there's any hint that we've been spotted, we'll be out of here."

Beau squeezed her tight, warmed by her concern for his family. He glanced at Natalie, one hand placed protectively on her bump, and thought of Carter, currently sleeping soundly in his bed. Just as he would never let anyone harm Emma, he would never let anyone harm the rest of his family. Because that was what Emma had become. Family.

"Right," he agreed, sharing a nod of understanding with Jack. If things went sideways, Beau wouldn't hesitate to whisk Emma away, but until then, Nantucket would remain their safe haven.

28

The next morning, after a fitful night's sleep, Emma sat at the kitchen island, chugging a mocha latte alongside Beau. She'd never been much of a coffee drinker, but in light of recent events and the sleeplessness they'd caused, caffeine had become a key ally. Plus, staying above a coffee shop meant unlimited access to the good stuff.

"Sweet enough for you?" Beau asked as he took a pull of his black coffee with just a splash of cream.

"Mmm," Emma mumbled, savoring the sweet drink. "They should always put chocolate in coffee."

Beau's low chuckle was interrupted by the ringing of his cell phone. He pulled it from his pocket and placed it on the kitchen island between them before putting it on speaker.

"Hey, D," he greeted his friend. "Whatcha got for me?"

"You're not going to like it," Diego said, the nervous edge to his tone putting Emma on high alert. Shifting on her stool, she uncrossed her legs to steady herself and grasped Beau's arm.

"Hit me," Beau said, any traces of lightheartedness erased from his tone.

"Williams found your bug last night."

"What?" Beau grabbed the edge of the island, his knuckles turning white as he gripped it. "Are you sure?"

"Unfortunately," Diego replied. "I listened to the tapes from last night early this morning, and everything was normal until, suddenly, Williams was swearing up a storm, then there was some static and crackling, then nothing. Complete and total silence. He must have crushed the bug, or put it in water or something, because it completely shut down."

"Shit." Beau ran a hand down his face, and Emma found herself rubbing his back in a fruitless attempt to soothe him.

"It gets worse," Diego said.

Beau silently waited for him to go on, his mouth set in a grim line.

"Williams must have been really pissed about the bug, because this morning he went over and roughed Earl up again, demanding any information he had on who may have been watching him. Earl squealed about your little visit to his house, Beau. How you asked him questions about Williams and had evidence of him being involved in illegal dealings. Williams put two and two together and realized you're the one who bugged his office. He has no way of knowing you've got Emma, but he knows you're onto him and his corruption, and now he's getting ready to come after you."

Beau's face grew harder and harder as Diego spoke until there was practically steam coming out of his ears. With a low growl, he raised a fist and smashed it down on the countertop. Hard.

Startled by the thud, Emma jumped on her stool. Realizing she'd unintentionally shifted herself as far away from Beau as possible, she sheepishly scooted back to the center of her stool.

Whipping his gaze to her, Beau's eyes softened as he shook his fist out. "Sorry," he muttered.

"Everything okay over there?" Diego asked.

Beau cleared his throat before replying. "Yes, sorry, just…a moment of anger. So, Williams knows I'm onto him, and he's coming after me, eh?"

His false sense of ease did little to soothe Emma. She understood damn well what it meant to have someone like Williams coming for you.

"It's good that you got out of town, but it's only going to take Williams one quick search to find out that your brother lives on Nantucket and get his address. You're not safe there," Diego warned.

Beau drummed his fingers on the countertop. "I know. We'll get out of here today."

Emma could practically hear the gears turning in his mind.

"We can't take one of the ferries because Williams could have people watching the docks. We'll have to get our own boat. I'll see if Jack knows anyone we can borrow one from. Once we get back to the mainland, we'll find a motel or something to lay low in. Somewhere Williams can't track us."

"That's a good plan," Diego said. "Now that they're not only looking for Emma, but you too, you need to stay out of sight."

Beau ran his knuckles over his jawline. "Fuck, how are we ever going to catch these bastards if I'm in hiding?"

Diego sighed over the phone. "This does mess with our plans a bit. We can regroup once you're somewhere safe. Right now, you need to focus on getting away from anywhere that Williams might suspect you to be."

"Right." Beau sat up a bit straighter. "Thanks for calling, D. We're going to pack up and find a boat. I'll let you know when we're on our way to the mainland."

"Thanks, man," Diego replied. "Stay safe."

"You too."

Beau hung up the phone and ran his palms over his thighs before turning toward Emma. "You ready for another trip?"

One hour later, they had packed their bags and said goodbye to Jack and Natalie, explaining what Diego told them and instructing them to vacate their apartment until further notice. Luckily, Natalie had a good friend who welcomed them into her home for the foreseeable future. Beau had contacted Fletcher to tell him to stay at Christa's as well.

Jack was able to secure a friend's boat quickly and drove them over to the marina where it was docked. Beau hid his truck in the empty parking lot at Madequecham, draping a tarp over it to hide the license plates. He couldn't leave it out in the open at the marina where Williams' men could see it and realize he'd been there. The less they knew about Beau's whereabouts, the better.

When they arrived at the marina, Jack showed them to his friend's boat and helped Beau launch it. After a quick goodbye, they were off.

Beau drove a few hundred feet, the only thing on his mind getting the hell off the island, before finally looking down at the steering panel. "Shit," he grumbled. "We're low on gas. Jackass didn't fill up the tank before docking it."

Emma looked over from where she sat at the stern. "It's not like he knew the next people to use it would be trying to escape quickly," she pointed out.

That earned a slight chuckle out of Beau. "True. But didn't he at least realize it could have been a possibility?" He knew it was ridiculous to be mad at a man for not predicting this sort of unthinkable scenario, but Beau was just stressed enough to feel that he should have.

Turning the wheel abruptly, he steered them back toward the marina to fill up the tank. He hated to spend more time visible out in the open, but they weren't going to make it the thirty miles to the mainland without getting gas. Plus, they still wore their disguises of hats and sunglasses. No one would spot them...he hoped.

There were several available pumps, and Beau pulled up at the nearest one. Of course, he hadn't spotted the *Card reader broken—cash only* sign on it until he'd already turned off the boat, but he wasn't going to waste time moving over to the next pump.

"Angel, I'm going to run inside and pay for this gas. Here." He tossed Emma his cell phone. "Can you please text Diego and tell him we're just about to leave?"

"Sure," she chirped, nodding her head quickly. Beau's gaze lingered on her for a moment, her eyes glued to the phone's screen as she fulfilled her duty with a serious expression, before he hurried toward the shack where the cashier stood.

"Two hundred on pump number one," Beau ordered. The cashier gave him a nasty look, but he didn't have the time or the patience for niceties. Slapping two one-hundred-dollar bills down, he leaned impatiently on the counter. He towered over the cashier, a short man with graying hair and large, round spectacles, and hoped his closeness would intimidate the man into moving as fast as possible.

Instead, the cashier—obviously annoyed with him—moved as slow as molasses as he inspected each bill, holding it up to the sunlight as if he suspected Beau had given him fakes. His foot tapped rhythmically against the ground as the man finally opened up the register and accepted his money. He cast a glance back toward Emma and was relieved to see she still sat in the boat, staring out over the water. Turning back toward the cashier, Beau met his eyes.

"All set?"

"Hold on." The man held up a hand in a *stop* gesture. "Did you want regular or premium?"

"Regular," Beau ground out.

"Are you sure?" the man asked, pushing his spectacles up

his nose. "Most folks these days prefer premium, and that's a beautiful boat you've got out there. Wouldn't want to tax the engine by giving it subpar fuel."

Beau heaved out a breath. "I need a full tank. Will two hundred get me a full tank of premium?"

He immediately regretted asking the question when the cashier turned toward his screen and began doing calculations. "Let's see here…" He tapped a few buttons but didn't produce an answer quickly enough for Beau.

"You know what? Doesn't matter. Regular is just fine. Thanks."

The man turned his bespectacled face up to Beau's, his eyebrows scrunched together behind the large lenses. "Oh, are you sure?"

"Yes," Beau hissed. "Regular fuel *now*, please."

The man paled a bit but hit the button for regular fuel. "You're all set."

With an indignant huff, Beau turned on his heel and headed outside. As soon as he caught sight of the boat, goosebumps raced down his arms, and the hairs on the back of his neck stood at attention. Because Emma was no longer in it.

※

The men had come out of nowhere. Three of them, all wearing ski masks, had popped out from behind a building and descended upon the boat in a matter of seconds. Emma, jarred by their surprise entrance, barely got the chance to pull out her self-defense moves. She did manage to get one guy in the groin, causing him to grunt and cup himself with his hands, before she'd been hauled from her seat and flung into a neighboring boat.

As soon as the three men were on board, it roared to life and took off at a breakneck speed. Too stunned to move or even say anything, Emma glanced around wildly, her gaze seeking Beau. If she could just see him, everything would be okay. He would come after her and rescue her. Again. He just needed to see her and see what was going on, even if she didn't quite understand what that was yet.

The boat was moving fast, too fast, and the marina got smaller and smaller in her field of vision. Eventually, though, Beau came barreling out of the cashier's shack. Though far away now, his large, menacing body couldn't be missed. She couldn't make out his expression, but she was sure he was as panicked as she was.

After a few moments, Beau disappeared from her sightline altogether, and she knew then that she was on her own. The three men in the boat chattered in low voices.

"Who are you?" she demanded.

One man ripped off his mask. His hair had grown whiter with age, but his hazel eyes, glinting with malice, looked just the same as the last time she'd seen him.

Detective Isaac Williams.

"You don't remember me? What a shame. And here I thought I'd made such an impression on you."

Emma's heartbeat pounded in her ears. He'd actually found her. Williams had found her and gotten away with her. The one moment Beau had left her alone, and he'd swooped in. Had she been doomed from the start?

"What do you want?"

"You, of course." Williams snorted. "I should have known McNally had something to do with you getting away, the bastard. Always taking my girls." He shook his head as he made a *tsk*ing sound.

Emma swallowed hard. She wanted to remark that Beau was *not* a bastard, and she was *not* Williams' "girl," but she knew it was probably best not to rock the boat. Williams was unpredictable—she'd learned that the hard way, years ago—and she had to be smart if she was going to escape him and the other men, who had also removed their masks. Emma recognized them as two of Mason's goons.

"Beau will find me again," she declared. "He won't give up until he does."

Williams turned to her wearing a snide smile that sent a shiver racing through her. "That's what I'm counting on."

29

Beau had never been so scared in his entire life. Eight years on the job, and he'd never encountered a situation that instilled quite as much fear as watching the small boat speed away with Emma on board. Helplessness clawed at his throat as he stood immobile on the dock, his mind racing with thoughts of what to do next.

The piercing sound of a boat horn snapped him back into action. He'd already paid for the fuel, so he quickly filled up the boat's tank before reaching for his cell phone, only to find his pockets empty. *Shit.* He'd given his phone to Emma. There went his plans to call Diego and figure out what the fuck to do.

Ideas whirled around in his brain until one stuck—get back to Jack's, call Diego, then book it back to the mainland to meet him so they could track these bastards down. Every single one of them had targets on their backs as far as Beau was concerned, and he wouldn't hesitate to take them out. Not only were these men responsible for Sofia's death, but they had hurt Emma and had now taken her away from him, and that was simply unacceptable.

Jack had left with the truck long ago, and it would be

quicker to get to his place by boat anyway, so Beau hopped in and revved the boat to life. He could hardly hear the motor over the roaring in his ears, and his heart pounded like a drum as he sliced through the water. When the building came into view, Beau gradually slowed down until he reached the dock, where he sloppily tied up the boat.

Jogging into Danny's Place, he found Jack leaning easily against the counter and chatting with a customer, the picture of calm, cool, and collected. Contrasted with Beau's frenzied demeanor, it was almost comical.

"Where's your phone?" Beau barked as he strode toward his brother.

Jack's brow crinkled with a frown. "What are you doing back here?"

Beau practically patted his brother down as he searched his pockets for a cell phone. "I need to call Diego. They took Emma. They've got her, man, and I have to get her back."

Jack's face paled as he tugged his phone out of his pocket, his hand shaking as he handed it to Beau. "Here."

Beau accepted the device and hurried out to the beach behind Danny's, where it would be quieter and more private. His hands trembled as he tried to navigate the keypad before he finally gave in and used the voice command, rattling off Diego's cell phone number.

His friend answered on the first ring. "What's up?"

Beau sagged against the wall of the building. "She's gone," he croaked, his voice hoarse. "They got her."

Diego inhaled sharply. "What? How?"

Beau took a wobbly breath. "I was at the marina, filling up a boat so we could get back to the mainland. I went inside to pay and…fuck, D, they took her. I stepped away for one goddamn minute, and they took her. Just like that. She was gone."

"I received her text that you were on your way," Diego

said. "Was that real? Or did the men coerce her into sending it to throw me off?"

"No, that was real. I gave her my phone while I went inside and told her to let you know we were about to leave. The next minute, she was gone." Beau thought back to the heart-stopping moment he had glanced over to find Emma missing. "D, I can't lose her. She's… I'm in love with her. She's everything to me. I don't know—"

"Stop," Diego ordered. "We need to focus right now, Beau. You say you gave her your phone to text me, right?"

"Yes," he answered, scrubbing a hand over his face.

"Any chance they didn't throw it overboard?" Diego asked. "Because if she still has it or it's in the boat, we can track it."

Beau sat up straighter as a seed of hope embedded in his heart. "I have no idea if they realized she had it or not. It's worth a try."

"Good." The sounds of Diego moving through his house filtered through the phone. "I'm grabbing my computer, and I'll get Isabella to drive me toward the Cape as I work on tracking her. Meet me there and keep in touch on the way."

"Will do," Beau said, already moving back toward his borrowed boat. On the way, he shot off a text to Natalie that he was taking Jack's phone and that he would be in touch when he could. He set the boat's GPS for the meeting spot Diego had picked out, untied the moorings, and set off through the Atlantic Ocean.

❦

It was dark and quiet, the air filled with only the sounds of Emma's ragged breathing. As they approached the shore, the men had blindfolded her and bound her hands behind her back, rendering her completely helpless. Though she hadn't been able to see, she had felt it as the boat churned to a stop and she was transferred into a car, then driven for an estimated half hour until they reached their current destination. She had no idea what sort of building she was in now, other than the floor seemed to be made of concrete because it felt hard and unforgiving when she stomped on the floor.

The men had dumped her in a chair, secured her bound hands to the back of it, then taken off, stomping up a set of stairs to the ground level. Emma used the time alone to gather clues about her location. So far, she knew the ground was hard, she was in a room that required going down a staircase to reach, there were few noises in the area, so it was probably pretty secluded, and there was a light breeze in the room that told her someone had either left the door open or there were no doors between her and the outside. She guessed it was some kind of basement, or perhaps a shelter of sorts.

She felt oddly calm about the whole situation. When she would have expected fear, unease, and flashbacks to the abandoned building, she only felt an unshakeable confidence that Beau would find her. He would save her again. She was sure of it. Plus, she figured if the men wanted to hurt her, they would have done it already. They'd had plenty of time on the boat to do whatever they wanted, and all they'd done was taunt her with empty threats.

Emma went on high alert as two sets of footsteps made their way back down the stairs, the sound bouncing off the walls. She remained silent, hoping to overhear something that might be helpful, but the men spoke in Spanish, and she couldn't understand a word.

The footsteps grew nearer until the blindfold was ripped from her eyes. Emma squinted despite the lack of bright light. Going from pitch black to the low light of the underground room was enough to jar her senses.

"Where are we?" she asked as she surveyed her surroundings. The room was mostly empty, except for the chair she sat on and a built-in stone bench that ran along the wall between the two entrances, each of which led to a staircase up to the outdoors. The two open archways at the tops of the staircases were the only sources of light. The walls were made out of stone, and she'd been correct about the floors being concrete. It was an odd little abode and seemed to serve no purpose other than getting someone out of the elements.

Or hiding someone they didn't want found.

The man who had removed her blindfold snickered. "Don't worry about it," he said in his thick accent.

"What do you want with me?"

The other man came around and tugged on the bindings on her hands, likely checking that they were still secure. "Don't worry about it," he parroted.

Emma was about to continue her line of questioning when a third man came thudding down the stairs. She assumed it would be Williams, as she hadn't yet spotted him in this new location, but it wasn't the white-haired detective that descended into the room. Rather, it was the short, stocky, dark-haired villain of her nightmares.

Mason.

His sharp eyes pinned Emma to the chair, his sick smile twisting her stomach.

Her earlier confidence evaporated as he watched her with his predatory gaze.

"Well, well, well," Mason chanted as he wrung his hands together. "Look what we have here."

His steel-toed boots slapped the floor as he made his way to the center of the room, standing with his hands on his hips in an arrogant display of composure.

Emma swallowed hard before repeating her earlier question. "What do you want with me?" The words squeaked out of her bone-dry mouth.

Mason stepped closer, his wicked grin widening when Emma reared her head back in an attempt to retreat. "What do I want with you?" he asked, reaching forward with one finger to tip her chin up. "What do I *want* with you? You ran away, dear Emma. All I wanted was to get you back. You're going to make me a lot of money."

Ignoring how that last part made her gut turn inside out, she replied, "I didn't run away. I was rescued."

"Rescued?" Mason's voice was incredulous. "By that little twat McNally? Williams told me all about him. That selfish bastard didn't rescue you. He just wanted you for himself."

"What are you talking about?" Emma asked.

Mason's eyes flickered toward the staircase he'd come down. "Isaac!" he called.

Seconds later, Williams came bounding down the steps like a dog given a command.

Mason turned to him. "Emma here thinks McNally rescued her from us," he said, his tone derisive, as if he couldn't believe she would be so naïve.

Williams scoffed. "Beau McNally is a selfish bastard."

Her fear was forgotten as the need to defend Beau rose up. "He is not!" she said. "He's been nothing but selfless. He saved me, protected me, and took care of me when you all tried to ruin my life."

"We didn't ruin your life," Mason said coolly. "Your daddy did that."

Emma shot him a glare. "And you helped him."

Mason just gave her a smug smile.

"He is selfish," Williams chimed in, clearly unimpressed with their side conversation. "First, he took Sofia from me, and now you, too. He won't get away with it again."

Emma frowned. "What do you mean he took Sofia from you? She died at your hand. How was that Beau's fault?"

"I'm talking about before she died. I'd had my eye on Sofia for years, and McNally knew it. She used to come drinking at the bar with all of us after shift sometimes, and he'd see us flirting. He knew I wanted her. I'd been gearing up to ask her out for months when, one night, I see her out with

McNally, hanging all over him like some desperate hussy. And then she went home with him. It was disgusting. A few weeks later, he went and broke up with her—what kind of asshole lets someone like Sofia go?—and drove her away. Away from *me*. I stopped seeing her at the bar. The best part of my day—gone. It was awful. I was dying to see her again."

Emma's eyes widened at the detective's tirade. It was obvious he'd had some sort of obsession with Sofia, and Beau's relationship with her had really set him off.

"I had to team up with Mason to find her again," Williams went on. "She'd run all the way to Mexico to get away from that son-of-a-bitch McNally." He smacked his fist against his palm, the violent noise making Emma flinch. His expression changed from anger to elation, then finally to despair as he finished his story. "When his men finally found her, I was overjoyed. They agreed to send her home to me. I was going to love her and care for her forever. But the shipment took too long. She died. She's dead, and it's *all. His. Fault.*"

Williams' vacant expression sent a shudder down Emma's spine. Wow. This dude was really messed up. She longed to knock some sense into him but wisely kept her mouth shut. It was not the time to defend Beau's honor or explain why he wasn't to blame.

"After I lost Sofia, I had nothing to live for, nothing to give me a purpose, until Mason asked me to join his operation. It wouldn't bring Sofia back, but I could help other men find their perfect woman."

Williams' dreamy expression revealed just how disturbed he truly was. This man really thought he was playing some kind of matchmaker by abducting girls and selling them off to the highest bidder? He had found his purpose in life by becoming a *human trafficker*?

Williams' gaze found its way back to Emma, his eyes hazy. "I'd had my eye on you since you were a teenager," he said. "I always knew you'd make the perfect match for someone, so I was delighted when Earl decided to sell you to Mason. I knew we'd make a pretty penny, and someone would get to enjoy you. It was a win-win."

Mason stood off to the side, watching Williams speak with an expression of approval. Emma wondered just how much Mason agreed with Williams' ethos of "helping" men and how much he was taking advantage of him and his connections with the police to get away with his crimes.

She silently shook her head, desperately hoping Beau would show up soon. She didn't know how much longer she could bear being around these men again. Her stomach was knotted into a pretzel, and her throat felt thick with a mixture of worry and repulsion.

She trusted Beau implicitly and knew he would eventually realize she still had his cell phone. She had managed to set it to silent and stow it away in the bra strap between her breasts, where no one would find it unless they removed her shirt, which she would do anything to keep from happening.

It was only a matter of time before Beau came to her rescue. She just hoped that when he did, he was successful once more.

30

The tires squealed as Diego's SUV skidded to a stop at a red light. At Beau's instruction, he'd been running as many yellows as he could, but they couldn't afford to be pulled over. It would slow them down too much.

"Fuck!" Beau roared as he smacked his hand on the dashboard.

"We're only five minutes out," Diego reminded him, his voice deceptively calm. He'd picked Beau up on the mainland, where they immediately took off in pursuit of Emma, tracking the cell phone that hadn't yet died or been shut off.

Somewhere in the back of his mind, Beau knew it could be a trap. The men could have found the cell phone and used it to lead them to their slaughter. But somehow, he didn't think that was the case. At least, he was fervently hoping it wasn't.

The light flipped green, and the car lurched forward, Diego's foot pressed firmly on the gas pedal.

"Make sure you slow down when we're close," Beau said. "I don't want to go in there unprepared, guns blazing. We need to survey the area for a minute to figure out what we're walking into."

"I know," Diego replied, sparing a smug glance at Beau.

"Do you really think I've forgotten how to work a case in the past few months?"

Beau rubbed his palm down his face. "Sorry, man. I know. I trust you. I'm just totally freaked out over this whole thing."

His friend patted his shoulder. "I know, and you have every right to be. But we need to stay sharp, and we need to trust each other. We're partners, remember?"

Beau grimaced at the reminder of his former job. "Not anymore. I quit, remember?"

One of Diego's shoulders lifted in a shrug. "I don't care about your job title. Plus, I'm still technically on leave, and I don't know if I'll ever return. We may not be official police partners anymore, but we'll always have that connection."

Beau warmed with appreciation at his friend's words. He considered the man to be like a brother, and he needed to put his faith in him like one. "I trust you more than anyone," he admitted.

The voice on the GPS tore him from the surprisingly sentimental moment, alerting them that they were a quarter mile away from their destination. They'd followed the navigation system off a main road to a back one, which had then led to a dirt path. Diego slowed to a stop in the highly vegetated area, tucking his vehicle behind some particularly tall shrubs.

"We should go the rest of the way on foot. The car would draw too much attention, especially in an area this secluded."

Beau grunted his agreement and hopped out of the vehicle, shutting the door as quietly as possible behind him. Diego joined him, and they quickly strapped on bulletproof vests, arming themselves before taking off in the direction of the cell phone. The tracker showed that it was right by the edge of the woods. It was difficult to know exactly what the topography was from the slightly grainy map, but there appeared to be some grassy hills surrounding it.

Beau and Diego snuck through the woods toward the spot, using only hand signals to avoid being overheard. The silence also allowed them to tune into any noises that might indicate they weren't alone. It was impossible to know how many men might be holding Emma, as Mason's network extended all over the country as well as Mexico, but Beau seriously hoped it was a small enough group for them to take down.

They hadn't encountered any people or anything out of the ordinary when they approached the edge of the woods. Diego held up a closed fist, and Beau halted to a stop. When Diego tapped his ear, Beau leaned forward to listen for whatever sound he was alerting him to.

A low, thickly accented voice floated through the air toward them. Beau nodded, confirming that he heard it, too, before a second voice joined the first. Beau held up two fingers, indicating that there were at least two men, and Diego gave him a sharp nod. With a single shared glance, they slowly made their way toward the voices.

The two goons were kicked back against a stone wall, wrapped up in a conversation and barely paying attention to their surroundings. *Fools.* Diego patted his handcuffs and jerked his head toward the men. Beau nodded his agreement. The first order of business would be to apprehend them before continuing to search the area.

Splitting up, they approached from both sides so there was less chance of the men getting away. They weren't spotted until the last second and managed to apprehend the men quite easily, cuffing their wrists and binding their feet with rope. They quickly covered their mouths with duct tape but not before the men made quite a raucous.

Beau silently cursed, wishing he had a better gag to keep them quiet. He briefly considered removing his socks to stuff in their mouths, but that idea was soon forgotten when the sound of footsteps caught his attention.

A few feet down from where the men had been resting against the stone wall was a set of archways. At least one of them must have led to a staircase, because the footsteps were getting louder and seemed to be ascending.

Diego headed to one side of the archway while Beau took the other. He was preparing himself to attack when none other than Detective Isaac Williams emerged. As the crooked cop and asshole extraordinaire appeared at the entrance to the stairway, Beau couldn't help his wicked grin. He'd been waiting for his chance to destroy the creep ever since Emma had identified him on the evidence board.

At the top of the steps, Williams whipped his head to both sides before realizing he was surrounded.

"That's right, Isaac," Beau growled, grabbing him by the arm and swinging him to the ground. "We've got you now."

Diego took his ankles and swiftly began tying them together. Beau stayed by the man's upper half and took his chin roughly in his palm, holding his face steady for the beating he was about to give him.

"You fucking asshole," he snarled as he forced Williams' gaze to his. "You are a good-for-nothing snake."

Beau's fist came down heavily on the detective's face, eliciting a yelp of pain. "That's for punching Emma when she was a teenager." He punched the other side of his face. "That's for holding her hostage right now." Back to the original side. "That's for being involved with Mason and driving this case off the rails." And one more to the opposite side. "And that's for Sofia."

Williams' eyes were shut tight as blood dripped from cuts on his forehead and cheeks.

"That's enough," Diego barked, pulling Beau off Williams' sluggish body. He produced another pair of handcuffs and shoved them into Beau's palm. "Let's get these on him and keep moving. Emma must be down there somewhere." He pointed to the dark staircase. Beau couldn't see to the bottom, and he dreaded what he might find down there.

Obeying Diego's order, Beau slapped the handcuffs on

Williams' wrists—not that he was in any shape to fight back at the moment—and stood.

"We going down there now?"

Diego nodded silently, clearly as worried as Beau was about what they might find. Their fear only increased when a menacing voice sailed up from the darkened depths.

"Whoever's up there, you'd better stay where you are. I have the girl, and I'm not giving her up without a fight."

Beau shot a worried glance at Diego, who nodded toward the other archway leading to a separate staircase. They would once again divide and conquer. If they weren't outnumbered, they should be able to take out anyone who was waiting for them.

Beau slunk down the stairs, keeping his footfalls as quiet as possible, and prayed that he and Diego were moving at similar speeds. If one of them got to the bottom first, they might be acting without backup. Even if only for a few seconds, the results could be catastrophic.

At the bottom of the stairs, Beau poked his head just slightly around the corner, where he got a momentary visual of Emma, tied to a chair and terrified, but otherwise looking alright. She was alive, and that was the most important thing.

The downside was that beside her stood Mason, the biggest snake of them all, wielding a gun and pointing it straight at him. A bullet flew past his face just as Beau pulled back into the staircase.

"I *said* stay up there," Mason snapped, his voice barely loud enough to make out over Emma's high-pitched scream.

"You knew that was never gonna happen," Beau replied with false bravado. "Give me Emma, and I won't kill you." He figured the brief exchange would alert Diego that he was ready to go and give him a chance to catch up if he had been descending the stairs more slowly.

Mason snorted. "What makes you think you'll be able to kill me before I kill you?"

"Because," Beau said. "One, I'm smarter than you. Two, I want her more than you do. And three—"

He burst from the staircase, and luckily, Diego had gotten the hint that he was counting down to an attack and jumped from the other staircase at the same time. Beau fired toward Mason, missing him by a few inches in his haste. Diego had better luck than him and landed a shot to Mason's chest, but not before Mason got a shot off toward Beau.

"Ah, fuck," Beau cried as he staggered backward into the wall, pain searing his right shoulder and making him drop his gun.

"Beau!" Emma cried. She attempted to lurch toward him, knocking the chair she was tied to over in the process. She was left lying on her side on the ground, still stuck to the chair. Her screams filled the room alongside Mason's moans as he lay in a puddle of blood a few feet away.

Beau clutched at his shoulder, where his own blood was seeping out, though not in amounts anywhere near as alarming as Mason's. Asshole couldn't have just aimed for his heart and hit him on the vest? Sure, it would still have hurt, but at least it wouldn't require surgery. This fucker felt like it was going to need surgery.

"Mason's down," Diego declared as he holstered his gun. The man's moans had quickly ceased, and Diego knelt down to take his pulse. After evidently determining that there was none, he rushed to Beau's side. "You okay, man?"

"Sure," Beau croaked as he leaned heavily into the wall. His shoulder felt like it was on fire. Flames licked over the area, radiating pain down his arm and over his chest.

Diego ripped off his vest and t-shirt, pressing the latter to Beau's shoulder to control the bleeding. Beau brought his own hand to cover the makeshift bandage and shot Diego a grateful smile.

"I've got this," he ground out, holding the shirt tightly to his wound, even though it hurt like a bitch. "Help her before she hurts herself, please." He pointed to Emma's writhing form as she fought the ropes that restrained her.

Diego studied him for a moment but must have determined that he was stable enough, because he moved to Emma's side as requested.

"It's alright, sweetheart," Diego said softly, and Beau's chest swelled with gratitude that his friend treated her just as gently as he would have. "Let's get these ropes undone."

Diego pulled out a pocketknife and hacked away at the thick ropes until Emma's limbs were free. Beau's eyes flared with contempt when he spotted the rope burn on her wrists and ankles. He only simmered in his anger for a moment before Emma crawled over to him, her tearstained face sporting a look of terror.

"Oh my God," she whispered as she lifted her hands, then lowered them, as if unsure where to put them.

"I'm fine," Beau assured her through gritted teeth.

A disbelieving laugh escaped her throat even as tears leaked down her cheeks. "You got *shot*."

He tried to put on his most charming grin. "Occupational hazard."

Emma shook her head as she lifted her hands again. "What can I do?"

Beau wanted to tell her not to do anything, that she had been through a much worse ordeal than him and she should be lying down and resting, but truthfully, he would appreciate not having to hold pressure on his own wound. Emma had proven her strength to him time and time again. It was time for him to trust that she could handle whatever was thrown at her.

"You can hold down this t-shirt over the bullet hole," he said. "Make sure you press firmly."

Emma did as she was told, using both hands to hold down the t-shirt. Beau tried and failed not to wince. She had a much better angle for applying pressure, which was a good thing, but it also meant it stung more.

"Am I hurting you?" she asked, her fierce frown so incompatible with her angelic face.

"It hurts, but it's also helping."

Emma turned her gaze toward Diego, as if for confirmation that she was doing the right thing. He nodded as he spoke in a low voice into his cell phone. After hanging up, he joined them.

"I called the local P.D., and they're on their way with ambulances for you and Emma, as well as cops to arrest Williams and the two goons. I let them know they'll need a coroner, too." Diego grimaced. Emma tried to peer around his body toward Mason, but Diego blocked the view with his body. Beau met his eyes, silently thanking his friend.

"You don't need to see that, angel," Beau said.

Her golden gaze met his again. "Is he dead?"

Beau reached up with the hand of his good arm and tucked some of her mussed hair behind her ear. "Yes."

She nodded solemnly. "And Williams?"

"Still breathing, unfortunately," Beau answered, chucking his thumb toward one of the staircases. "He's tied up upstairs. We'll let the cops take it from here."

On cue, sirens began blaring their shrill song up on the ground level.

"That'll be them," Diego said. "You two stay here, and I'll meet them. Keep pressure on that wound, Emma."

She nodded and watched as he sprinted up the stairs two at a time. When she turned back toward Beau, there were fresh tears swimming in her eyes.

"Oh, angel," he whispered, reaching up to wipe away the droplets that escaped.

"I was so scared," she choked out.

Beau cupped her cheek in his palm. "Me too. I've never been so scared in my life."

She scrunched up her nose in that cute little way of hers. "Never?" she asked, her voice laced with disbelief.

"Never," Beau swore.

"But you've been in so many dangerous situations."

"None that ever threatened the person I love."

Emma's eyes snapped to his, and suddenly, a spark of joy mingled with the tears there. She opened her mouth, then closed it again, so Beau decided he would do the talking.

"This is probably a really shitty moment to say this for the first time, but I love you, Emma. You are the sweetest, strongest, most beautiful woman I've ever met. You've shown me everything that's been missing in my life, and now that I know what it feels like to be around such goodness, I never want to live without it again. I was scared to death when those men took you from me." His voice broke as his throat clogged with emotion. "The thought that they could hurt you again was unbearable." He took a deep, steadying breath—as deep as he could with a bullet wound in his shoulder. "Thank God you're okay, because I plan on loving you for a long time to come."

Emma blinked back tears. She opened her mouth again, and Beau waited for her to tell him she loved him, too, but the paramedics chose that moment to come barging down the staircase.

Tearing his gaze from Emma's, Beau glanced at the nearest paramedic. "GSW to the right shoulder. She has unknown injuries, but definitely some bad rope burn to the wrists and ankles. Take care of her first."

"Sir, your injury is more pressing," the paramedic argued.

"Take. Care. Of. Her. First."

The paramedic shook his head but complied, dropping his kit by Emma's side. Another paramedic—a woman with raven-black hair and kind eyes—knelt down beside her. "I've got this," she said gently as she took over applying pressure to the make-shift bandage.

Emma sat back on her heels, her eyes a little glazed and

her hands shaky. Beau worried she could be going into shock, and he was grateful the paramedic had listened to him and tended to her first. The last thing he needed was to lose the woman he loved before he'd had a chance to properly love her.

He still had so many things he wanted to show Emma. He'd done what he could to broaden her horizons in the confines of his apartment while hiding from human traffickers, but now that the threat was removed, they were free to go wherever they wanted and do whatever they wanted.

Beau wanted to take her to her first baseball game—Red Sox, of course. He wanted to take her out for ice cream and find out if she liked to get a cup or a cone. He wanted to properly show her his hometown. He wanted to introduce her to his mom.

Unless Emma didn't want those things. Unless, now that she was safe, she wanted to go out and explore the big, wide world on her own.

He'd confessed his love to her, and she had seemed happy about it, but she hadn't said it back. To be fair, she was halfway to a state of shock. But what if she didn't want the same things he did? What if she didn't want to be confined to a relationship now that she'd had a taste of freedom? She had jumped right from being controlled by her father to being in a relationship with Beau—albeit a mega unconventional one.

He knew Emma was it for him. No one had ever or would ever appeal to him the way she did. He just had to hope she felt the same way about him.

31

Emma's butt was starting to go numb as she sat in the hard chair of the waiting room. The doctors had given her a thorough check-up and bandaged up her burns, then released her to Fletcher, who had arrived in record time after receiving a call from Diego about what was going on. He sat beside Emma in the waiting room while Isabella sat on the other side of her. Diego was still in a conference room somewhere, talking to the local police.

The paramedics had insisted on taking Emma and Beau in separate ambulances, and she'd barely had a moment to see him as they were unloaded at the hospital. Then, they'd been escorted to their separate exam rooms and hadn't seen each other again since Beau had been taken to surgery to remove the bullet and assess any damage to his shoulder.

Leaning forward, Emma dropped her head into her hands. She'd never told Beau that she loved him. He had given her a sincere, heartfelt declaration of love, and she'd given him a few pathetic sniffles. Now, she didn't know when she'd get the chance to return his sentiment.

A hand squeezed her shoulder lightly. "Hey, you okay?" Fletcher asked.

Emma sighed into her hands. "Yes. Just worried about Beau."

Fletcher squeezed her shoulder again. "He's going to be just fine. The doctors said it looked like the bullet missed any major blood vessels and probably bone as well. Beau was fully alert from the time the paramedics got to him until the time he went into surgery, which is a great sign. They're just going to go in and make sure they're not missing anything."

Emma lifted her head enough to meet Fletcher's gaze. "But what if they did miss something and his shoulder is permanently damaged? It'll be all my fault."

"Hey," Isabella snapped, her fiery passion blazing to the surface. "Don't you dare blame yourself for this. It is nowhere near your fault that you were abducted *again*. And Beau's a big boy. He made the decision to come after you, knowing full well the danger Mason's men presented. Not that I think any amount of danger would have kept him away. He's totally smitten with you, Emma. I've never seen him like that before."

Tears swam in Emma's eyes as she angled her body toward Isabella's. She was under no illusion that Fletcher couldn't hear their entire conversation, but it felt like a little girl talk was in order. "He told me he loved me," she whispered. "And I didn't say it back."

Isabella cocked her head to the side as she studied Emma. "Do you feel it back?"

"Yes. Yes, of course I do," she answered, unable to keep a tear from escaping down her cheek.

"I know," Isabella said with a shrewd smile. "And Beau does, too. It's obvious in the way that you look at him and talk about him. And you'll have a chance to tell him. Like Fletcher said, he's going to be just fine, and then you two can live happily ever after together."

Emma leaned into her friend's shoulder as she wrapped her up in a hug. Everyone, including the doctors, said that Beau was going to be alright, but that was hard to believe when she'd seen him get shot mere hours ago. She didn't think she could relax until she got a chance to see Beau awake and alert—and to tell him she loved him, of course.

The next couple of hours crawled by as they sat in the waiting room. Diego joined them eventually, assuring Emma that the local police had Williams and Mason's other goons held under lock and key. Her father had also been arrested. With Mason dead, his entire organization was sure to crumble, but the FBI had been brought in to round up as many of the remaining players as possible. The Boston Police Department had already begun an internal investigation to determine if there were any other crooked cops or if Williams had been a lone wolf. All in all, it seemed as if all threats to Emma had been eliminated.

Relieved by Diego's update, she had just started dozing off on Bella's shoulder when a doctor in navy-blue scrubs and a tie-dye scrub cap emerged into the waiting area.

"I have an update on Beau McNally," he announced, scanning the waiting room to see who to deliver his news to.

Emma shot to her feet. Fletcher, Diego, and Isabella followed close behind as they eagerly awaited the doctor's report.

"He did very well during surgery," the doctor said. "As we suspected by the mild amount of blood loss, the bullet missed any major arteries or blood vessels. It just grazed the clavicle, but mostly only hit fat and some muscle. He was extremely lucky. We removed the bullet and repaired as much of the tissue as possible. The rest should heal with time and physical therapy."

"Can we see him?" Emma blurted, desperate to get her eyes on Beau.

The doctor gave her an indulgent grin. "Yes. He hasn't woken up yet, but you're welcome to sit with him until he does. I would suggest just one or two of you go in at first, though. We don't want him to be overwhelmed right when he awakens."

Emma turned her gaze to Fletcher and Diego, knowing that Beau's brother and partner should really hold priority over her—a woman he'd met only a month ago.

Fletcher spoke first. "You go on ahead, Emma. I don't mind waiting a bit longer."

Diego nodded. "We'll wait out here until you've had a few minutes with him. We all know he'll want to see you first. If he has to see one of our ugly mugs before he gets eyes on you, he'll be pissed."

Fletcher snickered at Diego's reasoning but didn't disagree.

Isabella shot Emma an encouraging look. "Go see your man."

Emma thanked each of them with a quick hug, then followed the doctor back into Beau's room. She sucked in a breath when she saw him lying in the hospital bed, an IV sticking out of his arm and an oxygen cannula slung beneath his nose. He was so still, but the steady rise and fall of his chest filled her with gratitude.

"How long until he wakes up?"

"Should be just a few minutes now," the doctor answered, sliding a chair over beside the bed for her to sit in. "Make yourself comfortable."

Emma sat down and inspected Beau's shoulder. It was all wrapped up in clean bandages and held steadily in place with a sling. His arm rested on a pillow that elevated his shoulder slightly.

Not wanting to risk hurting him by touching anything near his injury, she ran her fingertips over his brow. He showed no signs of waking yet, so she sat back and took the hand of his uninjured arm in hers.

"You really scared me there, big guy," she said, just to fill the silence. Squeezing his hand, she added, "You'd better be okay like everyone says you'll be."

Despite his sizable muscles, Beau looked so vulnerable hooked up to all the medical devices. Normally, he was the biggest presence in any room. It was something Emma loved about him because it allowed her to shrink back into the shadows a bit, where she was more comfortable. In his unconscious state, she was left to occupy the space, and she longed for the moment when he would step back into his role.

"Please just wake up so I can tell you I love you," she muttered.

Beau's eyelids fluttered then, and his Adam's apple leapt as he swallowed.

"Beau?" she said.

He wrinkled his nose a bit, and his eyes opened into narrow slits. After a few slow blinks, his hazy eyes met hers.

"Hi," Emma whispered, savoring those beautiful brown eyes now that they were open. She brought his hand up to her mouth and placed a kiss on the center of his palm.

"Hi," Beau croaked back in a raspy voice.

"I missed you," she replied, hating how needy she sounded but unable to hold back the depth of her feelings.

Beau gave her a pained look and let out a grumbling noise, then cleared his throat and tried again. "I missed you, too, angel."

"You're awake. You're alive," she said, her tone laced with relief.

"Of course I am," Beau responded, his cocky smile slipping into place. "You didn't think I'd leave you that easily, now did you?"

Emma shook her head but found herself grinning goofily back at him. There he was. *That* was the Beau she knew and loved. And speaking of, she had that thing she needed to tell him…

"Beau, I—"

Her declaration was interrupted by the door opening and a nurse popping her head into the room. "Oh, you're awake! Good," she said. "Sorry to interrupt, but I'm going to need Mr. McNally's insurance card again. Someone must have typed a number in wrong, and our system won't accept it. I hate to ask right now, but insurance companies are a doozy."

"No problem," Beau said, his voice still a bit scratchy. "Grab my wallet from that table?" he requested, pointing to the small table in the corner of the room.

"Sure." Emma went over and rifled through the wallet until she found the correct card. As she pulled it out, a small scrap of paper fluttered to the ground. She picked it up and ignored it for a moment as she handed the card to the nurse, who thanked her and retreated back to the nurse's station.

Looking back down at the paper, Emma immediately recognized it as the fortune she'd received during her very first meal with Beau and Diego. *There is love in your near future.* At the time, that prediction had seemed so far from possible it was almost laughable, but it had come true after all.

Smiling to herself, Emma returned to the chair beside Beau's bed and tucked the fortune into his palm. He frowned slightly as he held it up to inspect it, then his lips curved upward as he realized what it was.

"Why did you save it?" she asked quietly, her head cocked with curiosity. It didn't quite seem like Beau to save something so sentimental.

He shrugged with his good shoulder, wincing as it inevitably pulled at the bandages on the other side of his body. "I think somewhere inside, I knew love was waiting for you. You'd had so much shit in your life for so long, I knew that something good must be coming. I wanted to save the fortune so I could remind you. Whether or not it's me, I want you to be happy, Emma. I want you to feel loved and adored every second of every day." He reached his good hand up to cup her cheek, and only then did Emma realize she was crying.

"I would be honored to be the one making you feel that way," he went on, "but if not, I understand. We found each other under the worst possible circumstances, and I don't want you to feel obligated to be with me just because I helped you out of a bad situation."

"Twice," she whispered as tears continued spilling down her cheeks.

This man. This man who had taken a bullet for her, who had cared for her so tenderly, and who so clearly adored her, was willing to give her up if it was what she wanted. His selflessness tugged at her heartstrings, and she covered his hand on her cheek with her own, wiping away her tears with both of their fingers intertwined.

"Of course it's you, Beau," she said. "It's been you from the beginning, and it will only ever be you. You make me happier than I ever thought I could be. You make me feel strong and safe and loved and adored. I don't ever want to be without you. I love you," she choked out.

His answering grin was dazzling as he tugged her in for a kiss. Emma had to lean over awkwardly to reach his lips, but she managed to give him a kiss that at least partially proved the intensity of her love for him.

She pulled back when he let out a pained hiss, and she realized he'd let his arm slip off the pillow it had been resting on.

"Shit," she muttered, gently repositioning his injured arm on the pillow.

Beau's eyebrows climbed his forehead as he stared at her, his pain forgotten. "You just swore."

A blush warmed her cheeks as she realized she had, indeed, let out an expletive. "I guess you're rubbing off on me."

One side of his lips tipped up. "I'd like to be rubbing off on you right now."

Emma's blush deepened. "I have a feeling you'll be waiting quite a while for that." She pointed to his injury.

Beau shook his head slowly. "Oh, no, angel. As long as we get creative so my shoulder doesn't get jostled, we're good to go."

"You saw what happened just from kissing." She pointed to the pillow where his arm now rested comfortably. "I refuse to do anything that might hurt you."

He pouted in a markedly un-manly way. "It will hurt me more not to get to have you."

She rolled her eyes at his puppy-dog face. "I think you'll live."

Beau reached over to grab her by the waist, pulling her in for another kiss. This time, though, she backed off before he could lose himself in the moment and potentially hurt himself.

"Are you sure you're going to be okay?" she asked, lacing their fingers together in her lap.

He scoffed. "Nothing a few months of physical therapy won't fix."

"Good," Emma replied. "Because I think I could use a few more of those self-defense lessons."

Beau sobered. "Of course. I'm sure Diego would be happy to assist with those as well. But you know it's not your fault you weren't able to fight those men off, right? It was three against one, and they're all way bigger than you."

"I know." Emma sighed. "But I still want to feel more prepared next time."

"There'd better not be a next time," Beau growled.

"Hopefully not," she agreed. "But if, God forbid, there is, I'd like to be able to defend myself *before* someone winds up getting shot."

"That's fair." Beau reached up to run his fingers down her jaw. "I'm so proud of you, Emma. You may not have had the physical strength to fight them off, but you had the mental cleverness to hide the phone in your bra, knowing it would allow us to track you. Despite having the odds stacked against you, you still had a hand in your own rescue." He swallowed harshly. "You're incredible, angel. I love you."

Emma's chest warmed at the casual way he spit out those words. It was a phrase she had heard so few times in her life, and coming from Beau, it meant everything.

"I love you, too."

EPILOGUE

After three days in the hospital while the doctors watched for any signs of infection, Beau was finally released home. His shoulder still hurt like a motherfucker, but painkillers were helping with that.

Emma hadn't stopped fussing over him since the second he'd left the hospital. Fletcher had driven them home, with Emma shooting him the most adorably angry glares every time they'd been jostled the slightest bit by a bump. Once home, she hadn't let Beau leave the couch, bringing him his meals and anything else he may need. Beau was convinced she would have used the bathroom for him if she could have. While he appreciated Emma's care, he was used to living an active lifestyle and was itching to move around.

After two days of being babied by his woman, Beau had had enough. "Angel," he groaned as Emma shoved an extra pillow behind his back as he reclined on the couch. "I'm really fine. I don't need to sit here anymore. I can get up and do stuff as long as it doesn't affect my shoulder."

Emma huffed a frustrated sigh in his ear from behind him, where she was *fluffing* his fucking pillows. "You need to heal. That's not going to happen if you're not resting."

"Can I at least rest somewhere other than this goddamn couch? I'm bored as hell of this room and all these ridiculous daytime television shows."

A frown creased Emma's brow. "Want me to run you a bath?"

He hadn't even bothered trying to shower yet, as his bandages and sling couldn't get wet, and it was too difficult to navigate the water stream around them. Instead, Emma had been running him baths, though—to his dismay—she'd refused to join him in them. Perhaps he could convince her to today…

Images of Emma's wet, soapy, naked body ran through Beau's mind, and a sly smile tugged at his lips. "Sure."

Eager to be of service, she hurried to the bathroom, and he heard the water turn on soon after. As if to prove his virility, Beau carefully removed his sling and took off his own shirt. Emma had helped him undress each time he'd had to since they'd been home, but he found it wasn't all that difficult to do it himself. He winced slightly when his movements tugged at his injury but was otherwise successful.

Without a second thought, he removed his pants as well. Emma wasn't likely to be seduced without a fight. Her nurturing side was too strong, and right now, she was treating him like a baby bird. But the less clothing he was wearing, the better his chances were.

Wearing only his boxers, Beau sauntered into the bathroom where Emma was just dumping some Epsom salts into the almost-full bath. It reminded him of their first bath together…and the results of that. Yeah, he was definitely seducing her today.

Looking up from her task, Emma blinked wide, golden eyes at him. "Oh," she murmured, her gaze coasting along his mostly bare body. Beau quirked an eyebrow at her visual study, and she quickly shut it down with a scowl. "You should have waited for me. I could have helped you take your clothes off."

He took a step toward her, loving how her eyes widened a fraction. "I would've enjoyed that. Why don't I help you take yours off instead?" he suggested.

Emma shook her head. "No, Beau. This bath is for you and you only. No funny business."

He sidled up closer to her, crowding into her space, then speaking into her ear. "But I like funny business."

Her breath hitched, and he wanted to punch the air in triumph because he knew he almost had her.

"I don't want to hurt you," she whispered. When she looked up at him, vulnerability and a hint of fear shone in her eyes.

Beau smoothed back her hair with his good hand. "You won't. I'll be extra careful," he promised. He trailed his hand over her shoulder and down her back before resting his palm on her ass. "Besides, I do still have one good hand, after all." He squeezed lightly and was rewarded with a beautiful blush that seeped into Emma's cheeks.

"You need to tell me if you're uncomfortable or if I hurt you," she insisted.

"You sound like me now," Beau joked, and she glowered at him. "I will," he vowed solemnly, bringing his hand to the waistband of her athletic shorts and pulling gently to indicate that he wanted her to remove them.

She leaned forward to place a kiss on his bare chest, then shimmied out of her shorts. Gazing up at him, she pulled her t-shirt over her head, and Beau was pleased to find that she wasn't wearing a bra. He bit back a groan at her oh-so-familiar and totally breathtaking body. He longed to kiss every inch of the expanse of creamy skin she'd uncovered, to tease and thrill and worship her, showing her exactly how much he'd missed her. But for now, he'd settle for joining her in the bath and blowing her mind with his good hand.

"I need you," he whispered, and with those magic words, their roles were reversed completely. Emma grabbed him by the waist and crushed her lips to his, finally giving him what he'd been longing for since before he'd even left the hospital.

Beau devoured her lips as his hand skated up to cup the back of her neck. "I love you," he murmured, pressing kisses to her cheek, temple, and forehead.

"I love you, too," she replied in a husky voice. "So much."

He grinned as he placed one final kiss on the crown of her head. "Get in," he said, gesturing to the now-full bathtub, fragrant from the scented salts. Emma stepped into the warm water, sinking down so she took up the front half of the tub, leaving space for him. He maneuvered himself in behind her, resting his injured arm on the ledge so it would stay stable.

"Come here," he rasped, pulling at Emma's waist so she would relax back into him. She was sitting ramrod straight in the most uncomfortable-looking position. Craning her neck around so she could judge her positioning, she gently leaned into his chest—right where she belonged.

Her soft sigh as she melted into him made Beau's chest tighten. This fucking woman. His woman. His angel.

The fingers of his good hand traced circular patterns over Emma's silky thigh. "I've missed you," he whispered.

She let out a small noise of disbelief. "We've been together all-hours for the past few days."

"I know," he said, nipping her ear. "But we haven't *been together*."

He didn't have to see her face to know Emma was blushing.

"I've missed this," he said as he lifted his hand to palm one of her breasts. "And this," he added as he circled her nipple with his thumb, then gently tugged it between his thumb and forefinger. "I've missed all of this." His fingers trailed down over her belly. "And I've *really* missed this." He cupped her in his large palm, and she rocked back, ever so slightly grinding into him.

"Oh, that hand *is* good," she said in a breathy voice that made Beau chuckle.

"See, I told you we could make this work."

Her gaze shot to his other arm, still safely on the tub's ledge.

"It's all good, angel," he assured her. "Not even a twinge."

She relaxed back against him again, and he began stroking lazily through her cleft and over her clit.

"When this shoulder's all healed up, I'll remind you how good *both* of my hands can be, but for now, this will have to do."

Emma squirmed as he paid a little extra attention to her tight bud of nerves.

"I still have so much I want to do with you, sweetheart. I'm going to show you everything," he promised. "These next few months will be a little touch-and-go with my injury and physical therapy and everything. It'll take me more time to heal than we've even known each other, but it's not a lot of time in the grand scheme of things. Because I'm planning on keeping you forever."

"Forever?" she squeaked, and he wasn't sure if the reaction was to his words or the fact that he'd just pushed one finger inside her.

"Mhmm," he hummed against her temple. "If that's alright with you."

"Y-yeah," she stammered. "Yes. Forever sounds good."

He smiled into her hair. "Good."

And then he gave her a taste of how good forever would feel.

WANT MORE?

Gain access to a bonus epilogue when you sign up for my newsletter! Visit my website www.mollymccarthybooks.com for more details.

If you enjoyed this book, I hope you'll recommend it to a friend and consider leaving it a review on Goodreads, Amazon, Instagram, or another platform. Indie authors rely on reviews and recommendations to get our work out there. Thank you!

DID YOU KNOW?

According to the US Department of State, 41% of human trafficking victims are trafficked by their own family members. If you or someone you know is a victim of human trafficking, call the National Human Trafficking Hotline at 1-888-373-7888 or text 233733.

ACKNOWLEDGMENTS

As always, I want to say thank you to my mom for her support in anything and everything that I do, and for reading my books even though the steam level is probably a bit higher than she'd like! And to my dad and brother for being excited for me even though they'll (hopefully) never read anything I write.

To all my extended family that bought my debut novel, talked it up, and coerced their friends to order it—you all should really be my marketing team. And a super special shoutout to my Aunt Jane for being the most…enthusiastic supporter of my writing career! I'll be sure to return the favor when you decide to finally write that book of yours.

To Lori, Robyn, and Miranda—the other 3/4 of the Fab Four—thank you for your support and excitement even though you aren't really romance readers. And a special thank you for the exuberant live readings of my steamy scenes on our girls' trips!

To my beta readers Alyssa, Laura, and Lexi—y'all ROCK! Your feedback was absolutely priceless, and I value each of your perspectives so much. And to my amazing editor, Jenn, and cover artist, Wilette—working with you both again was a pleasure.

And finally, last but most certainly not least, thank you so much to YOU, the reader, for taking a chance on my book! None of this would be possible without you. I write these books because I enjoy it, but my biggest wish is that others will enjoy them too.

ABOUT THE AUTHOR

Molly McCarthy is an avid romance reader and writer living just outside Boston, MA. She can often be found typing away in a café, drinking a latte, and dreaming of happily ever afters. Keep up with Molly on Instagram @mollymccarthybooks.

- facebook.com/mollymccarthybooks
- twitter.com/mollykmccarthyy
- instagram.com/mollymccarthybooks

WHAT'S NEXT?

Fletcher's hard-earned happily ever after is coming in spring of 2023!

Printed in Great Britain
by Amazon